# ALSO DARCY COATES

# THE
# HAUNTING
## OF
# LEIGH
# HARKER

# DARCY COATES

*Poisoned Pen*
PRESS

Published by Poisoned Pen Press, an imprint of Sourcebooks
P.O. Box 4410, Naperville, Illinois 60567-4410
(630) 961-3900
sourcebooks.com

Library of Congress Cataloging-in-Publication Data

Names: Coates, Darcy, author.
Title: The haunting of Leigh Harker / Darcy Coates.
Description: Naperville, Illinois : Poisoned Pen Press, [2021]
Identifiers: LCCN 2021018890 | (trade paperback)
Subjects: GSAFD: Horror fiction.
Classification: LCC PR9619.4.C628 H423 2021 | DDC 823/.92--dc23
LC record available at https://lccn.loc.gov/2021018890

Printed and bound in the United States of America.
VP 12 11 10 9 8

# THE SOMETHING

SOMETHING LINGERS OUTSIDE MY ROOM.

I am paralyzed. My hand-quilted blankets no longer feel like a warm cocoon but a straitjacket. They lace me to my bed. They strangle. My mouth hangs open as a breath dies in my throat, unable to reach my lungs.

And the something outside my bedroom creeps nearer. Just an inch, enough to reinforce its presence, to make sure that I won't begin to doubt my senses.

I don't dare avert my eyes. Nor am I foolish enough to move, not even to breathe. These straitjacket blankets will betray me. They will rustle. *It* will hear. I do not know what will happen then, and I do not want to learn.

My heart is so loud that I wish I could squeeze my fist around it just to make it go silent. Old oak branches, stripped bare by winter, jostle for space outside my window. They cut through the moonlight like knives, turning it into a lattice of sharp angles—a broken, shimmering glass discarded across my carpet and speckled up my walls. And over *it*. The four or five slivers of light that touch the dark shape reveal only tiny pieces of it, forcing me to glimpse it as though my eye were pressed to a keyhole.

It fills my doorway. Arms hang at its side. It gives the impression of grayness—grayness, with a tinge of sickly green. Skin or clothing, impossible to tell.

I cannot make out where the face ends and the hair begins, but there *is* hair, and it is long. I cannot see a mouth. Its eyes dominate its features. Round circles, too large, unnaturally huge, like an owl's. Sheer white, they catch the moonlight.

The eyes are fixed on me. They do not move. They do not blink. I know, innately, that the slightest movement will call it closer. My heart is too fast, too loud, too painful. That breath is held prisoner in my throat, my lungs aching.

It turns. It lurches. The terrible *something* disappears as it paces along my hallway. The knifelike shards of light glance off the edges of its form as it moves away and I see hair, gray, gritty, and unreal, flowing behind it.

Its legs are not visible, but it must have them, as its steps ring out. Heavy, laborious, each one falls like a gavel on the wooden floor. It moves slowly, but I have the unwelcome sense that it is only feigning sluggishness. That, when the time comes, I will have no hope of outrunning it.

*How do I know this? Have I been here before?*

My lungs begin to work again. Not well—they stutter with

each ebb and flow. The air tastes wrong. The perception lingers on my tongue, and I try to find words for what I'm imbibing. Dust. Age, like fabric left in the sun for twenty years or like a floor that has been swept but never mopped. There is something underneath those scents, too. Something disguised but insidious.

The weighty footsteps pause near my bathroom. It has to be looking inside, and I hate it, knowing its awful eyes will be staring into a room that never sees strangers, examining the half-empty bottles of conditioner, the cracks in the wall that harbor mold no matter how hard I scrub, the mirror that is a fraction too small for the area above my sink, and the discolored grouting between the aqua-green tiles. I feel as though a part of me is exposed, my secrets torn out of me, each one scraping painfully as they are extracted. I do not want the *something* to know me.

My arm snakes out toward the edge of my bed. The traitorous sheets crinkle like alarm bells. I fall still, breath suspended, waiting, but the *something* stays by the bathroom. I move again, dragging myself closer. The knives of light stab, repeatedly, over the quilted cover. They pluck out details. Eyes. A screaming mouth. Arms held up, clawing at darkness.

I created those designs. In the daylight, they recount myths from around the world. The designs are as familiar to me as my own face, but at that early morning hour, they feel evil.

My bare feet slide over the edge of the bed. Mattress springs groan and I clench my teeth. Over my shoulder, the bedroom door remains open, the hallway beyond empty. I watch the darkness, fearing what it might be hiding. My toes touch the plush rug in the center of the room.

My desk is underneath the window and catches the worst of the shattered light. It holds paperwork, stacks of it, meticulously ordered, piled in front of a penholder so full that it's a struggle to draw any implement out.

My journal is starting to gather dust across its leather jacket. A cup, empty, waits to be taken downstairs and washed.

Behind that clutter is a lifeline: my phone. The old-fashioned rotary model was bought as an impulse purchase for its aesthetic more than its practicality. I spent a quarter of my paycheck on it at a thrift store, regretted it before I arrived home, and then felt too embarrassed to return it, convinced that the thrift store staff would send each other knowing looks as I sheepishly pulled it out of my bag. In retaliation, I swung too far the other way: not using it as a glorified paperweight, as I'd initially intended, but plugging it into my never-used landline as though that might justify the indulgence.

It turns out that may have been the most vital waste of money of my life. I leave my mobile downstairs at night to prevent distractions. That antique rotary is the only phone on the second floor of my house.

My eyes stay fixed on the empty doorway as I rise from the mattress. My knees feel flimsy, as though they are built out of cardboard, unused to holding my weight. I reach through the shards of light toward the phone. A thudding footfall echoes from the hall. Has it tired of my bathroom? My fingers touch wood and I draw my eyes away from the gaping archway at my back.

The phone's dial is a circle of faded numbers. I lift the wooden earpiece, moving gingerly to stop the cradle from making noise. The dial tone greets me and I press it against my chest, muffling it, agonizingly aware of how far sound travels in the dead of night.

My first impulse is to call my sister, but she lives hours away. The only help she could possibly offer is to tell me to call the police, so I cut straight to that second choice. All that matters at this moment is to *not* be alone in my house, to *not* be trapped here with the something. My finger nestles into the well-worn metal circle and drags it around, the dial clicking in fragments. It will make a terrible ringing noise if I let it loose, so I don't, easing it back down to its starting position while I let air hiss through my teeth. Then I repeat the process.

The window above my desk was left open several inches. The night is bitingly cold, but I cannot sleep without fresh air. A breeze comes through, and vulnerable without my quilts, I shudder as its questing fingers worm through the gaps in my nightgown.

The third number has been turned, and as I ease the dial back to its starting position, I raise the receiver to my ear. It rings. I wrap one hand around the mouthpiece as I turn to face the doorway once again.

The *something* stands there. Only its flickering eyes are visible. Some part of it—its arms, maybe—shift.

"What is your emergency?"

The words come from the receiver, and I want to beg her to be quieter, but my voice has become a solid thing, frozen in my throat, a lump I cannot breathe past. My fingers are slick on the wood. My eyes burn, too dry, and when I blink, suddenly they are too wet.

"Hello?" The woman is patient, moderated, too serene for the situation. "What is the nature of your emergency?"

*Help me,* I want to say, but any noise will be the beginning of my end. The something watches, unblinking, hyperfocused, and I am cornered.

Again, the voice on the phone speaks. "Hello?"

My mouth opens a fraction wider, the blockage in my throat suffocating, my body set on fire by adrenaline even as fear grounds me to the spot—as though being still might save me. As though *it* doesn't know exactly where I am.

Then the something in the doorway tilts its head. I still cannot see its mouth, but I can sense it opening, and a terrible noise comes out.

"Hello?"

It is an imitation of what a human might sound like. The word is corrupted, a mockery of the patient woman on the phone. The unblinking, lifeless eyes bore into me as it repeats the noise, playing with the sounds, exploring the tones. "Hello? Hello."

The woman on the phone joins the chorus. "Hello?"

It breaks my nerves. The receiver slips from my hold. The sleek wooden piece twists on its cord as it falls, then hits the floor with a resounding thud.

The *something* moves. I was right; it doesn't need to shamble. It comes toward me with horrible speed, terrible power, its eyes as round as twin moons, boring into me, and I finally find enough voice to scream.

The back of my legs hit the desk's chair. I fall to the floor, sparks of pain rising from my elbow but immaterial in the face of what is before me. The *something* stands where I stood just a second before, the shattered light bringing it into terrible resolution, and I wish it had stayed in the fog of shadows.

The head rotates, the pupil-less eyes turning to stare down at me. I'm sprawled, braced on my heels and my lower back and elbows, and hyperaware of every vulnerable part of my body. My stomach. My inner thighs. My face. They are all turned toward the creature, exposed, and I may as well be offering myself up as a sacrifice.

The something's body rotates to match its immobile head. I scramble backward, feet kicking at the smooth floor, dust sticking to my palms, desperate to gain space from the shaggy thing looming above me. The receiver hangs, one end resting on the floor, the other suspended by the twisting line, and in the unnatural still of night, the voice floats from it: "Hello?"

"Hello." The something's voice is broken. It might be laughing, but the sound is as inhuman as the words. "Hello... Hello... Hello."

My shoulder blades hit the closet. I reach behind myself, arms stretching above my head as I blindly seek the doorknob. It clicks as it opens. I use my heels to kick my way inside.

The circular eyes flash. With no pupil and no iris, it's impossible to tell whether it's looking at me or looking *through* me. I pull the door closed and hear the latch click. Jackets and dresses and pants cluster around me, pressing on me, as though to smother me. Now there is only one source of light: a line of it, marking the shallow gap between the doors and the floor.

The something's footsteps are loud again. They thud, painstaking, as it drags itself closer to my hiding space. I cannot let it open the doors. My fingers are numb as they search for handles, but the inside of the wood is bare. There is no purchase.

A shadow cuts through the line of light at my feet. Metal groans faintly. I can picture its hands, heavy and disfigured, resting on the doorknobs.

I thrust my fingers, palm up, through the gap under the doors. The wood is rough there, raw, a shortcut the manufacturer thought would never be noticed. It grates on my fingers as I curl them up, gripping the base of the doors, desperate to hold them where they are.

Wood flexes. The line of light spears upward as the intruder tries to draw the doors apart. My shoulder muscles burn as I pull against it, and the vertical line of light shivers.

Then the external pressure releases, the doors snap closed, and I'm again swallowed by darkness.

My forehead touches the wood as I keel forward. It's not yet safe, and I don't dare remove my fingers from underneath the door. I wait, my hands cramping, my legs pulled up awkwardly as I huddle in my cloistered hiding space. If the intruder is still outside the door, it makes no noise, not even the whistle of breath. My eyes are wide-open but blind in the dark. My eyelashes graze the wood, my breath rolling back onto my lips from the proximity.

Then I hear it. Bones creak. Then crack. It is moving, lowering itself, coming closer to the floor. I look down. My hands are still hooked underneath the doors, my fingers braced outside, vulnerable. I cannot stand to leave them exposed like that. And yet, they are the only things ensuring the doors remain closed.

My fingertips feel electrified, the multitude of nerve endings sensitive, expectant. Warm, moist air brushes across my right index and middle finger. I imagine the something crouched and its open mouth close enough to my exposed fingers that twitching one outward would touch it.

It whispers, the word fractured and distorted: "Hello."

Something sharp stabs into my fingers. The muscles in my hands spasm and the sloppily carved wood digs into my palms. I jerk my hands back, withdrawing them, and clutch them close to my chest. They hurt, but fear both swells and muddies the sensation, making it indistinct. I could have been cut. I could have lost a finger. In the dark, it's impossible to tell. I bundle my hands together under my chin, squeezing them, and feel hot wetness seeping between the clammy skin.

The line of light underneath the door is speared through by nails. Long nails, ragged nails, creep their way through the gap, exploring the rough wood, touching over the areas where my own fingers were. My eyes are flooded and I tilt my head back, jackets and dresses lying cool against my flaming skin, hands clutched under my throat and knees pulled up against my chest.

The nails disappear from underneath the door. I already know where they will go next. There is no escape this time as the something reaches for the handles. I shimmy backward, letting the rows of clothing fall in front of my face. They cannot hide me. My legs are still exposed, and no matter how tightly I pull them against my body, they will be the first to be grabbed as the something drags me out of my hiding place.

The closet doors creak as they drift open. Through the shutters made of clothes, I can barely see the entity poised outside. A drop of warm blood falls from my palm and lays heavy on my forearm. My view is distorted by wools and cottons, loose threads so close to my eyes that they blur, creating layers of spiderwebs between me and the *thing* outside. I wish they were denser, dense enough to block out its awful eyes. They are its only visible part. Its form is painted all in ashen gray as the moon through the window backlights it. It fills the closet's entrance, its arms spread wide as they hold the doors open, its shaggy hair lying heavy around its form, its shoulders hunched as it stares down at me.

And I'm calcified to the wall, too afraid to even close my eyes.

The intruder looms closer, rising even higher above me. The doors groan. The band of light grows narrower, tightening into a ribbon, and then a sliver, and then nothing at all as the doors snap closed.

It is inside the closet with me. In that dark, narrow hole, close enough that I should have been able to feel its warmth, close enough that relaxing my position, even just slightly, would force my heel or my elbow to touch it. It makes no noise, but I can feel its presence. The air is heavier. Reeking of musty age and unwashed floors and that terrible something else.

My bleeding hand throbs with every pulse. The smell is overwhelming, and I cannot think, cannot breathe, do not dare move. The jacket to my left shifts, the wire hanger clinking as it turns on the rod. My wide eyes stare into nothing. My back aches from the pose I'm forced to hold, but I cannot relax, not even a fraction. I instinctively know that if I touch the intruder, it will be over. And the intruder is *so close*. It exhales, its rattling breath directly in my ear. I can all but taste its dead skin.

I burst forward in a spasm of energy that surprises even me. My hands hit the closet doors and they bang open as I charge through. There is no time to let my eyes adjust to the stabbing moonlight, no time to look over my shoulder. I run, bare feet slapping the floor. The phone's receiver twists on its cord as I pass it. The screaming faces on my quilt track me with their distorted eyes. But I am at the bedroom door, through the opening, and my shoulder glances off the wall as I twist myself down the hallway.

Footsteps boom in my wake. They are longer than mine, steady, gaining. I pass the bathroom. The stairs are ahead, a treacherous pit of black with a lone bulb that I have no time to think about. I close my eyes as I near them, trusting my familiarity with the house to judge my footfalls.

The first stair finds its mark. Then the second and the third, and I'm flowing downward so rapidly that I barely glance off each step.

My feet sting as I come to a sudden halt on the lower floor. I swing to put my back to the wall. The stairwell is impenetrable; only the closest two steps are visible, while everything above is perfect black.

The air no longer tastes foul. I am alone.

# THEY MIGHT BE FOOTSTEPS

THE GATE'S RUST IS RAW AND FLAKY. MY LEFT HAND RESTS ON ITS highest bar, a position it's taken many times, but lingering in a way that is unfamiliar. My right hand holds the keys to the sedan parked in the street behind me. Ahead is my house, set against the backdrop of the failing sun, its slate-tile roofing saturated by vivid, seeping colors.

Less than eighteen hours ago, something chased me out of this house. Now, during the day, it scarcely feels real. The encounter happened between those strange hours of two and four in the morning, where reality becomes distorted and dreams are intent on encroaching into the conscious world.

I lift my right hand. The key ring is hooked around my middle finger. A small cloth bandage is strapped to the index, running from between the first and second knuckles. That is my proof: a tangible rebuttal against the ethereal nature of those mid-dream hours.

Crisp air runs through my lungs. I push on the gate and it wails as it swings inward. That familiar greeting is my *welcome home* each night, the signal that I have left the outside world and reentered my dominion. It's also an alarm against intrusion. Visitors must announce their arrival well before they reach my front door.

Though, truthfully, the fence isn't much of a barrier. It barely comes to waist height, a constant that is maintained through regular dips in the rows of bricks to account for the way my street slopes. Anyone could hop over the lichen-fused fortifications with very little effort. They would need to keep to the grassed and gardened portions of my yard to avoid making the paving stones crunch, but within ten paces, they could be at my door, as silent as a specter.

The gate screams as it closes behind me. Spreading bushes and flowering trees dance to either side as the wind picks up, and the clambering mini rose bush that runs along the fence seems intent on snagging my knit jacket.

The four windows facing the street are all cold and dead, giving the building an air of abandonment. The ocher brick walls catch the setting sun. Spiderwebs live about the eaves and window frames on the second floor, too high for me to reach.

My sister once told me a house doesn't deserve to be called a home unless a family lives in it. That snide proclamation came three years ago, shortly after the birth of her second daughter; it was one of many finishing blows to our relationship.

She was wrong anyway. This is a home. No one could argue

against that. It felt like a home before I even moved into it as a first-time renter fifteen years ago. That feeling increased when I put down my deposit to buy it from its former owner, and it deepens with every passing year. I suspect it has become a home to everyone who has been a part of its near-century lifespan and will continue to be a home for others once I eventually move on.

Its flaws are numerous, from the problematic grouting in the upstairs bathroom to the badly angled corner cupboard in the kitchen, with its door that never properly closes. But its quirks are overcompensated for by its richness. Real wood paneling runs along the main hallway. The stairs' banister is thick and solid. The oak tree in the backyard must have been planted when the house was built, and its magnificent boughs overshadow anything else the street can offer.

Whatever happened last night is not something to be avoided, and I don't allow myself to feel fear as the loose paving stones grind under my feet. This is my home. No one can strip that from me.

The front door, unlocked, opens at a touch. When I left, I snatched up my key ring on the way out but hadn't spared the time to lock the door behind myself. The logic of the moment had said that if something was already inside, I would be a fool to seal it in there.

Now, I pause in the entryway. Bands of light come through large windows. They imbue the wood paneling and creamy paint with warmth. The hallway connects to the kitchen, running parallel to the stairwell that leads to the second floor. To the right is a rarely used living room that overlooks the front street, and to the left is the equally neglected dining room. I prefer to spend my time in the kitchen at the house's rear. I'd rather indulge in the solitude of my backyard than watch the street.

Keys go on the narrow table beside the front door. My satchel is thrown onto the brass hooks above. Then I follow the hallway past the stairs, flexing my shoulders as I begin construction of a mental checklist for that evening.

A doorknob rattles behind me. I stop, one foot in the hall and one in the kitchen, all thoughts disintegrating. There are not many doors on the lower level of my home, which favors open archways. I scan between those that are visible, listening. The fridge hums. Birds shriek as they fight over the backyard feeder that must be near empty. A car engine encroaches and then becomes more distant again.

Otherwise, the house is quiet. My eyes itch and I realize I've forgotten to blink. I retrace the length of the hall, back to the front door, and put my eye to the peephole. It gives me a fish-eye view of the flagstone path, the treacherous clambering rose, and the rusted gate. I touch the doorknob, wondering if perhaps I hadn't closed it properly, but there is no unexpected give to it.

As I turn, light catches off a bronze doorknob under the stairs, the only other possible source of the noise. That door is a part of my daily scenery but so little used that I'd long since blacked it out of my memory. Just like a spot on the carpet or a mug at the far back of the cupboard, it exists but is never truly *looked* at. I stare at it now, the tip of my tongue held between my teeth as I approach with measured steps.

What's behind that door? Storage, I'm pretty sure, but it's been so long since I used it that I can't visualize the space. As a single person in a five-bedroom home, storage has never been a source of stress.

The bronze doorknob is ornate, like most of the original fixtures in my home. A wreath of tiny leaves is embossed on the surface, surrounding the handle and a delicate keyhole, tiny berries clustered between the flora. It's well tarnished. The house's previous owners must have cared more about this door than I do.

My ear touches the wood's edge, where it merges with the paneling. The space holds echoes, and they play with my mind, teasing at the very edges of my hearing. My hand moves to the doorknob. It turns, but only for a fraction, before the motion abruptly halts. The door is locked.

It brings up a memory so vague that it could be a dream. I tried the door on my first day of renting my new home and found it was locked then, too. I must have intended to find the key or call a locksmith at some point but never did.

Over time, that door fell into the backdrop of my life, present but eternally overlooked. I smile. I've become so familiar with this dear home that it's a surprise to find a part of it I haven't yet seen.

I'll uncover its mysteries, but not just yet. My back is sore from work and my mouth is dry. As I step away from the door, a clammy sensation rises in me, like something alive moving from my lower stomach and into my chest. I look over my shoulder. Nothing has changed. The door remains discreet, catching portions of light that stretch through the tall living room windows, innocuous among the panels. It has been there for the last fifteen years of my life. So why do I suddenly hate having it at my back?

The kettle, heavy with water, thumps onto its stand. It will take exactly two minutes to boil. My favorite mug comes out of the dishwasher, and I drop a lemongrass-and-ginger tea bag into it.

The only part of this routine that ever changes is the sun's angle. Right now, it's low, the last traces struggling over my neighbors' roofs and through scattered trees to reach my yard. Winter is grudgingly giving way to spring, and its angle will rise every day for the next few months.

Normally I lean my forearms on the edge of the sink and stare at my yard for a minute and a half of meditation as I wait for the kettle, but tonight has something else on the schedule. Bandages and antiseptic come down from the cupboard above the stove, and I line them up on the laminate counter.

It only takes a second to unpick the safety pin holding the bandage around my finger. I unravel it gingerly. The finger is stiff and the bandages carry blots of red, and I'm surprised I made it through work without more trouble.

The gash runs from my first knuckle to the second. It's unlike the clean cuts that come from a kitchen knife or poorly handled scalpel. It's ragged, its depth irregular. It makes me think of a cat scratch, only deeper. If I bend the finger too far, I am liable to split it open and see tendons. Possibly even bone.

It might be worth visiting the ER, but not tonight. Everything about the past day feels too much like a dream. Tonight, I need to be alone to allow my thoughts to settle, to reconcile, to comprehend. And so I unscrew the cap from the bottle of antiseptic. The kettle cuts out, and in the abrupt silence following its furious rumbling, I can hear my breathing, too fast and too shallow.

The cut has fused over with dried blood, but I still clean its edges. Then I began weaving the fresh bandage around it, laying it carefully, binding it tight enough to hold the skin together.

Something moves in my yard. I'm a second too late to lift my head. The view through my kitchen window is serene; grass, due for a cut, sways. The old oak's trunk is unyielding, though its branches dance readily. The ceramic bird feeder, suspended from the closest branch, hosts two sparrows. They bicker over the seeds.

I'm certain the motion came from something larger. A figure the size of a man, or close to it. I stay still for another minute, waiting, but I can't be sure that I didn't just see a sliding shadow, so when nothing else moves I put my head back down to finish the bandages.

The safety pin seals the wrap. I stretch my arm out and move my fingers experimentally. As long as I don't try to bend the index, I don't feel much from it. That's good. A compromised hand would make it hard to do my job as an archivist at the natural history museum, and it's been years since I took a day off.

I'm not so egocentric that I would refuse to *ever* call in sick, but it would still irk me to break my streak. My fingers need to stay nimble for the labeling, transferring, and copious documenting that consumes the largest portion of my workday. The artifacts I work with are delicate. I can't risk fumbling them.

Steam still rises from the kettle's spout, but I don't like pouring it unless it's just finished boiling. I switch it on a second time.

The rumbles start quickly as the still-hot water jumps into action. My eyes close. The sound undulates, filled with pops and deeper grumbles and the faint hiss of escaping steam. And something else. Something that sounds like footsteps.

I let my eyes open, instinctively looking to the window, then behind myself and along the hallway. Flecks of dust twist through the bands of light, as though the air there was recently disturbed. The footsteps seem to be growing louder, but they're masked by the kettle, its own array of sounds growing to a fever pitch as it trembles on its base.

Then the kettle's switch flicks off, and the rumbles start to fade. The sound that might be footsteps lasts for perhaps a half second longer, then it, too, is gone. I am left staring along an empty hallway as my pulse throbs in my bandaged finger.

I pour the water. The tea bag spins, pale color flooding out of it, and I pull it out before it can leech too much. I roll my head, eyes half-closed as I stretch out my neck muscles, then pick up the mug and carry it from the kitchen. The tea will need time to cool, but I want to have it with me.

The stairwell has two light switches, one at the top and one at the base, but the lower switch stopped working two years ago and I have yet to call an electrician to repair it. Habit is an unyielding pressure, and once established, it is hard to deny. I'm in the habit of climbing the stairwell in the dark. It's a treacherous walk that I should fear more.

I take the stairs lightly, holding the banister for the first four before it turns at an angle and disappears into the walls. The steps are solid but old, and their wood strains under my footfalls, deep sighs that I'm compelled to echo.

Then I emerge from the cavern into the second-floor hallway. The doors are all sealed. I run my tongue across the back of my teeth as I take the sight in. I like to leave the bathroom door open to circulate air and ward off the always-present mold, and my bedroom door was left open against my will the previous night.

I adjust the angle of my mug. Heat seeps into the handle, warming my fingers, and I know the drink is hot enough to scald if thrown at an unwanted presence.

The bathroom door opens at my touch. Everything is where I left it: the towel on its rack, the bath mat, even the angle of my toothbrush in its mug. No amount of cleaning can improve the bathroom's impression of dingy neglect. It will remain this way until it is eventually remodeled and the heaviness of age is physically chiseled out of it.

The carpet cushions my feet as I pass the linen closet and stop at my bedroom door. Its handle creaks when I turn it.

The sheets on my bed are lightly rumpled. The corner is pulled back from where I crept out of it. In daylight, the quilt has returned to its more soothing form: it displays Aesop's fables. Rabbits and storks, foxes and grasshoppers, twisting and dancing as they tell their stories.

The phone on my desk appears normal, except the receiver sits in the cradle. I approach the closet. Its doors are also closed. I tug on them, and they swing outward easily, exposing rows of clothing arranged by season.

I place my mug on the desk's coaster. Slightly embarrassed, I hesitate, then crouch to look under my bed. There are no surprises, only the pair of soft shoes I store there, which I pull out and swap for the low heels I've been wearing all day.

My outfit, business casual and all black, came from my car: a uniform stored there in case I need fresh clothes at short notice. I switch out of it, transitioning from long skirt and knit jacket and into my comfortable evening clothes. As I pull the ibis clip out of my hair and tie it into a messy bun, I begin to feel slightly more human.

Something happened last night. It was real, even if the evidence is limited.

My house is too quiet. Peace is something I normally relish, but today it's more—not an island of solitude, but an ocean of it, enough to drown in.

I turn to the small black radio on my bedside table. It covers me in white noise on the nights my eyes won't stay closed. I turn it on and push the volume up. Music fills the room and I breathe deeply, the ache in my mind soothed by the thundering drums and furious guitar strains. If I asked my coworkers to guess what music appealed to me, most would probably suggest classical or jazz. I doubt any would consider hard rock, but as the beats envelop me, I am truly calm for the first time today.

The volume is high enough that I will hear it downstairs. I take up my cup of tea, which is not quite cool enough to drink but only a few minutes away, and return to the hall. The upper level holds two other bedrooms and a rumpus room, and I look inside them all. The doors were left closed, as they should be, and I cannot see any sign that they were disturbed.

The dark tunnel carries me downstairs. I turn into the kitchen and set about completing my routine: a microwave dinner from the freezer, heated for thirty seconds longer than the packaging recommends. Two foil packets come out of a drawer. One gives up a pain tablet to ward off the headache I feel prickling at the back of my skull, and the second gives a little pink disk. An antidepressant for anxiety. Both go onto the counter.

A folder of paperwork—none of it necessary from a professional view, but necessary for my own peace of mind—spreads out over the kitchen counter. The microwave beeps. I retrieve dinner and a fork, then pull up my favored chair, identical to the other three that make up the set sans the scuff marks and heavy wearing around its feet and cushion, and take my position at the kitchen table, ready to sink into the evening.

Only, I can't. My mug is missing. I must have forgotten it when I went upstairs.

Music drifts through the ceiling, too muffled for me to catch much other than the beat. I consider forgoing the tea entirely, then reluctantly scrape my chair out from the table.

The sun has set. Even with all of my delays, that seems too early. As I follow the hallway back toward the stairs, I swing past the living room to check the clock. Large white couches run along one wall and create a divide through the room's center, trapping a coffee table between them. Fifteen years in the sun has sucked some of the brightness out of their upholstery, but other than that, they could be brand-new.

The wall only bears two decorations: the simple black-and-white clock and the patchwork quilt suspended above the seating. The clock says it's six fifteen. I barely look at it, though, because the quilt has drawn my focus, the way it always does. Bittersweet sensations fill me, heavy on the bitterness. The sweet becomes harder to find every year.

Maybe it's time to take the quilt down. I've been thinking along that line for some time, but I never touch it. It took me hundreds of hours to sew, by far the largest project I ever took on, and I refuse to let the work go to waste.

I'm ready to turn away when I notice an abnormality. One of the couches has a subtle indent in its cushion. As though someone had been sitting there until just a moment ago. I picture the intruder from the night before hunched there, its shaggy hair sticking to the couch's back, its round eyes watching me walk through my home.

The indent seems to be growing shallower as the foam rises back to its normal state. I approach and place my hand on the fabric, half expecting to find warmth.

If anything, the seat feels *colder*.

My hand snaps back. My thumb moves in a small circle over the edge of the bandage as I look from the archway leading to the hall to the archway leading to the kitchen.

Music continues to flow from upstairs, but my favored drumbeats are missing. I tilt my head toward the sound as a waltz plays, slow and creeping. Under the melody is another noise: my bedroom door, creaking as it draws open.

# 3
# PAST THE BARRIER

I MAKE IT TO THE HALLWAY. WITH MY BACK TO THE WALL, I LIFT the flap on my satchel and retrieve my cell phone. The light comes on when I press the power button, but then immediately fades, the battery drained. The charging cable is tied in a tidy loop on the side table, near my keys, and I plug it in, whispering urgent pleas to it.

The waltz swells. Its lilting melody feels offbeat, its notes falling out of tune and starting to jumble, the dissonance growing worse. The wind picks up as though in response. I can picture the bushes and trees writhing outside, scratching at the other side of the front door.

My phone's screen is blank, even when I press the power button. I pull the charging cable out and then force it back in. Normally this causes the screen to light up, but not tonight.

There are footsteps above me. Heavy, slow, and dragging, they bleed through the layers of wood and carpet to paint a map of the intruder's path through my bedroom and into the hallway.

When I lean forward, I can see the base of the stairs that emerges from the smothering walls. I don't want it to come down those stairs. Instead, it turns, and the laborious footfalls track deeper into my home, progressing into the rear bedroom.

I fight with my phone again, urging it to come to life, even if just for a moment. When that fails, I turn to the door at my back. It's dark out, the moon compressed under suffocating clouds, the streets empty.

Going out there feels too much like abandoning my house, a tacit acceptance that the presence has more right to the building than I do. But I cannot face it alone. I need to call someone. And there is only one other phone in the building.

Hesitantly, I move toward the stairs. The intruder went into the deepest room, farthest from the front door. As long as I'm careful…

My feet are silent as I enter the stairwell, and I thank my luck that I changed shoes when I had the opportunity. As I turn the corner and enter the black tunnel, I watch the space at the top of the stairs. The off-white ceiling is barely visible in the low light.

Another step, followed by one more. I breathe through my mouth, my left hand hovering an inch from the wall as the upper hallway is revealed in slivers. The doors are closed and the space drowns in its own shadows.

The waltz is growing faster, the mistimed beats loud enough to drown out whatever small noises I might make. I take the final three stairs. The door at the end of the hallway is shut, hiding the thing inside.

The music is so loud, though, that the intruder could have moved quietly if it wanted to. Would I have heard it leave its room?

For a moment, I stay at the top of the stairs, my back exposed to the tunnel that plunges behind me. The light switch is to my left, and if I wanted, I could light the stairwell and clear the desaturation that drips from my home. But that would alert the intruder—the presence—whatever this unnatural force is. The end room, the room I hope it still occupies, is dark; it would notice if light came through beneath the door.

The music is cresting. It will only disguise me for a limited amount of time. I lurch forward, feet barely leaving indents in the carpet as I pass by the bathroom and near my own door. The handle clicks as I turn it, and I clench my teeth, my eyes fixed on the distant room to my left.

Opening my door causes sound to wash over me. The music is no louder than what I set the radio to myself, but it's unpleasantly thick. Static fills the infrequent gaps between beats. It travels through my chest cavity, using my lungs as an echo chamber.

The room looks untouched. My spare work outfit is folded at the foot of the bed, ready to be taken down to the car tomorrow. The closet doors are closed. The room seems empty.

I cross to the phone as the waltz struggles through its final bars. The receiver is cold against my ear. I turn the dial, counting each number, aiming for speed over silence. I can barely hear the unspooling of the dial as it returns home through the music.

Fingers tap at my bedroom window, and I know they are only dead branches but they still make me feel besieged.

The song crumbles under its own weight. Now only static is left. I had assumed the radio's channel had been changed, but there is no host, no following tune, no sound at all except for the crackle and hiss of dead air.

"Operator, what is your emergency?"

"Twenty-five Larch Tree Lane." Her question hangs ignored, but I don't know how long I have. "There is someone in my home."

The door of the final bedroom is rarely used and its hinges are quiet, but I still sense it open. I shy back, my thighs bumping the desk, my ear aching from how hard I press the metal to it. A heavy thump sounds as the intruder emerges. Like a mallet beating the carpet. It's followed by another, and I know there can only be a few more before it's at my threshold.

"Please send help," I say, and drop the receiver.

There should be enough time to run past the presence, to fly down the stairs, to get outside. I'm at the door in three long steps. But the intruder's pace elongates, too. I feel the floor shiver with each beat, and the hallway is suddenly so much shorter than I had believed. The presence is there, right outside, just around the corner, and I no longer have time.

Something reaches into the opening. I think I see skin, but it is gray in the shadows, its nails long, its flesh buckled and puckered.

I grab for the open door and force it forward. It slams into the frame, a gunshot that reverberates in my ears, and I put my shoulder against the wood.

The only sounds come from my gasping breaths and the oak branches outside my window. The former are fighting through my too-narrow throat. The latter scratch at my walls, clawing, picking at the gutters and the roofing.

The doorknob twitches. Turns. Metal scrapes upon metal. My weight is leaned into the door, but I use my right hand to hold the handle still. Blots of red appear through the bandage as the skin splits. The handle twitches against my palm, then falls still again.

The radio is silent now. No music and no static, though I can see a red light on its surface indicating that it is still turned on. The side of my head rests against the wood, sweat making the surface damp. I do not dare let go of the handle.

Something moves at the base of the door. Fingers, reaching under, exploring, scratching. I shuffle my feet away, putting my body at an angle to maintain pressure on the surface. The fingers feel along the space and then withdraw.

The idea that the intruder is feigning defeat, that it can easily get inside once it tires of our game, digs at me. I brace against the door with all of my strength, even knowing that it is still not enough. The phone's handset hangs by its cord. I hope the operator took down my address. I hope she takes my call seriously.

Pressure rests against the door's other side. It is subtle but undeniable, and I know the intruder is only separated from me by inches of wood. The smell begins to register. It sticks to my tongue: dust and old fabric and the intangible taste that I still cannot name.

Then it speaks. The word is stilted, every syllable corrupted, as it mimics a human voice. "Hel-lo."

What kind of throat would be needed to butcher speech so badly? It is baritone, interspersed with crackles of air moving through damp flesh. Like the recording of something long dead.

The door handle twitches, and I know it is holding on to the other side. Its throat makes another noise. A dry cough or perhaps something like laughter, then once more: "Hello." A pause. "Hello."

Does it expect me to answer? My mouth is parched, my head pounding, and even though the radio emits no noise, I feel as though its vibrations still travel through me.

"Hello." Again, the dry, hacking noise. "Hel-lo…"

The handle twitches. The pressure disappears.

Then it moves away, its path toward the stairs measured in its weighted footfalls. I feel like I have the flu, clammy, my cotton shirt plastered to my back and strands of hair adhering to my neck. My bedroom window, partially open, shudders under gusts of wind.

I lose the ability to hear the intruder somewhere near the stairs. If it was moving to the lower level, the old floorboards do not betray it.

Has it stopped? Is it moving silently? Impossible to tell. My shoulder is sore. I'm growing increasingly cold as my perspiration dries. If I had any confidence about where the intruder is positioned, I would close the window or find a warmer jacket in my closet. My hand aches, my back aches, the muscles held in an unnatural position for too long.

A rattling noise spreads through the house. It sounds like my window being jolted in its frame, but it comes from the wrong location. From below. Metal shuddering, jittering. It grows louder. *Angrier.* And I suddenly understand where it's coming from.

The door under the stairs. The one I had overlooked for years, the one I had been suspicious of earlier. The intruder is rattling the handle, trying to get it to open. Why?

I release the handle and slide my back down the door until I sit on the floor. Even though I now know where the intruder is, I cannot bring myself to leave the barrier undefended. The night is growing deeper. As the wind picks up and batters the branches outside my room, the radio replies, spitting out a session of pops before returning to silence. And the presence continues to rattle the downstairs door, fighting against the lock, trying again and again to open it.

My knees are pulled up against my chest. My head lolls forward to rest on them, exhaustion dragging on my eyelids. I still shiver, but I am too weary to fixate on the cold any longer.

Then my gate issues its warning. Someone has passed the barrier.

The intruder hears. It ceases work on the under-stairs door. I lift my head, my breath suspended, as I stare at the dangling receiver.

Knuckles hit the outside of my front door in three sharp raps. I pull myself to uncertain feet. The intruder is still out there, somewhere between me and the front door, and it has become alarmingly quiet. I feel a second of dread that this is a trap, that the malformed being is waiting for me to leave my room. There is no rebuttal for that possibility, no comfort, so I force the door open and step through before my doubts can cluster any more thickly.

The hallway's shaded depths have intensified. I reach a hand ahead of myself. It will be my only warning if something stands in my path. As I move toward the stairs, eyes unfocused into the black, I let my innate sense of the building judge the distance to the stairs. I'm less than an inch off; my right foot slides forward until it finds the edge of the top step.

Three sharp knocks repeat. My movements become faster as I race the shadows to the lower floor. I'm certain I turned on the hallway light when I arrived home, as I do every evening, but now the only source of light comes from the kitchen. Instinctively I glance toward it and catch sight of the hallway door. It is still closed.

I hit the switch to bring the entryway into relief. Then, pulling my jacket tighter around my chest and holding it there to disguise how unsteady my hands are, I lean close to the peephole. The fish-eye lens distorts two uniformed figures. I try to steady my nerves as I count to three, then flick the lock and open the door.

The officers are facing the street, watching cars traverse the path, and take a second to turn to me. They are both tall: one middle-aged, a peppery mustache holding up sagging cheeks. The other is young, his uniform immaculate and the right side of his face smattered with acne scars. Their smiles are disconnected, friendly but cautiously so.

"Evening, ma'am. How are you tonight?"

The older one addresses me, but he's not really looking at me; he gazes over my head, along the hallway, trying to read the environment beyond. I step to one side, tacitly inviting them in. "Thanks for coming. I think... I mean, I heard and saw—"

"We got a call about a possible disturbance." He continues to gaze into the house, not moving from the entryway, his smiling gray eyes shifting from the living room archway to the lit kitchen, and I sense that his wariness is more than mistrust built from having to enter an unfamiliar environment.

I force myself to lower my arms from where I hug my chest, to avoid looking so defensive. "There's something in my house. It was here last night, too. I don't know what. I wasn't able to see it clearly."

"Huh. Mind if we have a look around?"

"Please." I've left the entryway open, but they still hesitate before stepping inside.

The younger one pulls his hat off and drags his fingers through his hair. "Moved in recently, did you?"

"Ah...no." His tone is pleasant, as though we're old friends catching up, but I still feel uncomfortable correcting him. "I've lived here for fifteen years now."

He nods, leaning through the living room archway as his

companion does the same for the dining room. "It's a good neighborhood. Quiet. Low crime rates."

Is he implying that I must be lying about the stranger in my home? A sense of defensiveness emerges, but I contain it, knowing it won't do any good to argue with my allies. "I can show you where I saw the intruder. It was trying to get into the closet here, but the door's locked. It also came into my bedroom upstairs. I probably should have called you earlier, but—"

They both glance at the under-stairs door but continue along the hallway, toward the kitchen. I follow, feeling unpleasantly out of control.

We step from the wood floor to the tiled kitchen. The microwave dinner is still on the counter, cold, beside my stack of paperwork. The defensiveness morphs into humiliation. What must I look like? Wearing baggy clothes, a frozen meal for dinner, my hair shaken out of its bun by the night's exertion.

The older officer asks, "D'you live here alone, love?"

I'm a *love* now. Heat boils my insides. I pray they won't look at me, or they'll see the flaming color rising over my chest and face. I was able to contain the defensiveness, but this... I have no chance of keeping the stiffness out of my voice. "Yes."

"Big house for just one person."

There's nothing malicious in the way he speaks; he's just trying to fill the silence, but I am burning up inside.

Two pills sit on the kitchen counter beside my dinner; one white, one pink, they stand out against the mottled gray. There is no way the officers didn't notice them. The shame redoubles and I find myself paralyzed. They are only a painkiller and antianxiety medication, both commonplace and entirely legal, but they send an implication. I want to swipe them off the counter and shove them into my pocket where they cannot be scrutinized, but what would *that* look like to two officers?

I'm spiraling. I need to take control of what's happening, drag the situation back onto its tracks.

I cross the kitchen and pick up the tablets, then fill a glass at the sink. I swallow them as casually as I can, watching their faces, silently challenging them to ask. They pretend they don't see. The younger officer looks into the laundry room, then rocks back onto his heels, exhaling slowly.

"Let me show you where I saw the intruder." I place the glass back onto the draining board with a firm click and stride past the officers. "Upstairs first. Then, if you have a way to open locked doors, I'd like to see inside the door in the hallway. I haven't been able to open it myself."

They don't immediately follow. I wait at the base of the stairs as they circle back through the dining room. As I begin climbing, they share a look that they probably thought I wouldn't see. It's bemused, lightly entertained but also concerned. I have nothing to be ashamed about, but shame rises regardless, and I speak too loudly, trying to drown out my own fears. "It's possible they left through the kitchen door when you arrived. What do we do in that instance? Do I file a report? Can someone patrol the street through the rest of the night?"

"Do you have any family that lives nearby, love?" the older officer asks.

"No." The word is thick with seething frustration poorly contained. I reach the top of the stairs and again have to wait as they follow with painstaking slowness. I show them to my room, but they only explore it glancingly before moving further along the hallway.

"They're not here any longer," I'm forced to admit, "but someone was inside my house barely twenty minutes ago. What are we going to do?"

The older officer is looking into the farthest bedroom, spending more than a minute gazing at the bare floorboards and two shelving units that carry a surplus of quilting material that doesn't fit in my workroom. His younger companion leans in the doorway, smiling in a mild, curious kind of way. When the older officer steps back out, his tongue darts out to moisten cracked lips, and he looks as though he's made up his mind about something.

"Thanks for your patience, ma'am. We just want to make sure you're safe."

"I appreciate it."

"Everything seems to be fine, so we'll leave you to it. You can always give us a call if there's any trouble, all right?"

"Oh." I try to smile, but my mouth is caught in an unnatural position. There's my answer: they think I made it up. There won't be a report; there won't be any help beyond their sympathetic, indulgent smiles. I wonder if I would have been taken more seriously if I'd answered the door in my work clothes, or if there had been a proper cooked dinner on the table.

They're already retreating downstairs, and I'm forced to follow, ashamed and angry and filled with an abrupt sense of abandonment. I could ask them to stay longer, ask if I can show them my bandaged finger, but I know that will sound like the begging mewls of a lonely soul. And that is not who I am. I stand as tall as I can, my stomach in knots of humiliation but my face the picture of calm, as I see them to the door. "Thank you for coming, regardless."

"All right, love. You have a good night." The older officer ambles toward their cruiser.

The younger lingers for just a second longer, then throws his parting words at me. "Stay safe, ma'am." He replaces his hat and then he, too, has left.

As the door closes, I feel as though I am collapsing. My body stays upright, my legs stiff and my neck long, but inside, the blocks that make up my identity are crumbling, sucked into a hole that is too small to fit any of them but can never be filled up, and parts of me are stripped away relentlessly until there is nothing left but an empty shell. Their opinion of me shouldn't matter, but telling myself that never helped before, and it doesn't help now.

I put my back to the door. The presence, the intruder, whatever it is—it may have left or it may still be in the house, and in a self-destructive fit, I wish it would come out of hiding and hurt me, really hurt me, just so that the officers will feel ashamed for leaving me alone.

Though, suddenly, I am not so sure their behavior was entirely influenced by me. They were slow to come inside and swift to leave. Their search was conducted not in the way I would expect someone to look for a threat, but as an exploration. They gazed at the walls, the furniture, as though the house itself were a curiosity.

And the whole time they were inside, not once did they make true eye contact with me.

I cross from the door to the living room. Any sign that someone might have sat in the lounges is now gone. The room has returned to its true state: an emotionless shrine, saved from utter starkness by the many-colored quilt displayed on the wall.

The younger officer's words return to me: "Moved in recently, did you?"

As though I were new to the area. To the building. As though I should know something about my respectable home if I had been here any length of time.

Was that possible? Do they know something about my address that I don't? I've been the sole resident for fifteen years, and in that time, I've never before needed to call the police—or had them visit unexpectedly. If my home has history, it would need to be older than my occupancy.

Maybe their curiosity didn't have to do with my home, but with my street. Even if something remarkable had happened in my neighborhood, I'm not likely to hear it. I get on well with my neighbors. They don't often make noise, and I don't disturb them. We haven't spoken in years. And the officers made that comment about it being a good suburb, as though I needed to be reassured about that.

Regardless, I'm alone again. The clock on the living room wall says it's eleven thirty. The officers left me barricaded in the upstairs bedroom for more than an hour before responding to my call.

I fetch the microwave dinner from the kitchen and, too famished to care about its tepid state, eat as I walk through my home.

It is a good building. A safe building. No matter what anyone else thinks, it is my home, and I trust it, and I will not leave it.

The police already accompanied me through its rooms, but I follow the same path once again. Closets are opened. The spaces under the beds are lit up by my flashlight. Every window is checked and latches are engaged, even on the second floor. I hope that the intruder truly did flee when the police arrived because I could very well be locking it inside with me.

Once every other room has been explored to its fullest, I return to the only door that does not obey my will. Standing in the stretch of the hallway that runs beside the stairs, facing the shadowed door with its bronze decorative handle, a pit of misgiving sticks in my stomach. As though I should not be here. As though I had better leave well enough alone.

The handle is cold to my touch. Colder, even, than the thick metal base of the flashlight I hold in my other hand. I don't need its light, but I appreciate its weight.

I turn the handle. It shifts a millimeter, then sticks. I give it more force, then try the opposite direction, then push and pull alternately, until I'm fully certain that the door is locked and the only way to get inside is if I somehow find the key.

The floor creaks as I lower myself onto it. First to my knees, and then, with a surreptitious glance around me to be sure that none of my neighbors can see me through the windows, I lie flat on my stomach, my cheek resting on the smooth wooden floor.

The gap beneath the door is narrow. I hold the flashlight next to my head, my face close enough to the barrier that my breath blows back at me, and I close one eye as I squint to see underneath.

Dust soaks in the light, tiny threads and orbs that glow, obscuring my view. The wooden floor continues past the door. Everything else is a blur. I cannot tell how large the space is or whether anything occupies it.

The flashlight stays on the floor as I rise and jog into the kitchen, pulling open drawers and cupboards as I search for something narrow and reflective. I settle on a butter knife and polish it on my jacket as I return to the hallway.

Back on my stomach, my eye as close to the door as I can manage, I slide the thin end of the butter knife underneath, holding the handle by two fingers as I attempt to manipulate it. It catches the flashlight's beam, and I angle it slightly to the side, so it won't blind my view. Then, twisting the handle, I catch jittering, fractured glimpses of the space beyond.

A sliver of the door. A sliver of the wall—I think. A solid, horizontal shape. Something ragged. It's too dark. Bursts of cold air burn my nose as I try to push the flashlight closer to the gap.

Something hits me—an emotion so real that it could have been a physical impact. The skin across my arms and back immediately stiffens into bumps. My heartbeat quickens to a pulsing, rushing torrent. It fills my ears, and my head feels tight and cold, restricted, and I have some horrible sense, the idea that I am not lying on my wooden hallway floor but am somewhere lonely, sitting abandoned in the dark, deaf and blind and mute.

With those sensations comes a certainty: I do not want to open this door. I do not want to see inside. Lying on the floor with my face pressed so close to the concealed room, the dread increases, each squeeze of my heart sending it deeper through my veins like poison.

I roll away. The knife is thrown aside, and it skitters, reflecting the house lights across the walls and ceiling in bursts. The flashlight is still facing the door, and I rush to turn it off. Then I keep moving, crawling backward until I hit a wall.

Ten feet separate me from the door. I wish it were more, but for the moment, it will be enough. As moisture returns to my mouth, I taste something awful: sickness lying thick across my tongue and like glue to my teeth. My skin is cold. Everything underneath is too hot. When the sensations collide, they burn.

I have never felt anything like that before, and I sit, skew-legged on the floor, for several minutes before I can put a name to the experience—the fear of imminent death.

I don't understand it, and I'm not certain that I want to. My pulse still races out of control. My throat is clogged, my head buzzes. When sensation returns to my legs, I lift myself onto them, then shuffle into the kitchen to put the knife on the draining board and wash my mouth out.

That door has been a part of my life for fifteen years. That thought should be comforting, but I want to retch. Earlier, I asked the police officers if they had a way to open it. I'm grateful they didn't. If they had, something terrible would have happened. It sounds outlandish, but as the thought settles into my mind, it rings true.

I must not open the door. I cannot afford the consequences.

My hands are still shaking, and I crinkle the foil wrapper of a second pain tablet as I try to open it. I fill a glass and swallow it. The intruder has made two appearances now in the span of two days. There is a good chance they will be back.

Whatever *they* are. I have a growing feeling that, even if the police had opened the under-stairs door, they would not have found anything. This—whatever *this* is—feels personal. No outside help can so much as touch it.

My head continues to ache. I press against the temples as the abhorrent idea forms that this might be so personal that it is *entirely* a product of me. A phantom conjured by my mind. My own personal jail, each brick built by my own hands.

My mind is still too clear for me to imagine I am losing it. But what other answers are there? Any label I try to apply to the intruder—monster, specter, phantom—falls away limply. My life has been built around defining and categorizing every minute item that passes my desk, but this is one discovery that so far refuses labels.

The flashlight is still in the hallway, and I pick it up as I gather supplies. Clean blankets from the upstairs linen closet. Pillows from my bed. As I carry them to the ground floor, I realize this will be the first time I haven't slept in the upstairs room since moving into my home.

My cell phone registers as fully charged. It and the flashlight go onto the coffee table, which I drag to butt against the side of my nest. I chose the couch in the center of the room. It puts my back toward the hallway, but it is a three-seater couch, and I need the leg space.

Blankets form a cocoon around my shoulders, but they only seem to trap the cold against my body. I sit as I wait for the whipped-up froth of feelings to subside to the level where I can sleep. My eyelids are already heavy, but they are the one part of my being that wants to cooperate.

If I'd thought to bring my journal, I could use it to expunge my thoughts, but I'm not willing to travel upstairs again when it is so late. Instead, I mouth the words I would want to write. A transient record of my wishes that the encounter with the officers had gone better. How I wish I didn't have to be so isolated tonight.

The patchwork quilt hangs opposite me. The imagery was designed to be a balm, but as I take it in, it only inflames. The white horse. The brambles that caused me so much angst to sew. The distant, silhouetted woman. Every corner I look at is more uncomfortable, and when I feel as though I cannot take another second of it, the doorknob rattles.

I rise, my pulse skipping, then redoubling, the blanket draped around my shoulders like a deposed ruler's cape. Metal jitters, biting into itself, biting into wood, as the *something* fights with the door under the stairs.

Earlier, trapped in the upstairs room, I had believed the intruder was trying to open the door. I was right, but not in the way I'd expected. The hallway is empty. The intruder isn't trying to get into the concealed room. They are trying to get *out*.

The cell phone is in my hand before I can even think my choices through. The police won't want to be called back. They'll take hours to respond, and even once they arrive, the intruder will simply fall silent again, and I will be torn between telling the officers to leave and asking them to open the concealed door, which I'm already certain *cannot* be opened under any circumstance.

Battered from indecision and feeling more alone than I have in a very long time, I break a promise to myself. The list of contacts in my phone is short: work colleagues, a few distant friends from my school years, and a number I was certain I would never call. Meg. My sister. I select it and hold the mobile against my ear.

The door shakes as the something on the other side tries to force it open.

"Hey! It's Meg!" Her voice is good. When she gets excited the pitch rises until it begins to squeak. She's always close to laughter. On that, I'm torn between fondness and frustration. It makes it impossible to touch on anything deeper than gossip. Telling her about my anxieties leads to her giggling uncontrollably. But right now, that girlish upbeat hype is everything I need. That's why it hurts so much when her voice is followed by her husband's.

"And Justin."

Then, two more in succession, speaking so fast that I cannot tell which is which. "And Kaitlyn!"

"And Ashleigh!"

"And baby Elliot," Meg says, giggles in her voice. "We're not here right now, so leave us a message, okay?"

I end the call. The clock's hands move toward two in the morning. Ashamed, I slink into my seat, back to the door, even though the handle continues to shudder. The blanket bunches around my throat as I hike it higher and pull my feet under myself to conserve warmth. A cup of milk tea, untouched, slowly cools on the coffee table beside the flashlight, and as I stare at the film that forms on the surface, I idly note that I never did find the original missing mug.

Sleep will not be visiting me that night, but I know I won't be begging off work. It will be a relief to escape the house once dawn comes. Until then, I can only sit with my back to the hallway, eyes unfocused, as the door rattles for hours upon hours.

# AS LONG AS IT IS NOT INSIDE MY HOME

A WEEK PASSES, AND EVERYTHING GROWS WORSE. I COULD ESCAPE the house during the day and lose myself in work, but by the time six o'clock struck, I was back in my home and forced to prepare for the upcoming vigil.

I stayed downstairs both Tuesday and Wednesday. My once shrine-like living room was converted to a temporary encampment. The phone charging cable tangled with lamps I'd scrounged from elsewhere in the building. A pack of earplugs from the first-aid cabinet lay unused. I was getting very little sleep, but I still preferred to have my senses unhampered in the deep dark hours of the night.

The curtains stay closed. It makes the living room feel like a cave, dim and smothering, no matter how many lamps I space around. It has to be that way, though. The windows look out across the street and I dread what my neighbors would think of me if they could see my situation.

The under-stairs door rattled each night. It wasn't constant, not like the assault I had endured on my first night downstairs, but once or twice an hour it would shudder, and I would watch it until the handle fell still again.

On Thursday I reclaimed my bedroom. The living room arrangement stayed the way it was, a refuge in case my journey upstairs turned too hostile. Sleep was fleeting. My door stayed closed, but I could hear *it* outside, pacing the hallway, back and forth, from the stairs to the farthest bedroom, sluggish and persistent, for hours.

Friday night saw it open my door. The time on my cell phone, clutched in both hands under the covers that I'd pulled to my chin, flashed as three fifteen in the morning. The intruder had been pacing the hall for more than an hour when it halted outside my room. My mobile died, betrayed by a battery that was supposed to still be three-quarters full. I only had a heartbeat to see the abruptly blank screen before my eyes were pulled to the door as it was dragged open in minuscule increments.

The something filled the gap, and ragged flecks of moonlight traced across a frame of long hair. Its eyes flashed. Perfectly round, enormous, like mirrors in a pit of black. They were fixed on me.

I held my lips open as I breathed through my mouth, and my teeth ached from the cold air. I was on my side, face toward the door, limbs a dead weight as I feigned sleep. With my back to the window, it shouldn't have been able to see that my eyes were open, but I worried it did regardless. That it had lost patience. That it would come for me at last.

But its tolerance held for another hour. It was still, so well hidden in the partially opened doorway, that I began to wonder if it had slipped away unseen. My body hurt from being kept so motionless. Eyes, dry and bleary, stung, but I held on, kept myself awake, kept my attention focused. And finally, as the barest hint of predawn light flushed over the distant trees, the something turned and left. A moment later it was back at the under-stairs doorway, rattling it once more.

Now, it is Saturday, and I am afraid our tenuous impasse must crumble. I will be in my home for the weekend. The intruder and I have struggled to endure each other for a single night; forty-eight hours must force our hands in one way or another.

I lean over the kitchen sink as the kettle boils. Outside, the great oak tree is a steadfast reminder of how little the world has changed. Birds still flit over the feeder. I am guilty of not filling it all week. Many parts of my routine have been neglected.

My body is on the verge of collapse. It has not had enough sleep. Prolonged stress has drained its endurance. I feel flimsy, like an origami human, an approximation of a full person that is almost entirely hollow.

Even though it is light out, I am not granted respite. Through the boiling kettle I hear the door rattle, just for a second, and close my eyes. A headache gnaws. It is not yet serious but threatens to become so. As the kettle switches off, I drag open the first-aid drawer and dispense a pain tablet.

I pour boiling water into my cup—not the cup I lost, but my

second favorite—and rub at the irritated inner corners of my eyes as I face my home.

It is devolving in response to my broken routine. Abandoned items are strewn about: empty boxes of bandages that went toward healing my finger, crumbs gathering on the counter, cloths used to wipe up a spilled drink and then left aside for the laundry. And everywhere, dust. I didn't expect it to build so fast in just a week, but it clings to the wood paneling, to the corners of the countertops, to the floor.

That is what my weekend will go toward, I decide. I will not sit, paralyzed, waiting for the something to make the first move. This is still my home. And I will carry on as normally as the situation will allow.

I swallow the pain tablet and set to work. Overdue laundry is thrown into the machine, given slightly more powder than it needs, and left to churn. Then I pull on gloves and begin scrubbing.

Things are slightly out of place on the kitchen counter. At first glance, I thought the clutter was my own doing, but as I move the salt and pepper shakers back into their designated space in the pantry, I realize I haven't touched them all week. An empty glass jar was moved from the upper cupboard into a lower one. I hold it gingerly, my mind faltering as I try to remember the last time I used it, then shove it back into is place.

The dining room, at first glance, appears to be untouched, and I run a cloth over the six-seater table and the chair tops to clear the growing sheen of gray. As I'm finishing, I realize the chairs were moved. I like to leave them pressed against the table; all of them are pulled out, some by an inch, some by more. A couple were left at an angle.

It's a minute change, but it makes me queasy. The intruder wasn't content to merely walk my halls and look in at my life. It has touched my possessions, examined them, moved them, claimed them for itself. I shove each chair back into its place.

In the living room, the lamps are missing. I had at least five two days before, when I left that temporary base to return to my bedroom. Two on the coffee table, one on the floor near the hallway, and the other two used to light the darkest corners of the room. Only one is left—one in the corner, perched on the end table. I used to keep a lamp there, but this is not the same one. This one belongs in the spare bedroom.

I unplug the smooth blue base and take it with me to the stairs. Something about the ceramic feels wrong. Prickles travel through every part of my skin that touches it, spreading along my hands and arms. As though the intruder has poisoned it simply with a touch.

As I enter the stairwell, a cool breeze glides over my skin. There should not be any drafts in my home. The only latch that has been unlocked since the encounters began is the front door, and it is currently sealed.

I turn the stairwell's corner and the gloom welcomes me, swallowing my form. A floorboard shifts on the ground floor. I halt. Below, an arch of light marks the entrance to this dark tunnel. What I can see of the hallway is bare, but as I hold my breath to listen, it occurs to me that I must be standing directly over the locked door.

The idea is followed by a wash of sickness. The noise below me might have been nothing, but I don't trust it. I back up the stairs, lamp clasped against my chest, facing the descent. Only a sliver of the hallway is still visible, but something moves across it. A shadow.

I back up another step, near the top of the stairs. Something cool and slick brushes against the back of my neck. A tremor rocks through me as an involuntary response takes hold. I tip forward, and the stairwell no longer looks like a familiar part of my home but like a cave burrowed into the earth, sucking me into its depths.

My shoulder hits the wall. The lamp falls from my hands and bounces, the heavy base striking a rhythm against every third step, spiraling, the cloth lampshade flying off, before it collides with the wall at the turn.

I am still upright. My fingers press against the wall, picking up tiny bumps in the white paint. My shoes are half-suspended over the edge of a step; the heels are planted, but the toes reach into air. I shuffle back onto stable ground before I turn.

Only four more steps remain between me and the upstairs hallway. When I went downstairs that morning, I opened the doors to let natural light brighten the space. The doors are all closed again, and my eyes ache as I try to read the layers of shadow.

Something long and thin divides my path at head height. I reach for it. Smooth fibers run between my hands as I identify waxed rope. It hangs in a wide arc, which I follow. One end loops loosely across the faulty light fixture. The other disappears down the hallway.

My pulse is a slow, sluggish thing. I should feel shock. Maybe fear. Instead, all I can muster is a low, steady frustration. My emotions are too drained for much beyond that. If the intruder intended the rope as a trap, it failed. If it exists as a warning, message received. But, right now, all I care about is restoring my home to some kind of normalcy.

I follow the steps down to retrieve the lamp. Part of the blue ceramic is scratched, but at least it didn't break. I fit the cloth cover back on as I return to the rope. The closest end is draped, not tied, and it comes down easily. I wrap it in loops around my forearm as I follow it into the hall. Its other end is attached to my bedroom door—again, not tied, but looped around it multiple times.

I don't own rope. And if I did, I would not choose this disconcerting synthetic version. The coil rests over my shoulder as I take the lamp back to the guest bedroom and arrange it so that the scuff faces the wall. I have a small shed in my yard. Hidden from my kitchen's view by the oak tree, its dark green steel walls contain neglected gardening implements and weed killer. The rope can go in there until I decide what to do with it. Just as long as it is not inside my home.

But first I scope through the bedrooms. The breeze in the stairwell is worrying me. I find its source in the deepest bedroom, the one at the end of the hall. Its window has been unlatched and pulled open, so air circulates through the screen. The chilled wind is an unexpected caress across my skin, but I don't hate it. My house has grown stuffy and heavy since I sealed it up.

The windowpane's runners are rarely used, and the glass shivers as it scrapes along its track. I pull it fully shut and engage the latch, then face the room.

A rope surrounds the doorway. It was placed there with care, flush with the wooden frame, so that it would be invisible to anyone walking under it. Like a trap. Hairs rise on the backs of my arms as I imagine it as a second doorway and that walking through it has signed some sort of contract. Like stepping into a ring of toadstools.

That's only superstitious paranoia. I snatch the rope down, flicking it so it comes free, and coil it around my arm to join its counterpart. It's made from the same material but is less than half the length.

What about this room has drawn the intruder's attention? I try to tell myself that it has been in every room, that every part of my house has been subjected to its bleak touch, but that's not entirely true. It has ventured into my bedroom and this bedroom, but not the other three.

There's nothing here that should warrant its curiosity. Only two shelves bearing sparse boxes of quilting scraps and old supplies. They're too good to be thrown out and the guilt of wastefulness haunts me, so they must now sit in a purgatory until they are aged and outdated enough to be disposed of without remorse.

The window overlooks the oak tree, like most of the others

in my home, through sheer virtue of the tree being too large to escape. The closet is empty, but I check it just to be sure. The carpet, rarely trodden on, is plush and clean. I can see no reason for the intruder to be lured here.

A sharp ring snaps my attention to the hallway. I tighten my hold on the ropes as I move toward the sound, following it to my bedroom. It repeats as I nudge my door open.

I've never heard my antique phone's ring before. I'd expected it to be high and shrill, like something out of the movies, but it's deep and slow and throaty. Like a phone that would belong in a funeral parlor, its tone is reservedly sad.

The secondhand store didn't tell me where my acquisition came from, and I'm struck by the idea that my premonition may not be far from the truth. Few businesses would be interested in maintaining an antique rotary unless the industry indulged in a sense of wistfulness for older eras. And it had been used more than a household would justify, based on how worn down the numbers are.

It rings a third time. It must be a telemarketer or a wrong number. Few people have my mobile number, and none have my landline. But I am loath to turn away. This may be the only human contact I have all weekend, and while two days to myself would normally be a welcome situation, the prolonged stress has made me yearn to hear someone else's voice. I cross to it and snatch up the handset before the fourth ring. "Hello?"

The line sounds off. Hollow. Like my every breath is bounced through a vast, empty chamber. I am not alone. When I hold my breath, the echoes continue, emanating from some other presence.

"Hello?" I press the earpiece against my skin, a part of me certain that I will be able to hear the other party if I just listen hard enough. Tiny pops and crackles, formed by bad wiring, infiltrate the void. The echoes grow heavier, more intense, and I have the sense that I am in a tunnel and something enormous is coming toward me out of the deep darkness.

I slam the handset down. It was very likely an autodial from a telemarketing firm, not worth holding on for. My lower lip aches and I realize I've been picking a loose layer of skin off with my teeth. I lick it to sooth the raw patch as I move back toward the stairs. This time, I press the switch to activate the bulb. I'll have no way to turn it off once I'm back on the ground floor, but on a day like today, I think a slightly inflated power bill will be worth having the light behind me.

Back downstairs, through the kitchen door, and into my backyard. The oak's boughs shade not just my home, but parts of my neighbors' as well.

Sparrows scatter at my presence. At certain times of the year, I'll see migratory birds lingering around the feeder, but only my regular customers stay through winter.

The air has a peculiar tang: the charge that accompanies an approaching storm. The sky currently only bears streaky gray clouds, but I will be surprised if it's not raining by nightfall.

A brick path leads me past the clothesline and around the oak, and I duck to avoid the lowest branches. The shed is only really large enough for a few shelves and boxes, but it suits me. The door hasn't seen much use since I hired someone to take care of the lawns. Its wheels scrape painfully in dirt-clogged runners. Earthy, musty smells flow through the gap on heated air. I use my foot to kick at the door's base until it shifts enough to let me through and step inside.

The shed's floor is paved with porous tiles, but they were placed with no foundation and became unstable as the earth shifted under them. The space is large enough that I can stand in its center and stretch my arms out in all directions without touching the metal walls, but only just. Empty pots and bags of dried dirt cluster to my left. Rolls of netting to my right. A metal shelf, tilted badly on uneven tiles, lists at the back wall, and the spaces on and around it are filled with oddments and tools, many that I can't even remember buying.

Standing in the strip of light that comes through the door, I'm acutely aware of how many sharp objects are stored in this shed. Rakes. Shovels. Shears. Hoes. A push mower, its blades rusted.

They all face me. Crusted with dried dirt or spiderwebs. Dusty. But underneath that shawl of neglect, they are still sharp. Still ready to bite into hard earth, to tear through branches and stems. Through *me*.

The shed is cramped, but a walkway runs through the debris to the back wall. There's space on the shelf for the ropes.

I move forward, stepping high to avoid the bag of fertilizer that spills over the walkway, and something snags at my jacket. It's the lawn aerator—a ring of long metal spikes on the end of a pole, fallen out of its usual position to catch at my clothing. I'm careful as I extract myself. The aerator should be relatively blunt, but as I slide the jacket's threads off, it pricks my finger.

Blinking furiously, I back toward the shelf. The thick air, heated and filled with dirt particles, rubs the inside of my throat until I'm having difficulty breathing. My sweaty hands leave a sheen of moisture on the coiled ropes as they go on top of a box of wires.

Standing at the shed's back wall, it's impossible not to notice how the light catches on every metal object. The hedge trimmer. The edger. When did I get so many tools? This shed has become a graveyard for rusting implements at least a decade overdue for being thrown out.

A smooth slithering noise pricks my nerves. I dart away from it and something knifelike digs into my back, just below my left shoulder blade. Slowly, without moving my body, I turn my head to look. Just a trowel, poking out from a shelf, pressed near my spine.

One of the ropes lies on the floor in front of my feet: the source of the slithering noise. I hadn't paid enough attention to where I put it, and it fell.

A deep sense of unease runs through me. This shed is too pressingly narrow. It's more of a coffin than a room, and the tightness is grinding at me, keying up my desperation to be free from it.

I keep tight control of myself as I bend to retrieve the rope. Clumps of dust and dead insects cling to it. Grime crusts my fingers as I curl it back into coils and reach to return it to the shelf. The hairs rise on the backs of my arms, the skin prickling in warning.

Something shifts behind me. Metal scrapes. Loud, straining to move over clogged runners. I turn too late. The door is already closed, and I am blind.

# SPOTS OF 5 CRIMSON

I take a breath. The air is dense. Dry. Too hot, in the smothering kind of way. It leaves my mouth as a groan, my lungs still starving for oxygen.

The shed door is closed, but the only way I can be sure is by the swarming darkness. I can no longer see the exit, though I have a vague sense of which direction it lies in.

A second breath passes into my lungs, and it is worse, scratching at the sensitive flesh. I am light-headed. The rope drops from my arm, but I no longer care. I need to get out. The door is close. Only a few paces. It doesn't matter what might be on the other side or what presence shut the door on me. I just need to be *out*.

One hand reaches ahead of me. I step forward. Something metallic brushes my forearm and I flinch. The skin stings as though the top layer were scraped off. I can't guess what I touched; I can only adjust my aim and hope there is nothing else in my way.

The soft, meaty flesh of my palm presses into a spike. My mouth is too dry to make much noise, but a whistle escapes as I retract my hand and feel a drop of hot blood run toward my wrist.

The touch was only light. None of the tools in my shed should have been sharp enough to cut so easily. I run my thumb across the stinging flesh.

A third breath makes me gag. I need to get out, but I fear moving any further. Something touches the outside of the shed. Light taps, like a finger running over the metal, picking at the roof. I lift my chin to follow the noise as it moves from my left side and over my head. As I trace its progress to the right, a blunt edge touches my cheek. Reflexes jerk me away from the contact, and something like a nail nicks my ear.

I become still, lungs straining as I pull the toxic air into them. The exit cannot be far. I no longer remember its direction. But the shed is too small to be lost in. No matter which direction I walk, I will find a wall soon.

My willpower balks at the idea of extending my hand again, but I do. I cannot see, but I can feel my fingers quiver as they quest into the black. My reach increases a fraction at a time until my arm is straight.

Then I extend my left leg. Something unyielding presses into my shin, sharp enough to cut my pants. I adjust, shuffling to the right, and try again, this time only moving my foot forward by two inches. Then my other foot, barely leaving the ground, holding my balance as I creep it forward. My arm stays stretched ahead of me, waiting for the touch of metal.

It hits my throat first. Three sharp lines, like the tines of a rake or overgrown nails. The scratch extends from my collarbone to my jawline, stinging. I lean my head back until I am past it, then I use my left hand to touch the cuts. Liquid beads across the stinging skin.

My lungs are bellows, expanding desperately, then pushing the air out without gaining any benefit. Spots dance in front of my eyes like static. My senses are heightened, every limb, every inch of skin feeling brutally vulnerable. I lower my head and wrap my left arm across it as protection. My eyes are of no use now. The extended hand moves in a slow arc, left to right, feeling the space ahead of me, and metal bites into its pinkie finger as it goes too far.

I clench my jacket sleeve between my teeth to keep silent. Surely I am nearly at the door. My left foot scrapes forward again, and a blade—the blade of the hedge trimmer, I think—touches my right shoulder. I shy away from it, but something sharp hits along my left side instead. There is no choice, not without backing away. I bite my sleeve harder and press forward. The blade cuts through my jacket and into my shoulder, but then I am past it, gasping in the lifeless air, dizzy and drowning.

Still, there is no wall. It is impossible to have walked this far and still be inside the shed. Now that I am conscious of it, it shouldn't be possible for the structure to be this dark either. It would need to be near watertight. It feels that way. My lungs are aching, my body sweating from a need for oxygen.

Something is still outside, tapping on my prison, fingertips beating across the metal. It comes from the sides and from above. Too many directions for it to be a single presence.

What else can I do but keep walking? Another step forward. Something nicks my fingers. Forward again. And again. There is sharpness at my hip, but I contort my body to escape it. Desperation grows and I move faster, reckless.

My shin hits an object, and I'm no longer able to save my balance. As the sensitive skin tears, I plunge forward.

Falling doesn't hurt, but I know the landing will. I am surrounded by sharpness: metal edges, metal tips, metal spikes. All wanting to taste my blood. All waiting for my mistake. I do not have enough of a voice to cry out. All I can do is raise both arms in front of my face, hoping to at least preserve the most vulnerable parts of my body.

I hit the ground roughly enough to roll. The anticipated cut of metal doesn't materialize. I lie on something firm and scratchy, and it takes me a second to withdraw my arms from my face.

There is light again. Not as bright as when I stepped into the shed, but enough. I lie on my grassy lawn. The shed is just behind me, and my foot is tangled over the runner between the open doors.

The fresh air overwhelms my strained lungs. Dizziness swells as pins and needles spread over my body.

The tapping noise continues, but it's no longer as loud. I tilt my head back. The sky is filled with dense steel-gray clouds as my predicted storm moves in. Thick raindrops pound across the metal, the grass, and my body. They're causing the prickling sensation.

I sit gingerly. Through the open door, the shed seems undisturbed. The metal tools lay scattered about, some leaning against walls, some braced over bags of soil or empty pots. The walkway is clear. The shelf at the back wall contains one rope; the second is tangled on the floor. I will not be returning to replace it.

The sky was clear when I entered the shed. I shouldn't have been inside for more than two or three minutes, but the weather shifted dramatically.

I'm loathe to doubt my own senses, but what happened in the shed couldn't have been real. Did I somehow fall asleep? The heat could have caused a nightmare, and the environment—surrounded by metal, rain tapping on the roof—could have played into a dream. And it's true that I am sleep deprived.

But I've never suffered from narcolepsy or any other kind of sleep disorder beyond occasional insomnia. I don't want to believe it's possible for me to walk into a shed and fall unconscious in the span of seconds.

The rain is growing heavier. It soaks into my hair and trickles over my skin. I'm exhausted. I drop my head to stare at my hands, draped loosely in my lap.

Red-tinted rainwater falls from my fingertips. I turn my hands over. There is the puncture mark in the meaty flesh of my palm. And a second cut on my little finger. They bleed readily. I touch my throat, and the skin stings. Carefully, I stand and see the grass beneath me is painted in spots of crimson, steadily being erased by the thickening rain.

I sigh and the noise it makes is somewhere between vindication and despair.

My kitchen door creaks as I push it open. The sunlight's angle tells me it is late afternoon, with perhaps an hour or two left until nightfall.

Drops of tinted water fall onto the floor, but there is not much I can do to stop it. I fetch dish towels from their drawer and use one to wring my hair. The rain sticks to the window as it hits, blurring my view of outside.

I cannot find a way to make my hands stop shaking, so I let them rattle as I fetch the bottle of antiseptic, pain tablets, and fresh bandages. Then I sit on a stool pulled up to the kitchen table as I clean each cut and cover it to the best of my ability.

The cuts across my hands are the worst. They are deep, and my fingers cramp when I try to bend them. I wrap them first, and color bleeds through the bandages before I can even move on to dressing my legs.

Bandage backings accumulate over the table. The cold invades my limbs, and I know I should change clothes but I don't feel ready to go upstairs. Instead, I run the remaining towels across my wet skin while the kettle heats.

As I sit at the kitchen stool and brush the discarded medical supplies into a heap, I feel small. Things are happening that are outside of my comprehension, and as smart as I like to think I am, I am not intelligent enough to parse this situation. And I have no one to ask for help.

My cell phone is plugged into the hallway charger. I find it and scroll to my sister's number as I return to the kitchen. The rain has begun to fall in earnest, huge drops that blur together to wash away the layers of grime coating the world. Both the rain's noise and the rumble of my kettle fall into the background as I listen to the mobile ring.

Meg's voice mail greets me, and I deflate. It is Saturday, I reason. She is likely out with her family or visiting friends. I wonder if she even heard her phone ring. Or whether she took her phone out of her bag, saw my name flash up, and pressed the button to ignore.

The idea needles into me as the voice mail concludes with a beep. It's suddenly hard to find my voice.

"Hey. It's me. Leigh. It's been a while." I'm floundering. I want to tell her about what's happening, tell her I need help, but I can't sound clingy. "You can give me a call back if you want. It's not urgent. I hope you're well."

I end the call and drop the phone onto the table. The kettle has boiled, steam rising in contradictory angles to the rain on the other side of the glass, and I just stare at it for a moment. My body is heavy. I need sleep. I need a friend. Both needs will likely go unanswered. I pour my tea and wrap my hands around the warm mug, shivering as damp hair and damp clothes cling to me.

Across the kitchen are the chopping boards and knife block, next to the electric stove. My pulse quickens. One of the knives is missing. The smallest blade from the left-most slot, the one I use for fiddly tasks. I can't remember the last time I used it. Not this week, certainly; this week has been a blur of microwave meals and hastily chosen snacks. It can't be in the dishwasher. It has been taken, and the implications that follow are not good for my mental state.

Very few things are trustworthy, no matter how much they would like me to rely on them. My job feels stable: I have worked there for more than a decade, earning raises and performing my duties to the best of my ability, but even that could be pulled out from under me if the economy were to stumble. My home always used to feel safe—it was my sanctuary, my nest. But as this last week has shown, even that was not immutable.

There is only one thing I can rely on: myself. At least I have that. And now, I must ask more from my body than I want to give simply because no one else is in a position to do what needs to be done. Not my sister, not the police. It must be me.

I'm past questioning whether this is really happening. It is. My body is a tapestry of proof. Multiple cuts across my legs and hips ache as I stand. The pain tablets will still need some time to kick in, but afternoon moves toward evening and the storm is growing worse. I need to make preparations while there is still time.

Since the smallest knife from the block is missing, I take the second blade; it's the length of my hand but it still fits into my back pocket. There will be a confrontation between myself and the intruder. That was clear from the morning's outset, and as the weather grows thick, I sense that we must come to a confrontation sooner than I'd wanted. But I can at least make it on my terms.

I'd passed the stairs just minutes before to pick up my phone, but now a coil of rope runs across the banister. Slippery and white, it is hard to miss against the dark wood. I drag it free, wrap it into a loop, and throw it to the ground.

Then, up the stairs, and beneath the light that I know I left on. Darkness clings to the second floor. I switch the lights back on as I pass them: the stairs, the bathroom, the hallway light, and then, at last, my bedroom.

The wind has more power on the second floor. It shakes the windows' panes. The sound is joined by pops and hisses from the radio. I cross to it, pull out the plastic tab from its battery compartment, and knock the two AAs out. The abrupt quiet is merciful. I tuck the batteries into my accessories drawer, where I hope the intruder will not easily find them.

Then, fresh clothes come out of the closet. I like to dress up, but today my eye is trained for practicality more than style. Warm, breathable clothes, layers with elastane woven into them so they will stretch should I need to run or crawl. Nothing that can be snagged. Dark colors. I change, throwing the damp outfit into the hamper to be dealt with later.

As I pull a plum sweater over my wet hair, a hissing, popping sound breaks through.

I shake my hair out of the collar's grip and pick up the radio. The batteries are still missing, but that does not stop its noise.

Lightning blooms across the sky. Shards of it glance through my window and streak across the walls. I approach the desk as the thunder engulfs me and look outside.

A sharp wind drives the rain at an angle. It splatters across the glass, the droplets racing for the lower sill in a frenzy, their trails twisting over each other. Black clouds absorb the smeared residue of a setting sun. Within minutes, the outside world will be dark.

The grass ripples in the wind, forming waves like a body of water. The oak has seen many decades of storms, but the aged wood creaks under the onslaught, and it strikes me as sounding like an elderly woman, groaning as her bones cause her pain.

I wonder if I will sound like that one day. Wincing and crying out as I try to rise from my chair.

A line of water runs down the back of my neck, and for a second it is hard to remember that the house shelters me from the storm. I slide my arms into a jacket's sleeves and zip it up, but the layers are still not enough to warm me.

Lightning cuts across the sky, and I squint burning eyes. Something stands in my yard, in the middle of the rippling grass, just in front of the washing line, which rotates with abandon, shaded by the oak's straining branches.

I lean over the desk. The figure looks up at my window. Its hair is long and clumps of it lash against the wind. It is tall, arms resting at its sides, its back to the setting sun, and I cannot make out much more than its outline beyond the two round eyes that shine out of the gloom.

A screaming tone rises up from the desk. The antique phone

shivers as it calls for attention, and I step back from the overpowering noise. I don't trust the melancholy cries. I have no interest in knowing who is on the other side.

Fresh lightning floods the world, and this time the thunder follows so closely that it lines up with the phone's bleat. I lean over the desk again, my breath suspended.

The clothesline, agitated, spins faster. The figure is missing. I lean as close to the glass as I can manage, searching the ground directly below my window, and then I hear it: the distant but unmistakable whine of my kitchen door opening.

The phone rings a third time as I back away from the window. As the shrill tone fades, I hear footsteps. Slow and heavy, they move through my kitchen, past the scraps of medical supplies, into the hallway.

It saw me. It knows where I am. The phone screams, and I beg it to be quiet, to not drown out my hearing for as long as it does. By the time the tone fades, the footsteps are already on the stairs, rising, growing closer.

I touch the knife in my back pocket. The bedroom door is open, the hallway wall a blank canvas behind it, but I know it will not remain empty for long.

The rain feels as though it is directed at me, beating into the window at my back, the lightning painting me in harsh, desaturated light and distorting my room. The radio's hisses grow louder. The footsteps are in the hallway now, each one coming with enough force to shake the walls.

The phone screams. I wish I'd unplugged it. There is no time now. The something is almost here. I draw the knife out and hold it tight to my side, the sharp edge shaking against my thigh.

A weighted footstep comes from just beyond the edge of my door. My lungs ache. The ringing will not stop. One more heavy step, and the light above me flickers as the intruder enters my room.

# SALT

THE SOMETHING STANDS IN THE DOORWAY. I CAN'T SEE IT, BUT I know it's there. Its pungent scent surrounds me: dust and threadbare fabric and that something else that I cannot name. It breathes, and the inhale snags in its throat, wet and raspy and slow.

And I can feel it. Feel its eyes on me, its focus unwavering. Feel its presence, dominating, like its identity is a tangible thing that bleeds out from its form and stains the walls and floors around us.

The phone shrieks, a prolonged cry that goes unanswered. The bulb above us flickers again, and when it comes back, it is not as bright as it was before.

The intruder is there. I am certain of that. But I cannot see it.

My doorway appears empty. The hallway beyond is eggshell white, cast into shade until it seems almost purple. It holds on to shadows like stains, and I am convinced one of those shadows—the largest one—should not be there. The intruder's gaze is a weighted thing, pressing against me until the backs of my thighs bump into the table.

The phone's tone comes again, and I will go mad if it does not stop. Without taking my eyes from the doorway, I reach behind myself and lift the receiver. It seems too cold, and I flinch as it touches my ear.

The line is filled with the same hollow, hissing noise that comes from the radio. I refuse to speak first but hold it to my ear, my gaze unwavering from the doorway.

Sharp lightning cascades through the window, racing up the wall, sending dancing shadows fleeing into the corners. Thunder comes through the earpiece.

I still cannot see it, but I sense the intruder moving. Raising one arm. Reaching toward the light switch. My dry throat convulses as I try to swallow. The intruder moves slowly, challenging me, but I know better than to take the bait. And so it presses the switch. Lights die. Not just my bedroom light, but all of them—every lamp and bulb inside my home.

In the drowning depths of blackness, a voice comes through the crackling echoes of the phone line. *Its* voice: sick, twisted, unnatural. "Hello."

As dark as the room is, I believe it can still see me shake my head. I will not answer that hideous voice.

"Hello." A long pause, while the charge in the air thickens, stinging my skin. Then, again, "Hello. Hel-lo."

Lightning crests across us and paints the scene for one impossible second. The intruder is visible. It's no longer in the doorway but immediately in front of me, close enough that I could reach my fingers out and touch its gray skin. Round eyes absorb and reflect the light. As do its teeth. Many of them. Exposed in a grin.

I throw the phone receiver toward it and dart to one side. Thunder clouds my ears and I don't know if my projectile hit its mark; I only hear it snap against the desk's leg on rebound, as the cord drags it back toward its base. I raise my knife, holding it ahead of myself as I run, my head down. Something cold, like a burst of chilled wind, slices through my right-hand side, and I am left breathless. My shoulder hits the doorframe. I swing around it and race toward the stairs.

If there was any doubt left in me, it is now gone. This presence, this intruder into my life, is not natural.

Perhaps there is a word for it. A spirit. A supernatural being of some kind. I don't know that world well enough to label it, though I am certain it is something malevolent, something cruel, something that knows it will win this confrontation—and enjoys toying with its prey.

Whatever it is, it can hurt me. But it is not a flesh-and-blood human. And there, I hope, I have some kind of advantage.

I feel for the switch as I near the stairs. The mechanism clicks under my touch, but the bulb doesn't respond. I flip it up and back down again, but it has followed the path of the lower switch. Lightning splashes through the living room windows to illuminate the lowest steps, and I clench my teeth as I climb down.

At the bend in the stairwell, I look up. The something stands at the top of the tunnel, filling the archway, arms at its sides as it stares down at me.

I match its gaze. If it's hoping to frighten me out of my own home, it will be surprised by how resilient I can be...and how little I have to lose.

I hold my fingertips against the wall to guide myself until I find the entryway's light switch. It turns, but the lights stay off. Maybe the intruder is not wholly responsible. The storm could have tripped the power. It's worth trying to get it back on, even if going outside brings additional risk. My hope of getting through to dawn rests on having light.

Blind but familiar with my surroundings, I cross into the kitchen and turn into the laundry. I keep a crinkled blue raincoat on a hook by the door. A flashlight and spare batteries are stored in a drawer near the sink, and I feel through its contents until I find them. The flashlight flickers on, basting the off-white wall opposite with a sharp circle of gold. I pull the raincoat's hood up as I step through the kitchen door.

The storm is brutal as it snatches at me, making a mockery of my raincoat. I put my head down and cling close to the brick walls. A high wooden fence divides my property from my neighbor's, and my home stands close to it, creating a narrow channel leading toward the front yard. Water has already accumulated through the gravel, churning up mud that sticks to my shoes. I sweep the flashlight beam from the brick wall to the fence and back, and I hate how hard it is to see through the rain. Lightning breaks the sky and I taste it on my tongue.

A shrieking gust travels through the passageway, and my shoulder grates across the bricks as I try to maintain my balance. The meter box catches my flashlight beam, and I plant my stance wide as I pull the rusted metal hatch up.

The breaker was tripped after all. I hold the rain jacket's hood in place with one hand as I flick the switch with the other. As though in response, another flash of lightning floods the world. And I have the terrible sense that I am being watched.

I turn the flashlight along the passageway, first toward the backyard, then toward the front. Thunder comes so dense that I can no longer hear myself: not my breaths and not my heartbeats. I slam the meter box's hatch closed.

Despite flipping the breaker off and then on again, I cannot see any sign of light from my home. Not in the yard, and not from the windows on the second floor. I turn the flashlight off and squint against the rain. There are no lights in my neighbors' houses either. The storm took the suburb out.

Without the flashlight, I feel cut off from the world. I am adrift, tethered only to my home by the shoulder I press to the brick wall and the shoes that sink into the mud-clogged pebbles. The building and I float in a void; there are no neighbors, no street, and no cars. Just the house. Myself. And the intruder.

The sensation that I'm being watched is so vivid that I feel I am about to be sick. The flashlight comes back at my request, and as its circle of light catches across the tiles of the house next door, I begin to breathe again. I hunch against the cutting rain and gale-force winds as I stagger back into the rear yard. Spears of lightning arc behind the great oak, and its branches no longer seem majestic, but worn and fragile. As though it, too, fears this storm.

I move through the kitchen door and slam it closed. It may be able to form a barrier between myself and the rain, but I question how impenetrable it actually is. Rainwater pools across the kitchen floor, carrying leaves and insects borne in by the winds. The sounds are softened but not erased. I can still hear the wind. Still feel it at my back.

The rain jacket goes over the back of the nearest kitchen chair, where its drips will join those already invading my home. I swipe my sleeve across my face, which is saturated.

Power won't be restored until the storm abates. Perhaps not until tomorrow morning. There will be no lights tonight, save for my flashlight.

And I am trapped in this dark box until then. Not alone, though I wish I were.

My cell phone is still on the kitchen counter. It responds to my touch, but the power bar reads eight percent. It shouldn't be draining this fast; it was at ninety just a few hours before, when I unplugged it from the hallway.

It's enough for one call, though. Not a goodbye. The situation has not yet degenerated enough for me to consider leaving parting words. But I don't know exactly what the remainder of this night will bring, and there are some things I need to say in case future chances don't come as readily. I dial my sister's number. The flashlight picks out details from the hallway as I listen to the phone ring. The wood paneling that so neatly disguises the door I have grown to loathe. The archway to the living room. The edge of the stairs, where a loop of the white rope waits.

Meg's voice mail plays. This time, I'm grateful for it. I won't have to explain myself any more than I want. I move toward the living room as I wait for her family's voices to run through their routine. Standing in the archway, I pass the flashlight over the couches and the remains of my camp, and the circle of light touches the edge of the quilt as a tone tells me it is my turn to speak.

"Meg. It's Leigh again. I hope you got my earlier message."

The flashlight finds the goose hidden in the quilt, and I lower it before my throat can tighten too far.

"I've been thinking about you a lot these last few days. And I've been missing you. I'm sorry we stopped talking."

The impulse passes over me to debate the details—whose fault it was, who stopped talking first, whose transgressions were greater. But that will only pick open old wounds without actually providing answers. Because, I suspect, there *are* no answers. She would say it was my fault. I would say it was hers. And we would both believe ourselves to be correct.

But the last week, and today in particular, makes me realize just how petty that is. Does it matter if blame is never assigned? Will history remember the injustice if no one apologizes? We have both been punished through distance these last few years; does any more need to be meted out?

She may not feel the same way. She could very well ignore this call like she did the others. And I will have to live with that. But tonight, I would at least like to hear the voice of my oldest friend.

"I hope you're well. I hope the kids are behaving. There's a horrible storm tonight. It's probably not catching you in Metford, is it?" I lick my lips. "Are you still living in Metford? I know you wanted to move to a larger house—"

Metal grinds against metal, and I close my eyes. That noise has become so familiar that I don't need to look to know which handle is trying to turn.

"I just wanted to say that I love you, Meg. Always have. I hope we can talk more later."

I hang up. My phone has three percent battery left, but as I watch, it drops to two. I place it on the side table near the front door. There'll be no more use from it until power is restored. Then I drag my fingers through my hair, plastering back wet strands, as I face my home's hallway.

Because this is still my home. No matter what entity is trying to push me out.

I don't know much about hauntings, if this even truly is one. Questions stack as they outnumber answers. How ghosts are created. What causes them to latch on to buildings. Why my home in particular. And, most urgently, what it wants.

The way the police examined my home gave me the sense that something about it was a curiosity to them. If what I've gleaned from popular media is correct, ghosts are most likely created from violent or unexpected deaths. But I struggle to imagine someone dying in my home without me knowing about it. Especially not in the fifteen years I've called it home. It's possible one of the previous owners passed inside these rooms, but if this is their spirit, why did they remain dormant for so long? Did something happen to suddenly wake them? I scrape my mind for answers, but my life runs on routine, and I cannot recall any notable disruption to it. I took three weeks off over Christmas, as I always do. Since the break's end, I leave for work and return at the same times every day. The house hasn't been renovated since the second floor was added, before I moved in. Other than finding the under-stairs door, which happened after the entity's first appearance, the house has held no surprises for me in years.

Maybe it's not related to *my* home in particular. Is it possible one of my neighbors passed away within the last week? It would make sense for the police to be intrigued if they were summoned to a house next door to one they had attended just days before, especially if the death was notable.

But in that case, why would a spirit choose to invade my home over their own?

Ultimately, the entity's source isn't important. I simply need to know how to make it leave.

Memories stick in my mind: snatches of books and movies that talked about clearings or smudging or séances.

That's all outside my realm of knowledge, but I do remember salt being used in historical cases of suspected hauntings.

My pantry is kept well organized. The saltshaker seems insufficient, so I crouch to access the lowest shelves, where I store surpluses. As I reach between boxes of oats and flour, something delicate grazes the top of my hand. I pull back, wary, but the sensation could have come from shifting the cloth bandages strapped to my fingers. I duck my head to see into the shelf. Plain boxes and twist-tie-sealed bags form tidy lines. There's no sign of anything out of place.

I reach in again, and this time, I know it's not my imagination. The smallest sense of resistance forms against my fingers before breaking. I grab the material and pull it out.

My fist is filled with spiderwebs. Gray with dust, tacky and clumping. An involuntary noise leaves me. I grab the dish towel from the oven's door and scrub the cobwebs off.

How long have they been there? The flashlight beam glances between the boxes filling the lowest shelf before lighting the remaining strings of web in the back corners. Is this a sign of my negligence, or is it another symptom of the intruder's presence?

I use the towel to swipe the remaining cobwebs out and retrieve what I was looking for: a box of Himalayan rock salt. It's tinged pink from the minerals it's prized for, and I hope that won't cause problems. It's still salt at its core, but something about the concept of ghosts suggests that they care more about the ritual itself than science.

I put the flashlight between my teeth and hold it there as I pour salt into my open hand. How it's supposed to work isn't clear to me, but I believe it was used to bind presences and either keep them contained or refuse them entry. If there are rules for how to use it, I don't know them. I pour that first handful across the threshold of the kitchen door. It melts into the pool of water, but there's not much I can do about it without finding a mop. A second handful goes along the windowsill.

Wood creaks behind me. I turn to look over my shoulder, the flashlight still between my teeth, and catch the edge of the under-stairs door as it shivers. I wait, watching, until I believe it won't move again, then turn back to my task.

I draw salt lines across the laundry door and the archway from the kitchen to the dining room. As I skirt around the dining table to reach the hallway, a heavy footstep lands behind me. I turn. My flashlight picks up the simple drapes drawn across the windows. One of them shifts a fraction, and I imagine it was disturbed by a hand dragging across the fabric. There is no sign of the intruder, though, and no evidence that it is anything more than a draft of air.

I move into the hallway, drawing a line across the floor where the archway intersects my home. As I cross to the living room, my light catches on a foreign object resting on the coffee table. A candle, wide and short and dark blue, its wick unlit.

Lightning blinds me through the windows. The drapes are pulled back, exposing the glass, exposing *me*. With the world so dark, my flashlight is lighting up the room like a showcase, putting me on display for all of my neighbors. I cross to the windows in three long steps, salt box braced under one arm, and wrench the drapes closed.

The rolling thunder crescendos, and in its ebb, a hissing noise mars the stillness. The candle is lit. The wick quivers and darkens as the wax around it turns liquid. I take the flashlight from between my teeth and pan it over the room. Its ghostlike circle flits over surfaces and casts longs shadows. It catches on the quilt, and for a second, I imagine the cloth-rendered brambles are moving. I step closer. The hallway doorknob shudders, but its sound vanishes underneath thunder.

I catch motion in my periphery. Something large, moving along the hallway. It is gone before I can turn my light on it. My breathing is uneven, my extremities cold. The under-stairs door clatters, louder, seeming desperate.

My jaw aches from the pressure I've applied to it, and I force it loose as I bend over the candle. The pool of melted wax is widening, heated by and feeding the flame. I extinguish it with a puff. The thin strand of smoke spirals past me as I place the flashlight back between my teeth and reach for a fresh handful of salt.

Another line goes across the border of the living room and the hallway, and the lower floor is complete. I begin to climb the stairs, then stop. The doorknob to my right shudders, twitching, as something tries to turn it. I reach into the box and draw out a fistful of salt. The air is cold and grows colder as I approach the door. My skin feels electrified. Lightning encompasses my home, flashing through every gap in the curtains and under every door, and the thunder's reverberations run through my veins, vibrating my atoms, and I feel as though I am disintegrating. I loosen my fist and a cascade of pale salt pours free. It starts at the wall and I draw it out, pulling it into a curve, encircling the door, surrounding it. The handle shudders, louder, and the wood itself bows from pressure from the inside. I complete the circle at the wall, and as the last of the grains flick from my damp hold, a fist beats on the door. Once. Twice. Shaking the wood, sending tremors through the floor, as loud as the thunder.

My mouth is dry as I press my back to the wall opposite. The door is still. I can hear the rain again. Its melancholy tones blend into white noise, blanketing my home. The box of salt is running low, and I hope it wasn't foolish to spread it about my home. Perhaps I will have to face the coming week tormented by a restless spirit…and unsalted food.

The thought draws a wry smile, but my heart beats too quickly for me to laugh. The under-stairs door remains quiet. I watch it from the corner of my eye. It seems too easy that the salt barrier truly forced its silence; I expect it to shudder back to life, to dash my hopes, but as the seconds draw on, it begins to appear as it always was: a forgotten compartment. Nothing sinister, nothing malevolent. Simply a door that went unnoticed for too long.

I don't believe in half measures. There is enough salt to leave across the upstairs doorways, so I move the flashlight back into my hand and enter the stairwell. The circle of light undulates over each wooden step, highlighting the dust and fragments of dirt that avoided my cleaning efforts. I turn the corner and enter the darkest stretch of the climb, and as I raise my head, my steps falter.

In a house with no lights and no power, the upstairs hall is lit in flickering gold.

# THIS HALLWAY IS NOT MINE

I RUN MY TONGUE ACROSS MY LOWER LIP. IT IS DRY AND THE SKIN forms cracked plateaus, as though the salt I have been applying was absorbed into my own body.

Fifteen steps separate me from the second-floor hall. A hall that should be dark. I hold the flashlight at my side, bulb directed at my feet, but the off-white paint above me shimmers. It's cast in a golden hue. Splashes of red rise over certain sections, and although I am too low to see the source of the light, the way it waxes and quivers gives me a clue to its origin.

The box of salt is a poor comfort, but I hold it close to my chest as I climb. As the glow spreads across me, the outside noises become distant, the thunder and pounding rain fading until they seem to belong to another world. Only a sense of the gale remains. I feel it dragging at my house, as though my own bones are being assaulted.

Another step up, and the second floor comes into view. Side tables are placed along the walls. On them are candles, many made of plain wax, but some colored, and others held inside red-tinted jars with open lids. They light the hall less than the bulbs in the ceiling could have, and with less precision.

The wooden tables look old. Whorls and lines decorate the legs, some carrying the same floral patterns as the doorknobs. Dust covers them—more than mere complacency could account for. These are surfaces that have not seen a human's attention in years.

They carry more than just candles. Trinkets cluster over them. Tiny porcelain figures, painstakingly painted. Cherubs. Cats. Birds.

And there are photos. Not just on the tables, but framed along the wall as well. My flashlight conflicts with the candles too much, so I turn it off and push it into my pocket as I near a wood-framed picture. It shows a family of six. A mother in a faded dress, sitting. A father stands behind her, wearing a threadbare suit. Around them are four children: two sons and two daughters, between the ages of four and twelve. They're posed against a plain beige background. None of them smile.

The image unsettles me more than its mere composition should. It's old, blurred by either age or poor camera work. The edges appear faded, as though the figures are blended into each other, and the colors—applied by hand after the photo was taken—are muted. I cannot see any of their faces clearly.

Thunder cracks the sky, but I barely hear it. My world has

narrowed to this unnatural hallway and its contents. I step further along it, toward the door that leads to my room, and realize I'm walking on a runner that does not belong in my home. Like the furniture, the floor has drowned in the muffling dust.

The half table to my right holds a set of three sleeping porcelain cats next to the candle and, behind them, a pocket-sized photo encased in a metal stand. I crouch to see it better. The image is tiny and its details faded, but I recognize it as a replica of the first photo. The family stands in the same arrangement, wearing the same clothes, with the same unsmiling, indistinct features.

Wood creaks. I lift my head. Only one part of the hallway is not lit: the door at the end of the hall. It remains closed, but something moves inside. I step closer, then stop. My dry tongue clings to the roof of my mouth. I'm not certain I want to see what is behind that door. But do I have a choice?

This hallway is not mine. This clutter and this dust do not belong to me. Nor do the photos or the worn-down runner or the candles.

They are all someone else's. But they're inside *my* home. I reach beyond the pictures, across one of the flickering pillars of wax, and press my fingertips against the wall. Not even the paint is mine, but underneath…

Underneath is my home.

This entity—this presence that I now believe comes from before my time—will not drag my home away from me.

Cold sweat sticks my clothes to my back as I step toward the final door. The something inside moves again, heavy, slow. The porcelain figures watch me with painted eyes. Uneven pupils shimmer in the candlelight as they follow my progress.

The portraits flank me. They are all the same image. The same family, the same dead expressions, the same beige background. I feel unsafe as I pass them. I want to believe it's because they, too, seem to be watching me, but that isn't the truth. There is something else about them. Something that sends my blood cold, something that moves down my spine as a tremor. There is something inherently bad about the photos, with their blurred edges and indistinct faces.

The door is less than ten paces away. Floorboards shift beyond, and I know the something—the intruder, the presence—stands just inside, waiting for me.

On a desk to my right, one of the cherub figurines lays on its back, its arms spread at its side, and I have the awful impression that it did not simply fall over but that it was placed like that because it is dead.

The doorknob shifts, twisting around as though preparing to open, then falls still. My throat hurts. My lungs are empty. I am standing underneath the largest photo. Framed in dark wood, the family looms over me, the grainy picture magnified to be an arm's length wide, and the sense of *not right* is intensified. The edges are still blurred, but in a different way from the smaller replicas.

I reach toward the image but stop short of touching it. My fingers hover a fraction above the surface, but I can feel it. Like static, like the palest snowfall—there is something ethereal and delicate between me and the portrait.

Dust. Everything in the hallway is covered in dust. And so are the images. It muffles them, softens them, fades the colors and the edges. I push my fingers in and drag them to the side, and lines of powder scrape away like frost being rubbed from a window.

Underneath, the colors are deeper and the lines are sharper. I flatten my hand against the image and shear off layers of dust. My palm comes away tingling and gritty, and I step back to see the family.

I was right. They weren't watching me. Each face carries unsmiling, pale lips, bloodless cheeks, and two sightless eyes.

They have neither pupil nor iris. Their lids are open and their faces turned toward the camera, but there is nothing between the lashes—only white.

A hinge groans as the door at the end of the hallway drags open. I feel for the flashlight in my pocket, but I no longer need it.

A candle lights the darkest reaches of the hall. Bloodred and clasped between interlaced fingers. The intruder emerges from its darkened room.

The candles on either side of me gutter. Then, in waves, they fail. The set closest to me blinks out first, followed by the row behind, and then the ones behind that.

I take a step back, and the intruder moves forward. The final set of candles, the ones closest to the stairs, flicker and die, and I am stranded in a hallway that is pitch-black save for the intruder's half circle of light.

Thunder shakes my home's foundations. Ribbons of light accompany it, slicing underneath the closed doors, but they scarcely illuminate the rows of emotionless faces that fill the hallway's portraits.

The intruder appears to dwarf its surroundings. Its bent form blocks the hall and the candle does precious little to give its shape relief. The cowl of hair flicks, caught in a gust of air I cannot feel. I pace backward, desperate to put space between myself and the presence, but it matches each step, its own feet falling heavily on the dust-laden carpet.

A weight exists in my hand: I am still carrying the box of salt. I reach inside and close my fist around the granules.

The silhouetted hair shivers as the intruder's head moves. I know what is coming, but that does not make the corrupted sound any easier to endure.

"Hel-lo." A sick, gurgling breath is drawn in. "Hell… Hel-lo… Hell…"

I extend my fistful of salt and throw it in an arc, casting it across the width of the hallway. The grains glitter in the candle-light as they fall. They land just short of the intruder, a barrier between it and myself.

The intruder raises its candle in increments. The flame gives shape to its form. It is covered in some kind of cloth. Grays and sickly greens, the colors are faded as deeply as those in the dust-covered portraits.

I step back, and again, the intruder closes the distance. Its foot lands heavily on the salt barrier. Another step forward, and it has crossed over, seemingly indifferent to my defense. The candle rises higher. I can now see skin near its head. Gray. Creased and crinkled, thick, unnatural. Above, the circular eyes flash.

Thunder ripples through my bones. The light shoots in beneath the doors. My throat hurts. I reach a shaking hand into the box again.

"Hel-lo." The light rises higher, and for the first time, the details contained inside the intruder's shadowed form are exposed. I see teeth. Rows of them, exposed by pale lips that have been peeled back. I see its hairline. Gray hair, thick, rising out of the skin above its lamp-like eyes. Its skin is wrinkled. Bloodless. Chiseled with deep lines that gather around the unnatural eyes and bared teeth.

"You're a woman." My words are whispered, nearly lost under the pealing storm.

Her teeth part. A dark, shriveled tongue dances behind them. "Hel-lo."

The box of salt is nearly empty. I seize as much as I can find, draw it out, and hurl it at the intruder's form.

The grains spark off her coverings. They fizzle in the candle's growing pool of wax. They scatter around her, lost to the dark depths of the strange hallway.

But she does not stop. Another step pulls her closer, the passage marked by the impact of a foot that shakes the wooden boards and sends puffs of dust billowing about her.

She is close enough to touch. And that is too close. I step back again, my voice trapped in my throat.

One of her bent hands leaves the candle. The fingers are like claws. All knuckles, curled, twitching. It rises to her face. To the round, lamp-like eyes. It touches one of them. Digs behind it, as though to gouge the light out. My mouth is open but I cannot make noise. The eye quivers, the light inside it flashing, then fading. Then they both come away from the face. Peeled away, like a layer of skin dragged off a body.

Behind those round lamps are a second set of eyes. Human eyes. Except for one detail: they are fully white.

To either side of us, the family stares out of their frames, their eyes as dead and empty as those of the entity before me.

The box slides from my grasp. I stagger back. The intruder comes closer, filling the space ahead of me, her white, unblinking eyes fixed on me, the teeth held apart as the dancing tongue regurgitates a broken form of my own words. "You are a... You... woman... You are a..."

My foot reaches back. The toes land on wood. The heel drops into a void. Unknowingly, I have backed into the stairwell. I try to catch myself, but the intruder steps nearer, close enough now that I can feel the icy chill spreading from her, taste the rank scents on my tongue. My body recoils from her. I slide from the top step, falling backward, hands reaching out to grasp at nothing as I plunge into the black tunnel.

I have one final glimpse of the upper hallway in that midfall second when my body is held in suspension, cradled by nothing but air. The intruder stands on the top step, hands wrapped around the bloodred candle. Her round eyes are back in place, lamps that stare out of the formless face, rows of off-color teeth grinning as I plunge away from her.

A lot happens in the space of a second. My eyes close. My hands reach out, searching for any kind of grip. The bite of the stairs will come, I know, spearing into my back, cutting the rear of my head, before I crumple down the flight like a discarded doll. I am surprisingly ready for it. These weeks have been building toward our final confrontation, and I suspect this was always the way it was going to end.

The fall seems to last too long. As though I were plunging off a cliff. As though the stairs never actually existed. My mouth is open but I can neither breathe, nor cry out.

And then I land. Not on the sharp, jutting stair edges, as I'd expected, but on something flat and solid. The *bang* of the impact is louder than I could have imagined, drowning out the thunder, drowning out the howling wind, leaving endless echoes in my ears. My back aches, but it is the dulled pain of first impact, dampened by shock, and I know it will only grow worse as my nerve endings refire. My arms fall against the surface and I feel wood. The downstairs floor?

My eyes open. Above is not the ceiling, but a wall. Blank, off-white, but intimately familiar. I tilt my head to the side. There is an archway above and to the right. Through it I glimpse thick curtains, closed, and a lamp on a coffee table.

That is the living room. Which means I am in the hallway. But my world is tilted, and I struggle to make sense of it. I lie on my back, the weight of gravity holding me there, and the archway to the living room is above, in what should be the ceiling.

Abruptly, my sense of direction returns, and I understand where I am. My back is pressed to wood. My head, pounding from the impact, turns, and I see the ornate doorknob at my side, next to my hand.

I am given no time to react. The door under the stairs falls open. Not outward, as I always imagined it would, but inward, and I plunge through in its wake, falling into the space it concealed, the space that radiated that terrible, bone-twisting fear.

My arm reaches out, trying to grasp the doorframe as I pass it, but I miss. Above, a rectangle of light looks out into the hallway, then vanishes as the door slams closed, locking me inside the space under the stairs.

It is dark. Darker even than the shed. And it is cold—so cold that I am afraid my skin will split from it. I lie on my back on an uneven, painfully hard surface. My hands reach up. They touch the door. It is so close that I cannot so much as sit up without hitting my head on it. I scramble across the surface, seeking a door handle, but there is none. Every inch of the room is freezing: where my back touches, where my hands touch, and, I realize with horror, where my sides touch. This is not a room. It is barely a cupboard. So narrow, so tight that I can do nothing but writhe in the enclosed space, hitting the walls and the ceiling with every minute movement.

I finally find my voice. Screams tear out of me. They bounce off the walls, echoes that refuse to die, loud enough to deafen me. I push against the door. My hands quickly become numb as the cold invades, but I only push harder. The door opened once. I can force it open again, I am sure.

The cuts across my body burn. Every movement pulls them open again, saturating the bandages. I am suffocating. My screams grow thin as I struggle to find the breath for them. I can no longer feel my hands. Instead, I pull my legs up. I can use my feet to press against the door, creating leverage. The space is so narrow that I can barely get one leg up to my chest. I pause, lungs empty, screams still ringing in my ears, my whole body burning and sinking into numbness at once. Then, with effort, I pull my second leg up. The knee scrapes against the door, and I have to turn it at an angle to find room. It wedges into the corner, and for a second I think I am stuck, then I hook my arms under my knee and drag it up. The pants tear and a layer of skin scrapes free, but I have it up, both thighs pressed against my chest.

I had planned to put the soles of my feet against the door, and a stab of fear courses into my heart as I realize there is no space for that. The room has grown narrower. Or I misjudged. Either way, I am stuck. My shins are jammed against the door, my back pressed flat into the rough surface beneath me. I can move my arms, but only barely; the walls pin my elbows to my side. My hands push against the door, and I strain my whole body as I try to force it open. I feel it bow under my touch, but the effort saps my energy. I let my head drop, panting breaths burning my lips as tears freeze into ice on my cheeks.

"Please." I do not know who I am begging, only that I am willing to plead with anyone who will listen.

There is no one, though. Only me. And the walls are growing tighter. I can barely writhe. My hands stick to the door, frozen in place. There is no air. There is only dark. Only cold. Only silence.

The intruder has won.

# OBLIVION

A PHONE RINGS. THE SOUND IS ANTIQUATED, DEEP AND CONTEM-
plative, made from physical bells and metal strikers. I open my
eyes. The old bronze phone rattles in place as it rings, wanting to
be answered.

The sun has already risen. The blocks of light that break
through the oak branches seem larger than normal, as though
the tree no longer has the strength to slice it so thoroughly. They
scatter over the desk, shining on the polished bronze and wood,
then across my carpeted floor and, finally, onto me.

The quilt, resplendent in Aesop's creations, drapes over my
form. It keeps me warm and makes me reluctant to rise, even as
the phone calls to me again. The clock radio on my bedside table
says it is nearly ten.

Memories prod at me, disjointed. They carry a sense of deep
fear, but they are so faded that it is hard to give them much

weight. Like a nightmare, though not from a recent sleep, but from days ago: the emotions are still there, but they grow fainter with every hour, and soon they will be forgotten entirely.

I rub my thumb into the corner of my eye to clear the muck from it. The phone rings again. I won't answer it. No one has my home number. No one who knows me would try to call me here.

At once, memories clarify, and the sense of comfort evaporates. I see the shed. I see the hallway. I see the intruder, the woman, horrible and towering and grinning as I fall into the darkness of my stairwell.

Did I dream it all? The events were elaborately detailed, but they hold a sort of airiness that reality doesn't. Like the delusions that come from a raging fever or like events that occur after a night without sleep.

I rise, sliding my legs over the side of my bed. The phone has fallen silent. I sit for a moment, soaking in the details of my room, reassuring myself that, no matter what, I am awake now. My fingers run along the soft edges of my quilt, grazing the stitches that I planted one at a time. My bare feet sink into the carpet. Tickling threads burrow between my toes. Outside, the oak branches rub across one another, the most adventurous tapping at my external wall and picking at the edges of the window.

This morning is real. Of that I am certain. But now I must sift through my memories. How many of them actually happened?

Aches spread over my body as I stand. Bandages mark the places where I cut myself in the shed. A bitter taste fills my mouth as I am forced to accept that there is one experience, at least, which truly happened.

I approach the window. The bare oak branches move lightly in the wind. I thought there were fewer slices in the light this morning, and I was right. Fallen branches dot the yard below, debris from the storm complementing the shallow pools of water that gather around the washing line and the back fence.

The storm has spent itself, and the morning feels fresh and light, but I find it hard to revel in it.

My shoes were left beside my bed, where I always place them at night, and I slip them onto my feet. The door gives me pause, but only for a second. I push it open.

The hallway is my own again. The off-white walls are clean and empty. There is no dust. No porcelain trinkets. No portraits.

That part of my memory is fiction. I hope.

Back in my room, I go to my closet to find day clothes. It is only when I have picked out a top that I realize I am already wearing one. It is the outfit I selected last night: dark clothes, stretchy clothes. They are comfortable enough that I mistook them for my nightgown.

I change, regardless. As I peel the bottoms off, my knee stings. I examine it and find a scrape. More memories come into clarity: The space under the stairs. The door that would not open. Trying to pull my legs up; tearing the pants and grazing my knee.

One hand presses over my mouth. I feel sick. Out of everything jumbled into my mind, that is the one part I do not want to be real. Perhaps I gained the scrape somewhere else. In the shed or tripping on the stairs. Reliving the memories stirs an ache in my chest, and so I push the question aside.

I dress. Bruises mark my back, but I only examine them glancingly. As I tie my hair up, I feel along the back of my head. There is a bump, small, that hurts when I touch it.

The door creaks as I push through it and move into the hallway. To my right, at the end of the hall, the final door is open. I stare at it, daring the indistinct shapes beyond to move, but they don't. I turn to the stairs.

Something crunches under my shoes. I lift my foot, examining the sole, and find tiny grains of pink salt. I crouch. There is not a line of salt, not like I remember leaving, but there is still *some*. Perhaps a tenth of what I imagined I placed.

The light at the stairwell still doesn't work. I am not as willing to climb down as I once was, but I coax myself to move. It is no longer night. Daylight flows up the lowest steps, and the well is no longer pitch-black.

Several things catch my eye at the base of the stairs: The rope coiled on the floor, where I left it the previous day. The lines of salt are gone. I approach the living room and bend at the archway, examining the floor. There are still traces of the grains clinging against the wall.

The living room's curtains are pulled back. The light paints the space in pleasant colors, but my stomach turns as I see a burned-out candle on the coffee table.

Finally, I turn to the location I have most keenly wanted to avoid: the door under the stairs. It is closed. Unremarkable.

Almost invisible among the wood paneling. The salt ring I placed around it is also missing.

A heavy sensation fills my chest as I approach, something akin to dread: dense, cloying. My pulse spikes. I feel my pupils dilate. This must be how a prey animal reacts when it senses a predator.

I don't want to touch the door. Don't want to be anywhere near it. I'm now certain the door opened last night: opened to let me in, then slammed on top of me. How I got out, how I made it up to my room and still had the presence of mind to remove my shoes is a mystery. But I was on the other side of this door. I don't want to return. But I *must* be sure.

My fingers touch the doorknob. I try to turn it. It shifts a fraction, then jams. Locked again. Thank mercy.

I turn for the kitchen, eager for something to soften my dry throat. Despite the sense of unreality that clings to last night, I must accept that the events happened. Or at least, something *like* them happened.

The drawer at the kitchen counter scrapes open, and I pop pills out of their foils: two pain tablets for the throbbing headache and one antidepressant that I missed taking last night. I swallow the pills with a glass of water, then fill it a second time.

Last night, I saw the intruder's true face. A woman. An old one, with empty white eyes and long gray hair.

The salt didn't deter her. She is responsible for my fall. Responsible for me becoming trapped inside the room under the stairs. What does she want? She won our confrontation. So how am I still here? How did I wake in my own room, hurt but whole, only to face another day with her living in my home?

Perhaps this *is* what she wants. Not to kill me, but to keep me. To make me suffer again and again, every day, until I cannot take the torment for even a second longer and give up my own life willingly.

My hand shakes so badly that the glass rattles against the sink as I set it down.

Today is Sunday. I have another full day in this house before I can escape to work tomorrow.

That word, *escape*, lingers in my mind. I could leave my home. Relinquish it to *her*.

No; I'm not enough of a fool to imagine she would let me leave. If getting the house was her only goal, I'm certain she could have ended my life by now. She doesn't want the building. She wants *me*. If I leave, she will follow.

That is a heavy thought. I press my thumb into my temple, where the low pulse of a headache resides. How long has it been since I ate a full meal? Slept without being disturbed?

Is there anything that will make this stop?

I fold my arms around myself as I shuffle along the hallway. The door handle is still, but I give it a wide berth as I pass. My cell phone is connected to its charging cable by the door. It works again, and the battery is full. No messages. No missed calls.

I try not to let the disappointment hurt, but I truly thought that there would have been enough warm memories between us that Meg would call back. I would answer if *she* phoned *me*.

The rope lies at the foot of the stairs. I hate walking over it every time I need to traverse my home. The smooth synthetic fibers have an unpleasant texture as I take it up and carry it through the back door.

My yard endured the storm's beating, but it didn't come out fully unscathed. Leaves stripped from trees clump against the fence. The washing line lists.

My feet drag through damp grass as I cross to the shed. The door opens with some effort. I'm breathless by the time it's wide enough to see inside.

The space is as small as I remember. Four good paces would put me at the rear wall.

Metal implements cluster over the crowded walls. Sharp points, sharp edges, tines, and spikes. The scores across my body ache at the memory. I reel my arm back and hurl the rope toward the rear shelf. It crumples on the floor next to its companion, and I drag the door closed again.

The intruder can hurt me, but she doesn't appear to want to end me. Yet. I must see that as the advantage it is, even though the idea is tainted with dread. She has allowed me a weapon: time. Enough time to test her limits, enough time to try to understand her. With luck, it will be enough time to defeat her.

I stretch tired legs as I march back to the kitchen door. The intruder has been leaving hints as to her nature. Maybe that was deliberate, or maybe she has no control over how she influences my home. Either way, she let me see the hallway filled with portraits. That image, repeated so many times, must be important to her. It showed a family: a husband and wife, two daughters, and two sons.

The image was old. The colors weren't quite true but were hand-applied postdevelopment, telling me its original form was black-and-white. That makes it at least seventy years old.

The intruder is also old. She's distorted, unnatural, her face deeply creased and her hands frozen into claws.

It's possible the twisted visage that lingers in my home is the wife from the picture. Perhaps she lived here before I did, died in this house, and has been dormant until now.

The timeline feels shaky. The living room still has blankets from when I made my home there, and I take one and wrap it around my shoulders before retrieving my phone.

Back in the kitchen, I make a cup of lemongrass tea, strong, and hold it in my left hand for comfort as I sit at the wooden four-seater table. A piece of scored paper from my professional notebook sits before me, and I jot down theoretical dates.

It's possible to assume an approximate time frame for the photograph. When I first saw the photo, I was most focused on the family's eerily expressionless faces, but my subconscious—primed to read these clues thanks to my job—noted facets of their clothing. The wife's dress had squared shoulders, most common in the first half of the forties, but it might have been an old dress, as her hairstyle hinted toward the middle of the decade.

On the left-hand side of the page, I write *1945*. It's the closest estimate I can make without seeing the picture again. It's also around the time when color photography became cheap enough that a middle-class family would have no reason to opt for hand-colored instead.

On the right-hand side of the page, I write when I moved into my home, fifteen years ago. If someone died in this house, it must have been before that date.

I'd initially moved in as a renter before purchasing the building from my landlord when he retired. He was a pleasant man, shy, with thin ginger hair and a bony face. We only saw each other when he needed to make repairs or wanted to inspect the home, and my memories from that time are sparse.

The pen's plastic top scrapes the space between my eyebrows as I tap my forehead. When I signed the rental agreement, he told me it was the best building on the street—and he seemed to genuinely believe that sentiment.

The memory emerges slowly, but as it comes free from the recesses of my mind, I hear the words clearly: *It's a good house. I've lived here since I got married in 1966 and it's never given me problems.*

I write that date next to the year I moved in.

That gives me an approximate twenty-year gap from the time the photo was taken to the year my old landlord purchased the property.

The wife in the photo seemed in her thirties. At most, she might have been forty.

Assuming the photograph was taken right before hand coloring became impractical, and assuming the spirit belongs to the wife in the image, and assuming she passed immediately before my old landlord purchased the property, she would have been sixty at the oldest.

The pen hits the paper as I drop it.

The specter is old. Older than that, I'm certain. My clearest glimpse of her was candlelit and filtered through a haze of stress, but I would be surprised if she were younger than eighty.

What does that mean? I could have my dates wrong.

Or…the spirit tormenting me was not present in the photograph. It's possible they have a tangential relationship to it: an aunt, a sister. Someone who cherished the picture enough to manifest it, although it did not include them.

I wish I could see it again. To be able to examine its details, possibly eke some meaning from the background or recognize some trivial element. Anything that would give me a direction to move my research. A way to narrow down the identities of those present.

Because, I am certain, knowing the name of the specter will be vital to understanding how to remove her.

My tea is cooling. I push the sheet of paper away as frustrations rise and lift the mug to my lips.

An alarm sounds outside my home. My gate's rusted hinges complain as they turn, warning me that someone is coming. I rarely get visitors. Anxiety materializes. This could be a neighbor, someone who saw me through my lit windows last night. Someone who is visiting out of a misguided desire to help or, perhaps, pure callous curiosity.

My hair is overdue for a wash, so I tie it into a bun, where its ragged edges will be less noticeable. My home is a mess with salt residue and the supplies I have accumulated over the last week. Nothing I can do about that now.

Four quick knocks come from the door. As I pass from the kitchen and into the hallway, I glimpse lines of faded gray in the ceiling corners. Spiderwebs. Anyone who sees inside my home will think it has not been cleaned in months.

There are no windows in my front door, only the peephole. I keep my steps light, hoping they won't betray my presence.

As I near the door, the irony makes me want to smile. Just a moment ago, I was praying that I would not have to face this spirit alone. Now, I think I would gladly remain isolated if the alternative meant giving one of my street's gossips a front-row seat to my living nightmares.

I slow to a creep for the final few steps. Whoever is on the other side of the door is restless. The mat crunches. A jacket rustles as gusts tug at it. I hold my breath and extend my fingertips to rest against the door as I lean closer, my eye approaching the tiny lens.

A woman stands outside. Her back is to the door as she faces the yard, her head lifted as she surveys the vines bobbing across the low brick fence and the houses opposite. Her pea-green jacket flaps about her. It's not the kind of jacket you wear when you visit your neighbor: it's too formal, too expensive. The kind you don when you are traveling a distance.

Shoulder-length hair whips around her head. Fine strands tangle like gossamer, dulling what otherwise might be glossy. In the shade of my porch, it appears light brown. But it's not—not really. Under houselights, it's golden. In sunlight, it takes on a strawberry tint. At night, when the moon is large enough, it could be mistaken for silver.

I know, because that chameleon hair and the sloped shoulders and even the angle of her head are so deeply familiar. I lean back, my eyes burning, my throat aching. Meg came.

I'm wildly unprepared. My home is a mess. Once, I might have feared her judgment as much as I feared allowing the gossips and busybodies inside, but not today. Meg can see me at my worst.

My hands are unsteady and struggle to open the door. As it swings inward Meg turns, her hair dragging over her round face and barely disguising the hint of red lining her eyes underneath the mascara.

She's a crier. Always was. And today, I am as bad as her, on the edge of making a fool of myself, my eyes prickling no matter how fast I blink.

We stare at each other. She swallows, and a hesitant smile forms. It's different from the smile I know best. This is the one she reserves for strangers. I suppose that's what we've become. One hand rises, as nervous as her voice. "Hi. I'm sorry. I hope I'm not bothering you."

"Never." I don't hold back my own smile as I nearly throw myself on her. My arms go around her shoulders, my head resting against hers. She's shorter than I am, but we always fit together well. That chameleon hair fills my face and smells of fruit. Papaya and strawberry, I think, and it makes me want to laugh. We are so different. I never understood why I should want to put fruit in my hair, so my conditioners are odorless. She seems to pick them according to how hungry they make her.

I revel in the smell, though. It is so perfectly Meg. I hadn't realized how much I'd missed it. Her skin is a flushed kind of warm against my cheek. She's all softness and roundness, and she doesn't seem to be bothered by my relative boniness. My eyes blur, and I pull back and turn to my house in one movement so she won't be able to see the tears.

"I can't tell you how happy I am you're here." I sweep along the hallway to the kitchen, not bothering to close the front door, not bothering to even glance at the under-stairs door. It seems trivial now. Not worth my worry. "I have an unbelievable story to tell you. Let's get something to drink first. Do you still like coffee? I only have the instant kind, and it might be stale, but…"

The kettle begins to rumble as I switch it on. My own mug sits on the kitchen table, and I tip it out so I can make a fresh drink. The kitchen window's glass is clean after the storm, and the light is at just the right angle to reflect my own face back at me. I linger there for a second, swiping my sleeve over my eyes to clear them, before grabbing a second mug from the cupboard.

"I also have herbal teas. You must be thirsty. It's a long drive. Is Justin looking after the kids?"

I turn, expecting Meg would have followed me into the kitchen, but I'm alone. My smile falters as I move to the hallway. At the other end, the front door stays open, and Meg is framed in the light, her features unreadable. She fumbles for an object in her pocket, and I think she's saying something, but her voice is too soft for me to hear.

"Meg?" I walk toward her. The hallway never felt as long as it does at that moment. Something's wrong. This isn't how my sister should behave. She lifts her head, then drops it again, and it's like a knife into my stomach. There's pain pulling at her expression. She's trying not to let it show, but her perfect makeup is being ruined as her lips twist back and her eyes squint until they're nearly closed.

Meg is joy. Meg is always the brightest one in the room, the loudest voice at the party, the first onto the dance floor. She's the one who loves to bake even though her recipes aren't good, who loves to sing in an off-key voice, who will prattle on the phone for hours without getting breathless. The only thing Meg isn't good at is being sad. Or so I thought.

"I'm really sorry to bother you," she says. "I wouldn't, except it's important."

"What happened?" I am suddenly afraid. I offer a hand to her, but she doesn't take it. Doesn't let me lead her into the house. Doesn't seem to want to touch me. I'm left there, fingers outstretched, feeling that sense of smothering panic clawing at my throat.

"This is my sister." She holds out the piece of paper, a photograph, quivering between her fingers.

"Meg." The fear is sharper, so harsh that it hurts. There's something wrong with her. We're a two-sibling family. The sense that something terrible will happen if I let her continue—that her words are beckoning something dark and unendurable into my life—crests over me. "What are you saying?"

"She's very important to me."

I want her to stop. *Need* her to stop. But her words are coming too fast, and I have no air in my lungs to cut her off. I try to push the photo back to her, but she doesn't react—she just holds it out, as though waiting for me to take it.

And then I realize: she's not looking at me. Toward me, yes, but not *at* me. There's no eye contact.

My legs feel weak. My body, worn down from the week of stress and lost sleep, cannot adjust in time. I stagger back. My shoulder hits the wall near the stairs, and I lean against it for support.

Meg's gaze doesn't move. She stares along the hallway, focused on nothing.

No, not on nothing. On the intruder. The woman's shrouded form dominates the space. She must have been standing behind me, so close that I should have felt her cowl graze my back. Her wrinkled features are clearer in the daylight. They're hard, angular. Her round, owl-like eyes bore into Meg's.

And my sister addresses her. Offers the photo to her. "She went missing over a year ago." Meg's gentle eyebrows are pulled together, and they paint deep creases between her wet eyes. "The police think she left, but that's not like her. She's the most reliable person I know."

The intruder reaches out a hand. The appendage is frozen into a claw, and the knuckles strain as she takes the picture between two fingers.

Meg relinquishes it. "This used to be her house. She might still come back. Please, if she does, or if you find anything, will you call me? I'm so worried."

The intruder's jaw moves. It is horrible, unnatural, as it allows the broken voice out. "Of course, my darling."

"Thank you." Meg's voice catches on tears. She bows her head and begins to back away. "My number's on the back. Thank you so much."

The door closes. Her shoes crunch on the paving stones, then the gate wails as its hinges are forced to turn, and a second later, a car engine comes to life. My sister is gone. It is now only the two of us: me and the intruder, isolated in the long hallway. I press my back to the wall, not breathing, heart not beating, as the towering figure turns toward me.

Her crow-like hand rises, the fingers framing the picture. In it, a pale woman with long hair stares toward the camera. Her expression is serious, her eyes dark. It is an intimately familiar face.

"This is you, isn't it?" the intruder asks.

A scream tears from my throat. Howling, deep, sick with terror and anger. I clamp my hands over my ears, but it only grows louder. The walls are shaking. Photos shudder in their frames as the air turns to ice around me. My legs give out. The scream is unending as I slide down the wall to meet with oblivion on the floor.

# HAIRLINE FRACTURES

MY FINGERS REST LIGHTLY ON THE GATE. THE METAL IS BEAUTI-
fully old, aged past the point where it begins to look shabby and
into the era of dignified charm. The rust meets with lichen. Spots
of dirt are indistinguishable from spots of age. I could easily
afford to redo the fence—build it higher, maybe, and switch the
gate for something more modern—but I wouldn't relinquish the
squeaky heirloom for anything.

Though I'm reluctant to open it. Work allowed me to escape
the house for a few comforting hours, but now I'm not sure I'm
ready to be home.

I have to go in eventually, though, don't I? Neighbors will
notice if I stand on the sidewalk for too long. I close my eyes and
focus on the cool late-afternoon air grazing my face, the way the
thorny rosebush snags at my slacks, and push on the metal. The
gate cries out. I step through and let it close behind me.

This isn't right. I frown, turning to look behind myself. My car, its engine still warm, waits on the street.

Something happened yesterday. Something that changed me, that broke me in an imperceptible way.

Once, several months ago, I dropped a mug. It was one of my favorites: lovely red and gold geometric patterns laced across the surface. I felt a burst of panic as it hit the floor, followed by gratitude when it didn't break. Thanking whatever luck held that mug together, I placed it back on the counter and filled it with tea.

But while it looked intact, the fall hadn't left it unscathed. A hairline fracture ran from the lip to the base. It was so fine that I couldn't find it with my naked eye, but the water had no such problem. As it filled, beads of liquid appeared at that crack and began to run onto the countertop.

I feel like that mug. My hair is pulled into a tidy bun. My cardigan is clean and neat, although the clambering rose appears dedicated to snatching threads loose. My shoes are polished. From the outside, I appear fine. But I am as broken as if I had shattered into a thousand pieces.

Did I truly go to work? Yes, I know I did. I woke up this morning. I had breakfast. I drove to the museum and spent my day there. I know that all happened, but when I search my memory, I can't find any distinct recollection. I cannot say who I spoke to or what I said. I cannot recall how heavy the traffic was. Or what I ate for breakfast. It's like being on autopilot, except that the whole day has been absorbed in that fugue.

I look back at my car, and now, I am no longer certain that the engine is warm.

Loose grit cracks under my feet as I approach my front door. By all reason, I should not have gone to work today. How could I after what happened? And if I did, wouldn't I have said something to one of my coworkers?

What *did* happen yesterday? Meg visited. But what did I say to her?

The memories are like soup that has been cooked for too long, every distinct occurrence an ingredient that has begun to disintegrate, and the more I stir, the more they blend together.

The door lists inward at my touch. Routine is hard to break, and I sling my bag onto the hook on the wall. If this were any other day, I would move toward the kitchen and begin preparing something for dinner.

But this can't be a normal day, can it? My body wants it to be. It's trying, with all of its power, to make this feel mundane. It insists this means nothing, even though I'm standing in the same place Meg stood yesterday when she spoke to the intruder.

My sister didn't find that alarming. Neither the intruder's existence in my home, nor her appearance. Meg was upset but not because of that.

She'd brought a photo. A photo of me.

The intruder is still here. I know she is. When I focus, I can hear her: in the kitchen—something ceramic bumps against something wooden.

My legs feel leaden. My lungs hurt, and I realize I've forgotten to breathe… For how long? Since the gate? Since before?

The hallway leads me to the kitchen. *My* hallway. *My* kitchen. She is there. Sitting at the kitchen table, turning the pages of a book, a mug that I do not recognize held in one hand. She seems so much less terrifying than she does at night. Not as large, not as aggressive. Her creased, angular face appears almost placid.

Her head lifts to face me. The mug goes back onto the table with a gentle tap, and one of those awful bent hands closes the book. For a moment, we don't speak, and I can't tell what to make of the silence.

"I was hoping you'd be back," she says.

I drag my tongue across my lips. The kitchen is clean. The mud from the storm is gone. So are the cobwebs. The countertops seem to have recently been wiped down. I wonder how much she has touched and moved while I was gone.

Though I wasn't truly gone, was I?

My mind is hurting. I feel as though I've walked to the edge of a precipice, and it's my duty—my responsibility—to step over, but doing so will destroy me in more ways than I can comprehend.

Stepping over means opening myself to a truth I don't think I'm capable of enduring. I already know what it is. What *I* am. My body quakes, physically repulsed by the knowledge, desperate to squirm away from it and forget.

For a second, I nearly do just that: turn around and walk away. If I leave now, she can't hurt me. This monster sitting at my table, speaking to me, expecting me to reply, won't be able to crack through the mental barriers I've constructed unless I lower them myself.

Lowering them is what I'm supposed to do. It's the only *right* thing to do. It will alter everything, though, crumbling every part of my identity until I no longer recognize myself.

I would give anything to return to the bubble of delusion I was living in. But I glimpsed what was over that precipice, and now, there is nothing left to do except lean forward and plunge recklessly.

I rest a hand on the archway that bridges the hallway to the kitchen. Smooth paint, cool, its texture so fine that my fingertips can barely make it out. I try to keep my voice emotionless, to not let her hear the fear that churns inside. "Am I dead?"

She draws in a slow breath, and it whistles as it goes down. I expect words to come on the exhale, but they don't: she simply releases it. A sigh, tainted with sadness, and I know I have my answer.

My throat aches as I turn away. "I need something to drink."

"By all means."

Her blank eyes stay on me as I cross to the kettle. My hands are unsteady as I fill it, put it back on its stand, turn it on. Then I brace my palms on the edge of the counter as I stare through the window. The fallen branches, stripped during the storm, have been gathered into the yard's corner. Birds fight over the feeder. She must have added seed to it.

"I can't be," I manage at last.

She tilts her head to one side, and those horrible circular eyes flash. I can't stand having them fixed on me, and I make a show of brushing stray hair away from my forehead to put my hand between my face and hers. "I can't be dead. I—"

"Do you remember how it happened, sweet thing?"

"It didn't." I put my hand down with more force than I intended. My palm stings. I focus on that, relishing the pain, knowing it means that there must be some mistake, that this encounter cannot really be going in the direction it tries to. "The police. I called them. They came. I led them through the house—"

"I remember." She turns her mug with one clawed hand. "They showed up in the middle of the night. One of the neighbors had seen me rushing between rooms through the windows and called them. They came by to check I was okay. It took some convincing to get them to leave."

They never seemed to really listen to what I said. The realization saps my strength, and I hunch low over the sink as steam rises from the kettle. I asked them to look at the door under the stairs; they ignored me. I tried to show them through the house; they made their own way. They never actually met my eyes.

The kettle reaches its peak and switches off. My hands shake so badly that I am in danger of dropping my second-favorite mug as I place a tea bag into it and pour the water. The intruder remains seated and silent, her eyes still trained on me, but seeming content to just watch.

"What are you?" I ask.

"My name is Sarah." She turns the mug again, rotating it so

that the handle faces her. "I am eighty-four. A mother. Retired. I hope something in there answers your question."

I look her over out of the corner of my eye. Strangely, even in the well-lit kitchen, she is still hard to make out, as though the smudging effect of nighttime clings to her like a permanent cloak. And that is very much not natural.

The tea bag is hot enough to burn my fingers, but I don't bother searching for a spoon as I fish it out and drop it into a saucer by the kettle. "Why have you been doing this to me?"

"What *have* I been doing to you?"

I work my jaw, rankled that she would try to play obtuse.

"I've been trying to communicate with you," she says after a moment. "Ever since I realized you were here, the day I moved in. And you've made it hellishly difficult, if you don't mind me saying. Slamming doors. Closing curtains, making this place seem like a morgue. Sneaking up on me at night. And the salt. It *was* salt, wasn't it? You left it everywhere. Took fully half a day to sweep it all up."

Something chokes in my throat, and I'm shocked that it might be broken laughter. The salt was supposed to keep presences contained. I never actually did step over one of the salt lines once I'd laid it, did I?

That thought makes me abruptly sad. I put my back to the sink and fold my arms, as though that might keep my erratic emotions restricted. "Why do you look like that?"

"What do I look like, sweet thing?"

Is she going to play dumb about this too? Is she going to force me to say it out loud, to cross the barrier of tenuous civility we've established? No. I actually don't care any longer. So what if I sound rude? She's invaded my house. Tormented me. It's too late for her to expect me to pretend there is nothing to comment on. "Like a monster."

"Well." Again, the head tilts. "That's interesting. Especially coming from you."

"What does that mean?"

One hand twitches, waving my question away. "So I look different from the way a person should, do I? If I had to guess, I'd say you've created a fictionalized picture of me. If you were afraid when you first saw me, your mind could have crafted something to be frightened *of*. A veneer. In the same way that this likely still looks like your home."

"This *is* my home," I snap back.

"My sweet darling, I'm sorry. I bought it nearly three months ago." She draws a slow breath, her shoulders rising and falling with it. "I kept much of the same furniture, but there are more than enough changes."

"No." I extend a hand, indicating the kitchen. "There's dust and cobwebs, and that rope you put everywhere, but—"

Then, like a light being switched on, I see. I'd filled and boiled a kettle. But it's no longer the steel kettle I always used; now, it's bright red. I touch its side. Cold. The mug I filled is missing. I step back, staring about the room and feel moisture burning my eyes. There are cookbooks stacked beside the stove. Pots for sugar and tea. A vase with flowers. None of it mine.

She still sits at the table, the paperback novel discarded beside her, the mug held in one hand. She is still tall, still intimidating, but no longer supernaturally so. The fabric across her form is a sage-green dress. Her gray hair, which had seemed ragged and wild, is still long, but now it is plaited. Her face is creased, but only to the degree of anyone else her age. Only one part of her still appears inhuman.

"Your eyes," I say.

She reaches up. Her bony fingers feel around the edge of the terrible lamps, then slip *behind* them. Gouging them out. As they come away, I see her real eyes beneath. Regular eyes. Gray-green. In her hand is a pair of round glasses.

My legs shake, so I approach the table and draw out a chair. As I lower myself into it, her pale lips move into a slight smile.

"I really am dead, aren't I?"

"I'm sorry. You don't deserve to be. Not when you're still so young."

I want to cry. I won't. "Would you call my sister, please? Meg. You met her yesterday. She should know."

Sarah leans closer, her clawlike hand resting near mine, and in the silence that hangs between us, I sense reluctance.

"Please," I press. "Meg was in so much pain. At least give her some closure."

Sarah's green-gray eyes are heavy with sadness, and her voice is gentle. "What would you like me to say?"

I understand why she hesitated. What *is* there to say? My body can't have been found; otherwise, Meg wouldn't still be searching for me. And without a body, how can I expect Sarah to explain to my sister that I am truly dead?

A groan wrenches its way out of my stomach. I press my palms into my closed eyes.

"It wasn't yesterday," Sarah says. "Just so you know. It was a week ago."

"Are you sure? It *feels* like yesterday."

"Mm. You're not always here. Only sometimes. You'll disappear and come back days or weeks later. That's made it hard to speak to you. But…well, we managed it eventually, didn't we?"

My hands drop from my eyes. I flex my right index finger. It was cut—and badly. I wrapped it in bandages, afraid that the skin would split. But then I forgot about it. The bandages vanished. The skin returned to its unblemished state. Just like the cuts from the shed. Just like everything that has happened to me since Sarah appeared in my home.

I never even considered seeing a professional about the injuries. Because I couldn't. Some part of me knew I was gone, even if it wasn't conscious knowledge, so the idea of seeking help never even crossed my mind.

Sarah has left her glasses on the table, and her face is so much gentler without them. Still angular, still creased, but now appearing attentive.

"Are you sure you don't remember how you died?" she asks. "If you know how and where, I could give your sister closure. And maybe help you move on."

It's a strange question, made even stranger because I don't have an answer. My life has progressed steadily, with very few changes. Taking three weeks off over Christmas is the most notable thing to happen all year, and even those three weeks were uneventful. I rested at home. I worked on an ocean-themed quilt. I read. I cleaned the yard.

A person should remember their death. Shouldn't they? Unless I'd passed from an aneurism or some other undiagnosed condition when I was asleep—but, if that had happened, I should have been found in my bed when I didn't turn up for work. When Meg visited, she said the police believed I'd left. That meant they didn't find my body. Or have any clues as to where it might be.

But how could that be possible when I rarely leave my home, let alone travel far? How could I simply vanish in such a way that even *I* don't remember it?

"I don't know," I manage.

Sarah is no longer sitting opposite me. The shadows have shifted; evening has progressed into night. The cup Sarah drank from is sitting upside down on the washboard to dry.

I'm alone again. The lights in the house's lower level are off, making its details blend together. The cold floor drifts away ahead of me, leading through shadowed rooms.

An electric sensation trails over the sensitive backs of my arms, and I am struck by the impression that it is not wise to be alone right now. I rise, my eyes straining through the gloom.

Metal strikes metal. A door handle—*that* door handle— twisting in place. And the fear of being alone is abruptly much worse.

"Sarah?" I turn, putting my back to the kitchen counter as I stare down the length of the hallway.

Something is wrong with my house. It feels like a poison seeping out of the walls, corrupting every surface. A slick grease that gets on my clothing, on my hands, sticking to me until I can never be free from it.

The hairline fracture I thought was running through me has spread. It is not just inside me any longer. It is in the house. And it is bleeding.

# 10
# MEAT AND TENDONS
# AND BONES AND VEINS

THE MORNING IS OVERCAST, AND IT MAKES IT HARD TO WAKE. Without the sunlight invading my room and prodding at my defenses, I lie, content to be wrapped in the warmth of my quilt.

My bedside radio flashes the time: seven thirty. I didn't hear the alarm, and now I'll have to skip my morning shower if I don't want to be late.

Even with time escaping my clasp too fast, I still find it hard to get dressed. A cloudy day is a heavy thing, making me feel as though I weigh twice what I normally do.

Quarter to eight. It's time to go. I pull a cardigan over my shirt and move into the hall.

I'll eat one of the muesli bars I keep in my car's glove box for breakfast. That will buy me a few minutes. I take the stairs quickly, rubbing at the corners of my eyes, still feeling sluggish and irritated. Into the hallway. I snatch my bag off the hook by the door and unplug my phone. The crisp morning air greets me as I pull the door open. I'm two steps into my front yard before I stop.

My bag's strap falls from my slumped shoulder. I remember now: Who I am. *What* I am. How did it take me so long to recall my new reality?

That's the power of my routine. And, most likely, why I didn't notice anything was wrong for more than a year.

I try to smile as I return inside my home, but it hurts. I'm prepared for work. I won't actually get there. Never again will. I groan, pressing my fingers into my skull, messing up the hair that I put up so carefully.

My life was run by routine. But now it has infected me, and the loss of it hurts more than I ever expected.

The satchel is discarded beside the door. I step toward the kitchen with the vague idea of making a cup of tea holding in the back of my mind before I realize that, too, is part of a dead routine. A life that is now unattainable.

"Hello? Sarah?" I move into the living room, then from there to the kitchen. It feels strange to call someone else's name inside my home. But she has to be here, doesn't she?

I stop by the kitchen sink. She's at the listing washing line, green fabric spiraling in the wind. Her gray hair moves like a mass around her head: like disembodied fog, like seaweed trapped in a swell. Part of me is affronted to see her in my yard. Another smaller part of me is relieved.

I approach the washing line in long, steady steps, my arms

folded across my chest to protect against the wind and the awful vulnerability permeating me. She either senses me coming or is talented at hiding surprise. "Morning, Leigh."

She's hanging laundry. Mostly dresses like the one she's wearing: loose, moss-green or brown shades. I give her a curt nod.

"It's good to have you back." She shakes out a shift that edges toward burnt orange. "I've been impatient to get started."

"On what?" I didn't notice how thin her arms were before. She's a large woman, especially for her age—not overweight, but broad shouldered and stocky. Tall, too; maybe not as tall as I'd imagined her, but nearly the same height as me. Her arms are thin, though. The sleeves hang over her elbows but from there down seems like bird claws. The bones in her forearms are defined, wrapped by a thin layer of loose skin, and it's hard not to think of the mummified remains I've categorized over the years.

"I want to help you pass over, of course."

I can't see her eyes behind the flashing circles of her glasses, but I'm almost certain she's watching me sidewise as she pegs the dress. A red peg on the left sleeve. A purple one on the right. I always tried to match the pegs when I could. Did I really have so little of value in my life that I prided myself on how color-coordinated my laundry was hung?

"My grandmother said I had a gift." Sarah bends, moving painfully slowly, to pluck a pair of underwear out of the basket. She gasps as she straightens and reaches into the peg basket. "My mother didn't like that idea. Didn't want me to mention it, didn't want me to think about it, especially after Ruth. But that's around the time we moved in with my grandmother, and she had no such compunctions."

"I'm sorry, who's Ruth?"

Sarah draws a deep breath, then scoffs it out. "Never mind that. What I'm saying is, my grandmother said it was a gift and that I should use it for good. I just never had the chance before. You're the first one I've seen so clearly. The first one I've been able to really talk to."

"You think you're a spirit medium?"

Sarah laughs. It's abrupt and barking, its vitality at sharp odds with the birdlike arms. "Sweet thing, I'm talking to you, aren't I?"

"All right." I try to smile. Sarah bends to her basket again, and my inactivity rankles me. "Can I help with that?"

"I don't know. Can you?"

My tongue runs across the back of my teeth. I'm suddenly desperate to participate in the chores I once barely paid attention to. My hands plunge into the basket. Fabric, damp and cool, envelopes them. I take measured breaths as I draw a dressing gown out, almost ashamed of how much I relish being able to hold it.

"You're a lost soul." Sarah rights herself and braces one arm against the washing line as she watches me. "Now, forgive me, because I don't exactly know the nuances of how the afterlife is supposed to work, but I'm pretty sure you shouldn't still be here."

The words come out on impulse, perfunctory. "This is my home."

"It *was*. But I'm talking in more general terms. You shouldn't be…*here*. On this mortal plane. There's somewhere else you belong. Heaven, maybe. I'm assuming you're not sure how to get there."

I pin the gown. A green peg on the left sleeve, a green peg on the right. "No. I didn't even realize I was…"

"Dead?"

"No longer living. Not until Meg visited."

The memory of my sister brings down a slew of implications. I'd always pictured us reconciling at some point. As the separation graduated from months to years, it didn't hurt as much as it might have, and I never felt pressure to release my grudges because I always saw it as a temporary rift. But now it *is* permanent. And there's nothing I can do to reel back that lost time.

The basket offers relief from my own thoughts and from Sarah's scrutiny. I fish out more items, my movements snappy to compensate for how badly I wish I was alone to cry.

"That means, I suppose, that there's something keeping you here. Movies love to call it unfinished business, but I don't know if that's the best term for it. From what I've seen, lots of spirits are like you. They don't know they're already gone."

I pretend to hunt for space on the line as an excuse to hide my wet eyes. "Have you seen many spirits?"

"You're the fourth." The line creaks as she shifts her weight. "The first was in my grandmother's home. We moved there when I was twelve. My mother wasn't coping, and my father had left, and my grandmother was the only person who was prepared to look after three kids. Her house was small, so I had to sleep in the loft with my brothers, and on the second night, I saw a young girl. She'd crouched next to the blankets and pillows I'd used to make a bed. She asked me if I wanted to play hide-and-seek."

The story is helping. My throat is relaxing, my hands more coordinated as I pick out matching pegs.

Sarah chuckles. "I thought she was real, and that my grandmother had taken in another family. I told her I was too tired to play and she should go to sleep. She told me to count to a hundred. Then she ran off, laughing, into all of the storage that was kept up there, and I rolled over and dozed off. The next morning, I asked my mother why the girl in gray wasn't having breakfast with us. And my mother started crying."

I frowned. "Did she see the girl too?"

"Oh, no. Our family had just gone through a bad patch. She cried about everything, but especially about children. My grandmother waited until my mother had gone to lie down before she sat next to me and told me she knew the girl I was talking about. She'd rented out rooms to boarders when her own family was young and needed money. A girl got trapped in a trunk during a game of hide-and-seek and suffocated."

"That's horrible," I manage.

Sarah's head dips. Loose strands of gray hair gust about her face as she looks toward the bird feeder, where sparrows bicker over breakfast. "It's an awful way for a child to go, but worse for the parents, I think. I saw her for the rest of the year that we lived there. She always wanted to play. If I tried to talk to her, she'd run off, as though the game had started. And, you know, I never actually learned her name. My grandmother would have known, but I never thought to ask."

The basket is empty, but I don't want to return indoors yet. "Do you think she's still there?"

Sarah's bony shoulders rise and then drop. "I have no idea. I like to hope she found peace somehow, though neither myself nor my grandmother could help her. But in an odd way, she helped me. I couldn't talk to my mother about what I'd seen, but my grandmother was open to it. She said it was my gift, something precious that God had given me and that I must not waste it. And here I am, one foot in the grave myself, and I finally have the opportunity to do some good."

"I might be just like that girl," I say. "I might be beyond help."

"Well, we won't know until we try. If you can't see a way to move on, I'm guessing you have something holding you here. And I don't doubt it's related to your death—or, more specifically, that your body hasn't been found."

I don't appreciate being talked about like a slab of meat lost behind the counter, but I try not to show how badly it bothers me. In some ways, it's possibly not too far from the truth. I'm still here, nearly as much as I was when I was alive. The meat and tendons and bones and veins that made up what I imagined to be myself are just gristle on the butchering floor of life.

"I don't really care about finding where or how I died." I speak carefully, testing the words to make sure they're honest. "But I want Meg to have answers."

"Mm. That feels right." Sarah rolls her shoulders, then leads me away from the clothesline. "Your unfinished business, if we're going to call it that, is your sister. Let's get her some closure."

As I follow Sarah toward the kitchen door, I glance behind us. The clothesline holds a half dozen items. The rest are still in the basket, turning cold in the chill breeze, and my heart sinks.

"To start with, let me tell you what I know." Sarah moves into the kitchen to reach the kettle. "I looked you up online. News articles are sparse, I'm sorry to say, and only a few lines long. They quote the police as saying they have concerns for your well-being. They ask anyone who might know your whereabouts to get in touch."

"When were they published?"

"February last year. Nothing since then."

"So if there's an investigation, it's not active." I settle at the kitchen table with my back to the window. As much as I try to approach it from a pragmatic perspective, it's hard not to feel disappointed at how little my disappearance matters to the world.

"That's how it seems to me, too." Sarah selects a mug from the cupboard, then glances back at me. "Do you want something to drink?"

"I'd love some tea."

"All right. So, first of all, we need to narrow down the window of when you disappeared. I already have your sister's number, but I'm hoping you can give me a few more people to call—friends, relatives, anyone who can tell me when they last heard from you and when you stopped answering their texts or showing up for events."

I pick at my fingers. "Most of my friends were from work. I'm an archivist at the natural history museum. *Was* an archivist. You can visit the museum for free and ask to meet with Mariah Comstock. We were probably the closest out of the team."

"That's a good place to start. What about family?"

"Just my sister. And she won't be able to help. We haven't talked in years."

"Well now, that's a shame." Sarah stops by the table and places a mug of green tea at my side. I take it, grateful, as she settles in opposite. "Did something cause a rift?"

"Nothing that mattered." A thousand paper cuts given over a lifetime might be insignificant, but when none of them are allowed to heal, they fester into something awful.

Sarah lets her fingertips rest on the rim of her mug, framing the rising steam, as she watches me. She's waiting, expectant, as though there's more to the story. I continue to pick at my fingers. "Could you take your glasses off? They're unnerving."

She laughs, a throaty, deep noise that shakes her shoulders, before peeling the circular lights away. "That's something coming from you. Now—let's figure out what you remember from around the time you went missing."

It's easier to relax when I can see her real eyes, watery and gray-green and still filled with a steady warmth, though their lashes are thinning. I focus on them, forcing my hands still and my voice steady. "I never missed work. My coworkers should be able to narrow it down to a day, or at least a weekend. Unless it happened over Christmas break. The archivist team all had time off from the twentieth of December until the second week of January. I mostly kept to myself during the holidays."

"No Christmas parties? No friends over?"

"Like I said, my friends were all from work, and we'd seen enough of each other through the year."

She makes a faint noise, something between incredulity and sadness, and it stings.

"I *like* being alone." I didn't intend for my voice to be so curt, but I don't regret it. "I'd feel smothered otherwise."

"You think so?"

"What does that mean?"

She shrugs, lifting her head to look at the house. "It's a big place for just one person."

"Pot, meet kettle," I snipe.

"Oh, sweet thing, your barbs cannot break through this hide." Sarah reclines in her chair, a languid smile forming. "I have four good children. And they've given me nine grandchildren, with another two on the way. I bought this house specifically so that there will always be room for them to visit. And if I'm being honest, so that I can have a chance to escape them once in a while."

That means other people will be allowed into my home. I'm still coming to terms with Sarah's presence, and for a wild second, I imagine asking her not to let her family in.

It would be dangerous for them.

The thought comes from nowhere and flickers out like a

sickly flame before I can fully fix on it. I'd thought my home was harboring an intruder, and technically, it was, except I now understand that Sarah isn't a threat. Why would I believe my home is something unsafe knowing what I now do?

My eyes track across the ceilings, where they meet with the wooden paneling, and down toward the front door. I imagine cracks running through the paint. Hairline fractures, spreading, extending with each passing night. Still too fine to see with bare eyes, but widening. They cannot be real, and I know that, but they *feel* very real. If I put my hands on the walls, I'm sure I could find them.

"Leigh?" Sarah prompts me.

I shake my head, as though the thoughts can be chased away, and form a smile. "Sorry. Got distracted."

"Mm. That's fine. I just asked if you were likely to go anywhere over Christmas. Visiting another town or going on a hike or camping."

"I do like hiking," I admit. "It's been a couple of years since I planned one, though."

"If you don't remember your death, then it's likely you don't remember the days leading up to it either. A solo hike could be dangerous if you strayed off path or traveled somewhere remote. That could be something to look into."

She pushes her thumb into her canine tooth, as though testing it, and I swallow the impulse to ask her not to. Her skin seems so thin, so fragile. She'll cut herself.

"I'll call in on your coworkers, but in the meantime, let's create a list of trails you've visited before and places you might have wanted to go. It's possible your body is still out there, waiting to be found."

# 11
# THE HOUSE TILTS

I PICTURE MY BODY LYING UNDERNEATH A SPREADING TREE. WIDE branches, not unlike the oak outside my home, cast shadows over me. My form would be cradled by the roots, covered in a blanket of fallen leaves, and sheltered from prying eyes by long grasses.

If my body has to be lost somewhere, that is where I want to be. Peaceful. Secure. I'm able to rest, and rest, and rest, held by that tree.

Something moves in my mouth. Not my tongue. My tongue is dead and has been for a long time. This is living. It is smooth and cool. Solid. Insistent as it presses against the roof of my mouth, trying to force my jaw open.

My lips part. The beetle slinks through the gap between my teeth. Prickling legs snag on the skin as it passes over my chin, moving toward my neck, where a festering wound is alive with fly spawn.

This is not rest. It is not peaceful. I have no control over my body as it writhes, bloated with life that is not my own. The tiny creatures that now use me for nourishment. They never leave me alone as wave after wave of them come, running through my veins, creeping into my vacant eye sockets, picking at me until there is nothing left.

I sit bolt upright in bed, covered in clinging sweat. My breaths snag in my throat, which is crowded by screams that can't get out.

My arms move across my body, hands clutching, fingers searching, but I'm intact. No insects. No holes. I slump against the headboard.

Sarah did this to me: her talk of my body being forgotten in some nature trail coated my mind as I slept. If what I'm doing is even sleeping.

Moonlight flows through the window. It infuses the air with some cold, unpleasant scent. This is my room, but I don't feel safe in it.

A body moves on the lower level of my home. Heavy footsteps, shuffling. They progress from the kitchen to the hallway and back in a loop.

I wouldn't have expected Sarah to still be awake so late, but I'm grateful that she is. The dream left me feeling sick.

I slide my feet out of bed and rest them on the rug, relishing the sensation of rough fibers against delicate skin. I press the toes further in, then recoil. The carpet is damp. Not recently wet, but an old kind of damp—the kind that has been sitting there for weeks, festering, incapable of ever fully drying.

My fingers run over the sole of my foot, but I can't find any moisture on it. The carpet disgusts me, though, and I pull my feet back onto my bed as I reach underneath to find my shoes.

Sarah continues to pace downstairs. Insomnia, perhaps. I used to lie awake some nights, but never because of my house. Tonight, though, something feels unstable about it. As though the foundation were placed just slightly wrong and the house now tilts.

I put my shoes on before allowing my feet to touch the floor again. My dressing gown goes around my shoulders as I move into the body of my house.

No lights come from the lower level, and the stairwell is bitterly dark. I let my fingertips run across the wall as instinct guides me down. Sarah completes another loop of the ground floor and keeps moving. Perhaps this isn't insomnia but sleep-walking. I can't think of many other reasons for her not to at least switch a lamp on.

As I turn the stairwell's corner, something smooth and cold grazes my arm. I slap it, and my palm hits synthetic rope. I close my fingers around it and drag it down, my breathing just slightly too fast. At least three meters coil around my hand before I find the end.

Sarah moves into the space below the stairs and halts there. She must have heard me. I call out, "It's just me. Do you know where this rope came from?"

I take the final four steps to the ground floor. The living room curtains are open, but clouds filter the moonlight until it is only a whisper. I can see Sarah next to the under-stairs door, but only barely. If she were to stop swaying, she would be at risk of vanishing into the blackness.

"Sarah?"

She has to be sleepwalking. She wouldn't stare at me so blankly otherwise. Swaying, as though she can feel the house's unstable foundation as well, as though she's trying to find a footing.

The hairline fractures extend just a little further, and my body goes cold. This figure is not Sarah. As it sways, hints of its outline are revealed against the mottled grays and blacks of the kitchen. It's too thin.

I creep backward. The hallway light switch is just inside the door, near the hooks where I hang my bag. I keep my eyes fixed on the figure as I feel across the cold walls.

They're damp, just like the carpet upstairs. The kind of dampness that comes from inside the walls. Seeping out.

My fingers touch plastic. I find the switch and turn it. Light catches over my surroundings.

The figure is gone. I can visualize the exact point it was standing next to the under-stairs door. Water catches and reflects the light. Two footprints, bare soles and distinct toes, mark the location.

My stomach wants to turn over as I face away. The living room curtains are open. I cross to them in frantic steps and wrench them closed. Knowing that my fear, that my predicament, is on display for the street—it's abhorrent.

As I move through the lower level, I close every window and

turn on every light that I pass. I watch for signs that I'm not alone, but the house is now suspiciously quiet.

I finish my loop through the dining room to arrive back at the hall. The lower level is alight now, a blaze of lamps and bulbs, and I try to hold on to their bracing effect as I climb the stairs.

There is only one place I could expect Sarah to be. I pass every other door as I move toward the room at the end of the hall. The rarely used hinges sigh as I force them to turn. The curtains in this room are also open, and the moonlight tangles across a bed that is not mine. I press the switch, bathing us in light.

"What? Leigh?" Sarah, covered in a sage-green nightgown and her long hair in a plait, struggles to sit up.

I feel some of the tension slide away as I take in her room. She's decorated it in trinkets: porcelain cats, porcelain people, all glazed in white and with pastel details painted on top. Haphazard shelves and trunks and tables support the decor. It's a stark change to the plain storage room I'd maintained. As I step inside, I examine an owl figurine that calmly watches over the space. "Sorry to wake you. Is anyone else staying in my house?"

Sarah groans. She shuffles up in her bed, putting her shoulders against the cloth backboard, and rubs at the corner of her nose. "No. Why do you ask, sweet thing?"

"I saw someone downstairs." The owl's gaze is peaceful, and I focus on it, afraid that if I turn toward Sarah, she'll see the fear in my eyes. "I think I did at least. They vanished when I turned on the light."

She could have easily talked me down from it. I'd just woken from a nightmare. My mind seems to become more scattered, more erratic, when I fall out of my routine. And it wouldn't be the first time I've materialized something that didn't truly exist. Instead, Sarah reaches for a gown that hangs beside her bed and pulls it over her arms, her legs still covered by the blankets. "What did they look like?"

"Tall. And thin." I glance at her, then away again. "Pacing through the lower level of the house. Why did you pick this room?"

She shakes her head, uncomprehending, and I know I'm jumping through ideas too quickly.

"This isn't the master bedroom," I amend. "Why did you pick it, instead of the one down the hallway?"

"Ah. When I moved in, the house still had all of its—your—original furniture. And that larger room clearly belonged to you. It would have felt odd to take it over. Besides, I prefer the view from this one."

She hasn't minded taking over the rest of the house: changing the decorations, opening curtains that are supposed to stay closed. But I appreciate this gesture. "This may be an odd question, but did you bring any rope into the house? Rope hanging from the walls or from the ceiling?"

"Oh, yes. My macramé. I used to love making it, and it took so much time that now I can't stand to throw it out."

She chuckles, and I feel a smile of my own creeping up. "I know what that's like. My quilt—" A fear, sudden and sharp, cuts me. I've failed to notice many changes in my home until they're pointed out to me, and the quilt in the living room doesn't match Sarah's style of decorating. "Don't throw it out. You didn't, did you?"

"No." She sighs and sinks slightly lower on her bed. "I realized I wasn't alone in this house on the day I moved in. And I thought I had better not anger you by throwing out anything that was so clearly important."

My shoulders bow with relief. I've been thinking about throwing out that quilt for years. Now, I can't stand the idea of losing it.

"Speaking of angering spirits, I'd like to know more about this middle-of-the-night awakening. You said you saw a figure, but they're not there any longer?" Sarah rubs at her nose again, and I realize she's still fogged with sleep.

"No." I don't know how to tell her about the fractures or about the growing sense that there's something very wrong with my home. Instead, I try for a joke. "Maybe I'd feel less edgy if you didn't open the curtains all the time."

"The place feels like a morgue," she fires back. "You kept it so gloomy."

"I like my privacy, that's all."

"Sweet thing, this isn't your home any longer."

My mouth opens, but I force it closed before I can say anything unkind. It still *feels* like my home. From my perspective, nothing has changed—except that I now have to contend with an intruder.

But she's right, isn't she? I no longer pay the bills. Or maintain the building. Or have much control over it at all. She left most of my furniture in place as a kindness. She lets me keep my room also out of kindness.

I still live here, but it's no longer truly mine. And I hate that.

Sarah smiles. One of her clawlike hands pats the edge of her bed, inviting me to sit. I do, feeling uncomfortable but also grateful. She's close enough that I can count the creases around her eyes, rolls of loose skin covering bags, mapped by spots of burst capillaries. Age has fought her, strained her joints and damaged her skin, sapping the strength from her body. But it has not doused her spirit. She gives no leeway and, despite how long it has dragged on or how inevitable it is, does not back down from the fight.

She's the kind of person I would like to be when I'm eighty.

Would have, if I'd been given the opportunity.

"This house is special. The moment I stepped into it, I felt like I was home." My hands knit together as I struggle to put emotions into words. "I rented it until my landlord wanted to sell, then battled to get together a deposit before anyone else could offer on it. I never doubted that I wanted to spend the rest of my life here. It's just…unlike any other house."

"That's something I can understand." The truth in her words strikes me. She would have bought this building for the same reason I did: because it felt like her home.

"Sorry," I manage. "I was so preoccupied by having you in my home that I forgot it goes the other way, too. You probably weren't thrilled to find someone already living in your new property. And you can't even evict me, can you?"

She laughs. "I wouldn't try. It's not so bad having some company in this old building. I suspect I'd be lonely otherwise."

Maybe it's not so bad. I glance across the painted figurines, trinkets that must have been accumulated across decades, and my gaze lands on a small photo. It's sized to be handheld, framed in bronze, and I leave Sarah's bed to examine it.

"Are you in this?" I cradle the photo as I return to sit on the edge of the bed, and Sarah's knuckle-heavy finger indicates the image.

"Yes. My family. That's me."

She nods to the elder of the two girls. I tilt the photo. It's far smaller than the versions I saw in the distorted hallway, and the details are harder to make out, but I want to believe the family's expressions are less grim than in the nightmare version.

"My mother did odd jobs." Sarah sinks back into her bed, her eyelids heavy. "Washing. Cleaning. Ironing. Anything our neighbors wanted to pass to us. My father worked in the local steel factory. That's gone now, of course…demolished more than fifty years ago. He left, too. About a year after that photo was taken. Left for work one morning but never came back. His coworkers say they saw him get on a Greyhound, and that was it. Never even picked up his last paycheck."

"I'm sorry."

She chuckles. "Do you know what the strangest part is? I still imagine I might hear from him one day. He must be long dead by now. But, see, my mother always believed he'd come back eventually. Even after she passed, I held on to that idea. He was out there somewhere. Maybe with a new family, a new job, a new home. But we would have to be weighing on him—the family he abandoned. Surely his conscience wouldn't let him sleep until he came back and made it right. And even though he'd be over a hundred if he were still alive, it's hard to let go of that idea."

"You'd want closure," I say. "It must be hard not knowing what became of him after he left."

"That's it exactly. We struggled; my mother's odd jobs couldn't keep us afloat, even if she'd had the strength of will to keep up with them. And…I suppose I would have liked to know. Did he struggle, too? Did he die young? We didn't have much in savings, and he didn't try to take any of it, so he could have ended up on the street. Or maybe he did all right for himself. Maybe his life was better without us in it."

The idea is like a barb in my mind. "He wouldn't have deserved it."

Sarah's eyes are strangely fond as she regards me. "Oh, don't worry. I'm well past resentment. I was young enough when he left that I can remember only the best parts of him, and that's the way I want to keep it."

"What about your family, though? He left four young children…"

She takes a deep breath and releases it in a rush. "We struggled, sure. But our neighbor's charity kept us from starving. And then we moved in with my grandmother. And we lived there until my brothers were old enough to leave school and get jobs of their own."

I turn my gaze across the two boys: one who had to be close to twelve, one who looked around eight.

The picture strikes me as something deeply melancholy. It had captured a family on the verge of collapse; within a year, they would be fragmented, never to be reunited. The details are tiny and blurred under the hand coloring, but I imagine I can detect traces of restlessness in the father's eyes. Perhaps, even when that picture was captured, he was building dreams of a different life.

Sarah's eyes are heavy. I rise to carry the picture back to the dresser where I found it only to realize my hands are empty. It's back in its position between the porcelain figurines, as though I'd never touched it. Which, I now know, I hadn't. It was just my mind hard at work building delusions. Those beautiful figments designed to lull me into the belief that life still continues—that I can still hold and lift and move things—only last as long as they're not examined too closely. The moment I question them, they evaporate like shadows under a harsh light, leaving me empty once again. A sigh rises in my throat. I suppress it. "Sorry again for waking you."

"What's the point of having a ghost in my home if she doesn't disturb my sleep on occasion?" Sarah's smile fades. "Did you have a bad dream? You can stay longer if you like."

"Thanks. But I'm okay." As I move toward the door, images return. My body, writhing, alive with insects. My mouth turns sour. As I stop by the door, fingers hovering above the light switch, a question swims across my tongue before I can halt it. "Do you think my death was peaceful?"

Her eyes glitter in the light, wetter than they should be. Sarah is quiet for so long that I begin to think she's refusing to answer, then her shoulders hunch closer to her chin. "I'm very sorry, my darling. I don't think it was."

I turn and rest my forehead against the cool doorframe. My throat is tight, but Sarah is patient as she waits for me to speak. "Why do you think that?"

She no longer meets my gaze but pulls the blankets higher, signaling the end of our talk. "We'll find out what happened to you. Good night, my darling."

The switch clicks under my fingers. Another figment, I realize a moment too late: the lights were never on to begin with. I close the door gently, then rest against it, listening to the crinkling duvet as Sarah curls up in bed.

There is something wrong with me. My feet are light on the runner as I follow the hall to my bedroom. I put the light on, breathing deeply as I cross to the closet and pull the door open. Its internal side has a full-length mirror, an uninterrupted pane of glass that's tarnished by age and with a reflection that never seems quite in focus. I stand in front of it, arms spread at my sides, as I examine my body.

Tall, pale, a figure like a rectangle. Dark brown hair runs like a cascade on either side of my face. Moles dot my body, but I don't spend enough time in the sun to gather freckles. I lean close to the glass to examine my face. There is some darkness gathered underneath my eyes. My lips seem pale. My pupils constrict in the light.

I am as I always am.

What does Sarah see?

Once again I imagine my body filled with insects. My stomach bloated from them, my fingers twitching as they eat through muscles, my mouth held open as they travel down my throat.

The door bangs as I slam it closed. My lungs ache. I put my back to the door, hands held over my face, as I wait for my racing heart to slow.

Sarah says we will find out what happened. I hope she is right. And I hope the answer is not more than I can bear.

# 12
# CREEPING UP
# THE WALLS

"Leigh?"

The voice comes to me from a fog. I'm asleep. No…it's something like sleep. I'm not in bed. I'm not sure *where* I am, except that I am inside my home, and I don't want to be disturbed.

"Leigh, are you about?"

It's Sarah's voice. After waking her last night, it's only fair that she's allowed to disturb me, too, I decide. I reluctantly push myself to consciousness.

Midday approaches. It's easy to tell from the sun's angle as it cascades through the kitchen window. A momentary pang of panic—did I oversleep? Am I missing work?—must be dismissed. Then I look down at my hands and see they are resting on the kitchen table. I'm in my favorite seat, facing the window, where I can watch the birds fight over the feeder. The day is warm and smells like spring, even though the season will not break properly for another month. I stretch, rolling my shoulders, feeling the knots and stiff muscles.

"Leigh? Ah, there you are." Sarah appears in the archway bridging the kitchen and the dining room. She's given more thought to her clothes than normal; the dress and cardigan match, and a scarf—too light to do much against the cold—hangs across her shoulders. She's twisted her plait into a bun, but the bobby pins poke out at odd angles.

"I'm glad I caught you." She moves through the kitchen with quick, eager paces, pulling a half dozen plastic cups out of the cupboard. "I have a few things to tell you. First, some updates on your situation. Second, my family is coming to visit."

She opens the oven to examine a tray. More smells register. Herbs. Cheeses. She closes the oven door, apparently satisfied, and gathers the cups to her chest. I follow her into the dining room, where the table is half-set. Something registers deep in my stomach. Panic. "Your family?"

"Yes, sorry. I would have given you more notice, but they only phoned to say they were coming yesterday afternoon. I've been waiting for you to pop up again but you've been rather shy these last few days."

She places the cups next to the table settings—not in any random order, I notice, but picking out colors to match the napkins. I count seven settings. Three using grays and whites, presumably for the adults, and four with bright primary colors.

My tongue runs across my teeth as a tangle of words catch on it. *Maybe they shouldn't come here. Are you sure this is wise? Is it too late to stop them?*

"I wanted to make sure you knew, since this is still partially your house after all. So that they don't surprise you, or vice versa." She regards the table, nods, and shuffles back to the kitchen. "I don't expect any of my grandchildren to be able to see you. Not like I can. So you're welcome to hang around if you like."

"Grandchildren?" The word comes out weak, anxious. I feel the house's cracks under my feet, sense them above my head. Something dark seeps out of them. Something horrible. Something no one, especially not children, should be allowed near.

"Yes! Four of them. Millie, Avery, Ryan, Kayleigh." She opens the oven again, flicks out a towel, and wraps it around her hand before removing the tray. It's filled with herby cheese toasties. Three are regular slices of bread. Four have been painstakingly cut into shapes. I recognize a flower, a treasure chest, a book with the herbs arranged to form the title, and a blobby shape I can't make out.

"That's supposed to be a dragon," Sarah says when she catches me looking. "It went a bit wonky, I'm afraid."

"Their favorite things?" I guess.

"I keep notes in my book." She pats her front pocket. "I wish my brain was stretchy enough to remember it all, but I have nine grandchildren, and their interests change so quickly. I just do my best to keep up."

"They're lucky."

Sarah is busy at the fridge, pulling out a pitcher of juice, and doesn't notice my anxiety. Her steps slow to shuffles as she attempts to carry the jug to the dining room, her arms shaking under the weight. As she leaves my line of sight, I move into the hallway and stare at the under-stairs door.

The cracks I know can't really be there shiver and widen. Just a fraction. Still too much. I put my arms around my chest, fingertips digging into my ribs, my teeth clenched.

"Sorry, Leigh. I keep forgetting." Sarah comes from my left, from the archway near the front door. She uses one hand to guide herself along the wall, and that's when I realize she's not wearing her glasses. "We've made some progress. I went to the museum like you suggested and spoke to Mariah Comstock. She confirmed what you said. You were never late, and you never skipped work. And thanks to that, she was able to confirm when you went missing. It was over the Christmas break, after all. She said you seemed normal on your last day of work but didn't show up on your first day back."

"Okay." It's not the best outcome—this gives us a three-week window when I went missing, rather than one or two days, like we were hoping. But at least it's a step forward.

"That's not all, though. I—"

A phone rings. The tone is unfamiliar—bright, timed like a waltz—and I flinch. Sarah makes a faint noise and passes me, one hand brushing my shoulder, as she returns to the kitchen. The rings cut out and Sarah answers the call.

I follow, stopping in the kitchen archway, watching as Sarah holds a handset to her ear. The warm sunlight paints her in gold, catching on the beading of her dress and the askew bobby pins in her hair. She paces, her voice animated, then stops at the sink, facing the window, as her words lose some of their luster.

"Of course. Of course. No, don't worry about it. That sounds good. I'm looking forward to it. I love you."

She puts the handset onto the counter. I step toward her, then stop, feeling like I'm intruding on something very personal.

Sarah looks over her shoulder, sees me, and smiles. "They can't make it."

"Oh." Relief floods me, quickly followed by guilt. "I'm sorry."

"My daughter's a cardiologist." Sarah crosses to the stove top, where she'd left the tray of cheesy bread. "A very successful one. I'm so proud of her. But oftentimes she's busy."

Sarah takes one slice of the bread, puts it onto a plate, then stares at the remaining six. She takes up the tray, and I feel like I'm watching her age a decade as she crosses to the trash and carefully scrapes the hand-cut toast into it.

"She was called into work. A last-minute emergency. They're going to try again next weekend."

"Sarah…" Words feel inadequate. I want to hug her. But when I move toward her, she rolls her shoulders and smiles.

"This just means we have more time to focus on you." Sarah slides the tray back into the cooling oven. "Let's—we'll make a cup of tea. Do you want one? I'm sure you do. Let's—"

"Sarah, I'm so sorry."

She is resolute, already filling the kettle, her eyes watery.

"I have plenty to tell you. So it's all right. We'll have a busy afternoon."

"Okay." I don't know what else to say. "I'd love some tea, please."

As Sarah puts on the kettle, I return to the dining room and look across the place settings carefully built out of her grandchildren's favorite colors.

Part of me is grateful. This is not a house for children. But Sarah has been here for months, and from what I can gather, this would have been her first time seeing her family since moving in.

The first time seeing anyone, now that I think of it. She made sure to warn me that they were coming, so that I wouldn't be alarmed. But there's been no cause to do that before. No friends, no other relatives. No one to visit. Just her, alone, in this huge house.

I stack the settings and, moving quietly, carry them back into the kitchen so that Sarah won't have to. She stands facing the kettle, unresponsive, as I pack the plates and cups away. As I close the cupboards, I glance back to the dining room, and my heart sinks. The settings remain untouched on the table.

Sarah's not completely alone, but I will be the first to admit that I am not the best form of company. She needs more.

"She bought this house for me." Sarah's voice snaps me out of my reverie. She smiles as she places tea bags into two cups. "Just so you don't think she doesn't care. She does. But her work is important. It's not like an office emergency. She can't just…put it off until Monday. Her job means saving someone who might not last until tomorrow. So it's not her fault when emergencies come up."

Sarah seems to want to talk, so I follow her lead. "What's your daughter's name?"

"Sylvia. She's top of her field. Her father and I had to cut our budget down to scraps for years to make sure she could get her education, but oh, she's so wonderfully skilled at it. She won an award last year. I got to go to the ceremony and eat shrimp and talk to a lot of people who I have nothing in common with."

I chuckle. Sarah pours the water into our mugs, steam billowing to catch on the window's glass.

"So she bought you this house?" I prod as she moves our mugs onto the table and sinks into her chair.

"That's right. My last one needed more repairs than it was worth, so Sylvia said she was going to buy a home where I could be closer to her. She sat next to me as we went through some listings online, and I saw this one, and I asked for it without even going to a showing."

"It must have felt like home as soon as you saw it." It was the same for me. All mental lists of what I wanted in a house vanished as I stepped through the front door.

Sarah nods. "Always has. Now, let's get back to what's important. I visited Mariah Comstock. You never came back to work after Christmas break. The police started investigating you as a missing person a few weeks later."

"She must have contacted them." Mariah was a good woman. She got on well with everyone at the museum and was a stickler for details. She was the one who brought in cakes for birthdays, who organized flowers and ready-made meals when Lucille went on maternity leave, and who threw a going-away party when Steven moved to France.

Sarah's lips work against each other. She rotates her cup, using her fingertips to turn it in a circle, and I know there's something more.

"Mariah…didn't call the police?"

"I'm afraid not, sweetheart. I spoke to her, and I spoke to many of your old coworkers."

"What did they say?"

"They thought you'd quit without giving notice."

"What?" Something cold sinks into my stomach. "But…I never missed work. I never took sick leave. I was the most reliable person in the office. Why…"

Sarah's green eyes are deeply sad. Her head is down, but she watches me over her mug, her thin eyebrows knit together.

"It's okay," I manage. "Tell me what they said."

"Sweetheart, they saw you as antisocial. You never went out to the bar with them. Or went to their parties. Or sat with them at lunch break."

"It was easier to get work done when they were at lunch," I manage.

"And they thought that meant you didn't like them." Sarah gives her mug another rotation, then sighs. "A lot of them said they weren't surprised when you didn't show up. They believe you got an offer for a better job in another town and left without telling them."

"But I did like them." It's a feeble protest, but it's true. I thought of them all fondly. Called them my friends—not to their faces, but in my journal, in the privacy of my home. And I thought they did the same in return.

Though, I'm forced to admit, intentions don't make an iota of difference at the end. I'm to be remembered as the frosty employee who left as soon as she had a better offer. Just like my sister will evidently remember me as the one who held her grudge forever. And it's too late to change. I am Scrooge, except the story ends before the ghosts arrive. I don't get my redemption arc.

"So, that's why no one noticed that I was gone for over a month." I try to laugh, but it comes out bitter. "Someone must have reported me missing, though."

"Your neighbors." Sarah nods toward the street. "That has been the most enlightening part of this. In my experience, every street has at least one individual who watches the comings and goings and keeps on top of the gossip. So I went searching for them. And we are in luck. Your street doesn't have one, but *three*."

"Oh, I think I can guess." I scrunch my nose. "Patty Galbreath, Cliff Kasack, Jenn Howard."

Sarah lifts her cup in a mock cheers. "That's them."

"Jenn once knocked on my door and asked me if I was well because I'd left my Christmas tree up into the middle of January, and she'd seen it through a gap in the living room curtains. I've kept them closed ever since."

"Mm-hmm. And that incessant nosiness helped you quite a lot. Patty Galbreath observed that your car hadn't moved for several weeks and mentioned it to Jenn Howard. Jenn checked your letter box and saw bills stacking up. She went to Cliff Kasack, and the two of them tried to get into your house."

An involuntary shudder runs through me. "They didn't."

"Oh, yes, sweet thing. But you'd locked both your front and back door, and thankfully they stopped short of breaking a window. They called the police for a wellness check instead. That was on the ninth of February."

Sarah takes her notebook from her pocket and turns through the pages. I glimpse many scribbled notes, separated by sharp lines.

"I didn't get the chance to talk to Jenn until this morning, but she was the most helpful. She hung around while the police were investigating and got quite a few details out of them—things that I suspect weren't supposed to be released to the public. You'd left your car, but your keys, purse, bank cards, driver's license, and passport were missing."

"Really?" It's hard to imagine what I needed them all for.

"There was no sign of foul play inside your house and no witnesses to anything unusual, so the police believe you just left your old life one morning. Their interviews with your coworkers supported the idea that it was something you were likely to do. From their perspective, you didn't have anything tying you down here. The primary theory is that you caught a bus or took a taxi to an airport and bought a ticket with cash."

"I wouldn't." My hands feel cold. The fingers rest on the table-top, and I move them, just to prove to myself that they are still a part of my body. "I've never wanted to do anything like that. Why would I? I loved my job. I love this house. I would have been happy with things going on the same forever."

"Don't panic, darling." Sarah places her hand on top of mine, stopping the anxious twitches. "I believe you. If we needed any proof, your mere existence here would be enough. You perished some time ago. And I suspect it happened close to home."

"Thank you."

She tilts her head back, as though to examine the ceiling. "It does strike out my earlier theory, though, that you met with an accident or foul play while out hiking. Your passport is gone, and there would be no reason for you to bring it with you on a day trip."

"No. I don't think I've touched it in years—not since I needed to apply for a mortgage to buy this." I'm faintly relieved. The idea of my corpse tangled in a prolonged dance with insects under some spreading tree has filled me with horror.

"Which leaves, from what I can see, two possibilities. You left home voluntarily, intending to travel somewhere that required a passport, and met with misfortune on the way. Or someone attacked you within this home and stole your documents. Perhaps a burglary gone wrong."

"How can *either* be possible? I don't like to travel, especially not over Christmas, and if I were attacked in my home, why wasn't my body found?"

"Mm. I have to agree, the latter has some holes in it. There was no sign of a disturbance in the house, and it was fully locked up when your neighbors tried to gain entry."

The tea scorches my tongue as I try to drink it, but it's a welcome relief from the fire in my mind. If there was any one person I should understand, it is myself, but now I am stuck trying to guess what could, or should, be within the realm of my normal behavior. "If I died outside the home, wouldn't my ghost stay at that site?"

"I wouldn't know. It's possible. On the other hand, you have such a strong attachment to this building that it feels most likely that you'd wind up here."

"Routine," I murmur. Sarah leans closer, one of her birdlike arms resting on the tabletop, and I clear my throat. "I think I'm so...*present*...because of the routine I built before death."

"Yes, that would make sense. You're not held here by the ties of injustice or a need for revenge, but simply because death could not interrupt the march of the familiar."

We stare into our respective cups, both lost in the outlandish scenarios of what might have interrupted my life, my last Christmas. At last I say, "I'll give you my bank log-in details. You can check the last transactions. If I called a taxi or bought a Greyhound ticket, I may have put it on that card. Even if I didn't, they should help narrow down the window of when I went missing."

"That's an idea." Sarah flips to a fresh page of her notebook and writes while I dictate. She finishes by drawing a line beneath the numbers. "While I look into this, you could search the house. It's still possible you met with an intruder. The police didn't note anything taken beyond your personal papers, but they didn't have you to consult. It's possible items are missing. I've changed relatively little since I moved in, so you should be able to account for everything—or close to it."

"Thanks." I stand, bringing the mug of tea with me. Light enters through the living room windows—open again, despite my best efforts. I approach and feel the air pressure change subtly as I leave the kitchen.

This might be good for me. It's the first time I've examined my home critically since Sarah moved in. A part of me didn't want to see the changes to the degree I purposefully overlooked them. Now, I force myself to see my surroundings as they truly are.

Sarah kept her word. She removed very little of what belonged to me; instead, she added on top. The living room still holds my three white couches, and my quilt hangs on the wall. But now, I close my eyes, and when I reopen them, I see the angel figurine on the coffee table. Brightly colored, patterned cushions on the couches. An old-wood display cabinet fitted into the empty space behind the seats. It holds rows of fine china teacups.

I was never much swayed by material trappings. The most valuable things in my home are the furniture, too large to easily move, and the quilts, whose worth is measured in hours rather than coins.

Still, there are a few places I can check. I turn, intending to visit the second floor, but catch myself.

A shoulder-height display unit is propped against the wall beneath the stairs. On its surface are photos: Sarah, appearing slightly younger than she is now, holding children on her lap.

The table has two shelves built in, and they're stocked with old paperback novels, their spines heavily creased.

"Sarah?" I feel unstable, like the floor is shifting under me, even though I know my house is perfectly still. "Did you put this here?"

She emerges from the kitchen archway and glances at the unit. "Yes, that's mine. There's a door behind it, but it's locked. Always has been. I figured I may as well put something pretty there instead."

"Right." Maybe it's for the best. Cover the door, hide it, never think about it again. My hold on the mug is tight, and the drink is still warm enough to make my skin prickle as I press it to my chest.

The unit must have been there since Sarah moved in. Have I really been struggling with, avoiding, and fearing a door that I cannot even access? So much time spent dreading that the door might open, watching it and avoiding it, and the whole time my mind was so focused on maintaining its delusions that I couldn't even see the cabinet in the way.

Abrupt anger blooms through me, heating me up more efficiently than the tea. Anger at myself. Along with something thicker and heavier: embarrassment. I turn aside, my stomach growing sick with the sensations, and take the stairs in rapid-fire paces.

The first entrance off the landing leads into the bathroom. I close the door behind myself and place the mug onto the sink.

Old tiles surround me in shades of off-white and aqua green.

They came from when the house was last remodeled in the seventies and would have looked better before the grouting became its crumbly, repulsive gray. The room festers mold, and no product has been able to uproot it. A crack runs along the wall by the mirror, the tiles failing to line up as the black, jagged line carves its way between them.

The vanity is as old as the tiles. Time has patiently pried it away from the wall, and a line of shrinking silicon fails to bridge the gap. Fake-gold knobs adorn two white cupboard doors and a stack of three shelves hold spare towels and bottles. The floor is technically clean, but it doesn't look it, so I try to avoid letting my clothes touch it as I crouch.

The cabinet doors always offer a slightly gummy resistance to opening, but once they come apart, they expose two shelves arranged around the underside of the sink. A pipe comes down from the gray underside of the basin, loops, and descends into the floor, unpleasantly reminiscent of a digestive tract. Bottles of conditioner and shampoo are arranged neatly in any space tall enough for them to stand, with boxes of soap beside them.

On the underside of the lower shelf I taped a plastic bag. It's impossible to see unless your head is nearly at the level of the floor. I feel under the shelf and cringe as I find spiderwebs clinging to the bag's edges. I tug it free, flicking it to disperse any unwanted hitchhikers, and bring it into the light.

Filing cabinets and desk drawers are obvious targets for thieves. Freezers, cushions, and fake sockets are more subtle but still frequently searched. Relatively few people would think to dig into the recesses of a grungy second-floor bathroom. At least, that was my hope.

The bag releases a breath of stale air as I breach its seal. Inside is an envelope. Thin. Empty.

That paper sleeve was plump with cash when I last stashed it away nearly two years ago. It was my emergency fund, a backup in case I lost access to my bank's savings account. Four months' worth of living expenses. Gone.

Whoever took it didn't simply discard the bag: they returned it to its position, carefully taped where the casual observer wouldn't notice it had been disturbed. That's something I would do. If I were forced to leave my home at short notice and didn't know where my next paycheck would come from, this emergency fund would be my lifeline.

The alternative is that someone else went through my home with such desperate thoroughness that they even looked underneath my bathroom sink. Not impossible. But implausible.

The crouched position is uncomfortable, but I hold it while I turn the question over in my mind. The missing money suggests that I did truly leave my home. Willingly. But the same question continues to dig at me: Why? What could make me leave a beloved house and job so suddenly that no one realized I was missing for more than a month?

And following that, how did I die?

The aqua-green tiles are nauseating. The color is solid across the floor, as though someone spilled the wrong paint and never found the time to wipe it up. From there it creeps up the walls in terrible increments. Two lines of solid color, a line of off-white, repeated. By the time the pattern transitions to solid white at shoulder height, my eyes are overwhelmed. Crouching near it is making me feel sick.

Creature of habit that I am, I fold the plastic bag over itself and use the same tape to stick it back into its position. As I rise, dust itches at my throat. My left forearm covers my mouth as I cough, and my right hand reaches for my drink. The mug is no longer smooth and warm, but cold, covered in a thick cloud of grime, repulsive and alien to my touch.

# 13
## HER SIGNATURE

GREASE-LADEN DUST COVERS EVERY SURFACE IN THE BATHROOM. It cakes the towels, weighing down their fibers. It paints a gray tinge across the vanity. It dampens the nauseating aqua-green floor. I lift my foot, and the space underneath my sole is the only clean part of the room.

My mug bears the same coating. The tea is gone—dried into a cracked layer at its base. My reflection is blurred into indistinct shapes. The mirror has always shown its age, with black spots marking the edges where the reflective sheen has been scraped up, but now it's brought into ruin by what seems like decades of neglect.

Something moves behind my reflection.

I turn, but I'm alone in the room. The door remains closed. The green tiles, smothered in grime, are abruptly too much. The sense of queasiness that has dogged me since entering the bathroom redoubles into nausea. I close my eyes, hands finding the filthy edge of the sink as I fight to regain my composure. It's gone in an instant. I retch over the sink, emptying myself into the basin, and the more I bring up, the more my stomach twists itself into painful contortions.

Shakes assault my limbs, and I'm left damp and cold as I slump against the wall. My mouth is foul, but not in the way sickness should leave it. The taste is metallic, thick, and slimy. I force myself to look. The sink is painted scarlet with my blood.

Something has gone very bad. I want Sarah. Even if she cannot help, even if she is incapable of doing more than sitting beside me, I don't want to be alone.

No. More than that. I don't want *her* to be alone. My hand finds the sink's tap and turns it. The pipe shudders, and I hear those echoes repeated through the house. My own blood no longer frightens me: I am beyond the point of being hurt. Sarah is not.

The pipes are loud. A banging, rattling sound spreads deeper into the building. I imagine the pipes are like tree roots—not straight and direct, but twisting, weaving around each other, splitting and spreading as the thicker main roots spear into separate rooms. Following the cracks that run through my house. Forcing them wider.

I turn the tap off. No water made it out, so there is no way to clean my mess. I wipe the back of my hand across my mouth, smearing away a line of red, and cross to the door.

"Sarah?"

My call repeats through the empty halls. Deep night has fallen, and I can't see farther than the bathroom's light allows, but the decay of passed time has spread. Dust holds to the walls like cotton candy to a stick. It gathers on my fingers as I guide myself toward the staircase. The familiar light switch appears under my touch. I turn it without much hope and am still disappointed.

Something pale and thin blocks my path. A rope. My eyes fight against the gloom, and the pattern of white acrylic is repeated, again and again, like some hallucination floating from the abyss. There isn't a single rope blocking the staircase but dozens, tangled over and around one another. A spiderweb of man-made fibers. Chaotic. Repulsive. I back away, and one of the loose rope ends caresses my cheek.

"Sarah!" I turn for the room at the end of the hall, and my paces lengthen until I'm approaching a run. She can't be downstairs; it's too dark. But she must still be close.

The hallway is shorter than I remembered. My outstretched arm hits the door and I gasp. As I feel blindly for the handle, I hear something behind me. Something akin to slithering. Smooth ropes, sliding against each other. Growing closer.

I find the handle and turn it. The door gives way and I stagger inside, slamming the barrier behind myself, and feel for the light.

"Sarah, I'm sorry, I—"

The bulb comes to life. This is Sarah's room, but Sarah is not in it. Hasn't been for a long time.

Her bed is made neatly, two pillows enveloped by the cover,

crease free. The figurines are arranged in clusters across the tables and shelves.

All are wrapped in the cocooning dust.

I put my back against the door. The age has begun to cling to me as well. I feel it in every crease of my skin, every pore, as though it wants to invade my very cells. Something moves outside the room: a slick, light thud against carpet. One of the ropes falling from its tangle.

Eyes are on me. Their weight is palpable, but it takes a moment to locate them. Six sets, inside the bronze frame on the table near the bed. During daylight, when the world makes sense, those eyes have pupils and irises. Now, they are only white.

Another soft thudding noise in the hallway, just beyond the door, as a rope falls. I pull my hands into fists, feel the tacky dust in them, feel the weight of lost decades building over me. I can't stand the eyes for another second. Five long steps carry me to the photo. I slam it down, putting those faces against the wood of the table.

But then, against my better judgment, almost against my will, I lift it back up. Something about this picture feels unpleasantly familiar. As though I know it better than I should. As though it tangles with my existence in a way that goes deeper than my association with Sarah.

I wipe the dust away from the portrait. Six faces stare back. The mother, sitting; the father, standing just behind, one hand on her shoulder. The four children. A plain beige background. Plain except for a tiny black spot that might be a scuff in the paint or might be an error in the photography. And except for the molding at the base of the wall.

My stomach, empty, turns again. I hold on to the table's edge to keep upright. Flecks of light move across my vision as the vertigo clears.

The wood under my hand is clean. I straighten. The bed is still there, still made; the tables hold the same positions and the same arrangements of figurines. But the dust is gone. Sunlight runs through the window; early morning, angled to creep halfway up my body.

I rub my fingers together. The dust still lingers there, as though I dragged it through the decades with me. But my house is my house again.

Six faces stare at me from the portrait. I hate them, but even when I turn the photo away, I can feel their presence.

But I don't put it down. I carry it against my chest, loathe to let it touch me but unwilling to let it go, as I leave Sarah's room.

The ropes are gone from the hallway. My footsteps only slow when I near the bathroom. The nauseating green tiles are familiar. The mirror is unchanged. I might have never even entered the room except that the sink is smeared with my blood.

The pipes respond as I turn the tap, and I use my palm to scoop water across the bowl. The red washes away readily. I imagine it being carried through the pipes, like blood through veins, and for a second I picture the house as a living thing, with me as its heart. The image vanishes. The sink is clean...enough. I still carry the picture.

I head down the stairs and into the hallway. Sarah is in the kitchen. I can't see her from my angle, but her footsteps have become familiar, and I try not to feel the sense of betrayal bubbling in me. Not yet. Instead, I pass through the living room and through the door to the study.

She hears me and calls, "Leigh, is that you?"

My mouth is too dry to reply, even if I'd wanted to. My back goes to the study's window as I face the wall opposite. Plain beige save for a rusted hook in the wall that was intended to carry a picture and the floral molding tracing along the edges of the floor. My shadow interrupts the sunlight spreading up the discolored paint. I hold the bronze-framed photo ahead of myself to compare.

My mouth is filled with the tang of bitterness, my throat suffocating me. A second ago, I only wanted to be vindicated. Now, I wish I had been wrong.

"Leigh, are you there?"

Those familiar footsteps shuffle through the house as she searches for me. For a wild second, I imagine myself vanishing. I must be able to do it. She says I go missing for days at a time.

Instead, I let her find me. She comes through the living room doorway, a tea towel rubbing water from her bent fingers. Her head tilts, questioning. In response, I turn the photo toward her.

It takes a moment for recognition to fill her features, then her eyes squeeze closed as a soft groan escapes, and I can't stay quiet any longer.

"You lied to me."

"Not intentionally."

"You—" My voice chokes off. I'm holding the portrait so tightly that the glass is at risk of breaking. Sarah extends a hand, mutely requesting it, and my anger deflates as I give it to her.

"Come into the living room, my sweet thing. I'll tell you about it."

She leads the way, placing the picture onto the coffee table before lowering herself onto one of my white couches. My blood is too hot for me to sit, so I pace instead, taking a path from the study door to the window and back.

"My family lived here when I was a child," Sarah says. "Before…things went wrong."

The window's curtains are open. I feel too vulnerable, too exposed, and drag them closed. Sarah doesn't object, but she works the tea towel between her hands, worrying at a frayed edge.

"You said this house felt like your home since you first saw it." Her watery eyes flick across the walls, and I feel as though she's seeing it in a way that I cannot. "I was the same. Always. When my father left us and we could no longer afford the rent, I felt like I was being torn away from a friend. But then I moved on. I married. Had my dear children. Built a home in other places. If you'd asked me at the time, I would have told you *those* were my true homes. But it would have been a lie."

I stop behind the chair opposite her, the tapestry of a quilt at my back, and brace my hands on the soft fabric.

"My daughter wanted me to move in with her. She said I'm getting too old to be on my own, but the way I see it, I'm too young to be smothered like that. Don't mistake me; I love my family. My grandchildren especially. But I need a break from them occasionally. So we agreed to compromise. She would buy me a home near her." A smile flickers over Sarah's features, warming them. "We looked at real estate listings. And this house was available. And I knew—I had to come home."

My energy is depleted. I round the chair and sink into the cushions. Grit rubs through my fingers as I lace them, but I barely care any longer. "You should have told me."

She laughs. "Oh, my dear thing. Maybe I should have. But it felt so…personal. Those years had such joy in them, but so much pain and sadness, too. The kind that's hard to talk about."

Losing her father. Losing her home. Her mother becoming a broken woman. I stare into the portrait between us and feel a fraction of the sadness Sarah must be experiencing. More than anything, I'm surprised she's been able to be so natural, so pleasant, during these weeks. She even left my furniture in place.

"Sorry for being angry," I manage.

"Perhaps that's not such a bad thing." Her hand lingers on the photograph. "Look. You brought this to me. And it didn't vanish when you let it go."

The shock is brief and bittersweet. Carrying a hand-sized picture should not be something to celebrate under normal circumstances. "How? And why this, and not anything else I've touched?"

"Perhaps you have some small abilities when your emotions are heightened." Sarah's smile is gentle. "You close the curtains when you're upset. You scattered salt across the hallways. You're still impacting the world, even in small, unpredictable ways."

I flex my hands. It's something. Not enough, but not nothing, either.

She inhales deeply, and her fingertips dig into the corners of her eyes. She's not wearing her glasses again. I'm grateful to avoid the flashing, owl-like eyes. Abruptly, a thought surfaces. Is she removing her lenses for my benefit, or for her own?

The question tumbles free before I'm certain it's wise. "What do I look like to you?"

A beat of silence passes between us, then Sarah says, "Why don't we talk about your bank account instead?"

I don't fight the diversion. Sarah moves to sit beside me as she takes the notebook out and flips to the later pages. She's meticulously noted down amounts and dates.

Most of my spending is in cash, which I withdraw from ATMs a few hundred at a time. The most recent withdrawal was also the largest, made five days before Christmas.

"I do that most years." I indicate the transaction. "I'll take out enough to last me a few weeks, do a large shop to fill my cupboards, and spend the time at home."

"So we know you were alive at that point, but your death could have come at any time after it." Sarah closes the book, her lips pursed until creases spread in a halo around her mouth. "It's too broad. There must be some other way to narrow down the day."

The sight of the notebook held in her fingers jogs an idea. "My journal. Wait here."

I'm at the stairs in a second, taking them two at a time. My journal had nearly fallen from my mind; it must be months since I last wrote in it. But I used to keep it religiously, adding an entry every night to help clear my mind for bed, even if it was only a few words.

My room is beginning to show signs of neglect. A hint of dust. The bed looks colder than it should. The old rotary phone no longer appears charming, but forlorn, as though it is trying to sink into and become one with the desk.

The journal is where I left it, near the phone, a basket of pens positioned close at hand. I take it up and flip through as I follow the familiar route to the ground floor.

"Eighteenth of December. Nineteenth. Twentieth. Twenty-first." I count the dates as I descend the stairs. My eye catches on phrases as I turn the crisp paper.

*Begin work on a new quilt... Knocking at the door last night... At the window again...*

I don't recall writing any of them. This could be a stranger's journal. As I enter the living room I reach the first blank page, and turn back to the final date.

"Second of January." I sink into the seat next to Sarah, my fingertips grazing the paper. Its entry is short.

*Making good progress on the new quilt. I'll need to buy more taupe fabric.*

"Is that the normal way you write?" Sarah asks.

"Yes. It just means nothing significant happened that day." I shrug. "I write in the evening, so my death must have happened between the night of the second and the night of the third."

I begin flipping back, reading the messages in reverse. Most of them were similar: commenting on a new book or my quilts, or catching up on work during my free time. Nothing stands out until the twenty-seventh of December.

> *Had lasagna for lunch. It needed more salt. I heard knocking at my door again last night, at nearly one in the morning. The doors and windows are all locked, but it felt like he had a way to get in.*

I read the entry aloud, knowing Sarah isn't wearing her glasses. She has her notebook out again, her pen flying over the page. "Who is *he?*"

"Not sure." I turn the pages back, scouring them more closely, hunting for anything abnormal. I find it on the twenty-fourth of December, Christmas Eve.

> *He was outside again. This time he walked along the street, pretending to exercise his dogs, but every time he passed, he stared into my house.*

Something is in my stomach. Thick and heavy, warning me, crying for me to stop turning back the entries. Dread.

But I can't stop. I find the edge of a page and pull it back to the twenty-third of December.

*I caught Cliff outside the living room window. He was standing knee-deep in the bushes, face pressed to the glass, hands on either side of his head to block out the glare. When he saw I'd caught him, he walked away. Not a run. Just a walk. Back to the brick fence, stepping over and disappearing along the street. Do I ignore what happened? It's too late to call the police, surely?*

"Cliff." The word is thick and repugnant on my tongue. "Cliff Kasack from number eight."

"I spoke to him last week." Sarah's eyelids flutter as she looks up toward me. "He's one of the gossip network. The one who tried to get into your home when you were noticed missing."

The realization comes slow, but that does not rob any of its force. Cliff Kasack likely killed me.

"He was one of the people who reported me missing," I manage. "More than a month after I was gone. That gave him plenty of time to clean my home and remove any evidence—if he really did kill me here. He must have, right? I wouldn't have followed him back to his home. Not after seeing him creep around like that." I indicate the pages.

"It's too soon to conclude anything. But I do wonder, if he truly is responsible and if he truly attacked you in your home, how did he hide your body?"

Our houses are on opposite sides of the street, twelve buildings apart. More importantly, the second member of the gossip network, Patty, lives opposite me. Her eyes are always prying. It would be a challenge for Cliff to enter my home, let alone park outside or carry my body out, without her noticing.

"Maybe he did it in the middle of the night," I manage. "And…it wasn't long after Christmas. People were distracted."

"Perhaps. Even if we don't know the *how* or the *why*, it does seem the most viable avenue to look into."

Something in her phrasing makes me hesitate. "Not by you. Call the police. Let them take care of it."

"Dear thing, the police won't listen to me. Or if they do, they'll be placating and nothing more."

"But you have *evidence*." I snap my journal closed and hold it up to her eyes. "These entries came just weeks before I went missing. They *have* to pay attention to that."

Sarah draws a slow breath, and as she releases it, some of the energy seems to drain from her. "There is no journal."

"No, look—" I push forward, intending to place it into her lap, to erase her irrational doubts, but my hand is empty. I stare at the fingers that held the thick leather-bound book just seconds before. "But…"

"You seem to manifest things occasionally. Cups. Pegs for the washing line." Sarah's eyes are fogged by sadness. "It appears to happen when you *believe* a thing should exist. Just like you saw me as something nightmarish before you properly met me. And just how you failed to notice the furniture I'd moved into our home until it was drawn to your attention. You believe things should be a certain way, and so, they are."

My hands lay in my lap, vacant, useless. A part of my mind cries out that the journal is still in the house; maybe I didn't carry it downstairs. Maybe it's still on my desk and all I need to do is run upstairs and fetch it.

But that is fantasy. Sarah's words are already sinking in. There is no journal—not any longer.

"If it's not here, what happened to it?"

"The police would have taken it for evidence. Along with any other personal effects—laptops, phones, and so on."

"But then…" Were the entries real? Did I actually see Cliff Kasack outside my home? Or did my mind fictionalize those events, just like it fictionalized the journal itself?

Sarah seems to guess my thoughts. She reaches across the space between us and pats my limp hand. "Don't be disheartened. From what I can see, there are two possibilities. You remembered the journal as it actually was, and in the weeks leading up to your death, Cliff spent a concerning amount of time around your home. If that's the case, the police probably already questioned him and discounted him as a suspect—correctly or not."

"Or I could have made it all up." The words burn, liquid humiliation spilling over my tongue.

"Or your subconscious could be trying to send you a message."

Another pat of my hand, then Sarah tucks her own notebook away. "Let's say those journal entries weren't real. Your mind still zeroed in on one person. It named him and him alone."

"You think my subconscious might be trying to relive something?"

"It's possible. Either way, it gives me something new to do."

"No." The word tumbles out. Sarah is rising, her joints cracking as she stretches them, and I stand with her, my heart thundering. "Don't talk to him. If this is real—if he actually did something to me—"

Sarah ambles toward the kitchen. "I already spoke to him last week, and he seemed a nice fellow. He may be able to shed some light one way or another."

"He could be dangerous. Sarah, promise me you won't go near him again."

"We'll see," she murmurs as she steps into the shadows of the hall. "We'll see."

# ILL OMENS

## 14

THE GATE'S ALARM RISES LIKE A DYING ANIMAL, FADING INTO A sky smattered in violent reds and sickly golds. Clouds hang thick above my house like an ill omen, soaking the sunset into their depths, chilling the air prematurely.

As the gate closes behind me, I pull my jacket tighter. Wind has sprung up, snapping, and the lawn is showing frost damage. As I follow the cracked stone path toward the door, I cannot help but look toward the living room window. The curtains are open. A lamp inside infuses warm color into the glass.

Of course. Sarah is inside. I'm not coming home from work. I stop, only halfway through the yard, and wait for the mental disconnect to subside. This habit—this mental routine—may be the only thing tethering me to the world. Sarah believes I have unfinished business. But I don't feel as though I do. I want to provide answers for my sister. I want to know what happened to me, even if the truth isn't pleasant. But those thoughts, although present in the back of my mind, are not driving me. Pure dumb habit is.

A bitter smile curls my mouth. The wind is growing colder. I shake the jacket up, unfurling the collar around my throat, and move forward.

The golden light in the living room windows draws my eye again. I picture a man standing in the yard, knee deep in the plants, leaning against the glass, hands pressed to either side of his head as he looks inside. Shudders rattle me.

Sarah has spoken to him. The thought comes abruptly, ringing with truth before I can even question it. She spoke to him a second time, even after I told her not to. *Begged* her not to.

The proof is at the front door. A pair of shoes are lined up on the mat. Men's loafers, an unassuming brown shade.

Fear sticks to my tongue, to the back of my throat, thickening in my stomach. I break into a run. Hit the door hard. It's unlocked; it bursts open, slamming into the doorstopper. Then I'm inside, wild and breathless, clutching the leather straps of my bag.

Two figures sit in the living room. One is very familiar—Sarah, underneath my quilt, her long gray hair braided and hanging over her shoulder. She wears a shawl across her shoulders to ward off the chill that has invaded even my home. Her eyes, circles of flashing light, turn on me as I enter.

The second figure has his back to me. He is still familiar. Horribly so. Cliff's sandy hair has a peculiar cut, too long to match the decade, not quite long enough to be a relic from the eighties. It's parted down one side and the strands sway over one another whenever he moves his head.

He turns, slowly, toward me, and I cannot breathe. He would have looked thirty if his skin hadn't aged so prematurely. It's pocked and creased, thickened from being in the sun, drooping slightly around the jowls and throat. Deeply pronounced sockets halo his eyes. The eyes are white, like those in the portrait, missing both iris and pupil, and I know it is a figment of my mind, but I also know this is another ill omen, a hint of corruption, a warning sign that will earn me punishment if I dare ignore it.

Those empty eyes are looking toward me, or through me, and I am desperate to step out of their path but dare not move. The corner of his mouth twitches. Something between a smile and a sneer.

Sarah, opposite him, picks up a mug from the coffee table. "Something the matter, Cliff?"

"Oh, no." His eyes remain fixed on me for another hateful second, then he turns back to her, his slumped shoulders rolling as though the cold has picked its way through his layers of knit clothes. "I thought I heard something, that's all."

My tongue darts over parched lips. "Did you invite him in? You need to get rid of him. He's not safe."

Sarah's eyes follow me as I move into the living room, but she speaks to Cliff. "The house groans and clatters sometimes. It keeps waking me at night. If I didn't know any better, I'd think it had a ghost."

"It wouldn't surprise me, honestly. When Leigh went missing, I did some digging into its history. It's a *strange* place." Cliff's clothes are like his hair: a tribute to an era that never actually existed. Slacks hold a prominent crease running down their front, forming an X where he crosses his legs. A starched shirt collar pokes out underneath a cardigan. It is a good appearance, one I always took at face value: it says that he is harmless.

"All houses over a certain age will have some dirt in their past, and this one has to be at least ninety years old," Sarah says.

"Oh, absolutely. But this one's... How to put it? Different. I don't like to believe in coincidences as a rule, but even if you do, this place has a little too much buried in its past to make me think it's wholly benign."

He's fishing, wanting a prompt that will allow him to launch into a detailed account of his knowledge, but to my surprise, Sarah doesn't give it to him. Instead, she shifts her mug between her fingertips and asks, "Did you know Leigh well?"

"Not much at all, I'm afraid." Cliff's lips twitch, the only sign that he isn't a fan of the subject switch, but he recovers from his disappointment quickly. "I probably liked her better than most people in the neighborhood did, but she kept even me at arm's length."

My fists clench spasmodically as I circle the seats to look Cliff in the face. The blank eyes are terrible, but like an insect in my room or mold on my food, I would rather see it than not. "Sarah, get him out of here."

Her eyes flick toward me, but that's the only acknowledgement I get. "She was standoffish, I gather?"

"Sure, that's how people liked to talk about her. It bothered them. Especially Patty across the road; a sweet lady, but she'd badmouth Leigh any chance she got. I thought it gave Leigh a nice kind of mystique, though. Like she had secrets."

I'm revolted by the glitter in his eyes. The way he rolls his tongue across the words, testing them, tasting them.

Sarah leans forward, her face reflected in the tea she brewed, and drops her voice. "What kind of secrets?"

"That's just it. No one knew." He mimics her posture, and it closes the distance between them. My hands itch. My head throbs. I need him gone—out of my house—away from Sarah. He reaches for his own cup and I'm struck by how enormous his hands are. The hairs across his knuckles are sandy, like on his head, just the right color to be invisible against his skin until the lamplight catches on them. "Maybe she was just peculiar. An introvert, you know? Or maybe there was something deeper. Something worse. Something…not entirely right with her."

It's barely sundown, but the clouds are thickening, heavy with rain, and Sarah never turned on more than one lamp. The room has become dark, and what colors exist are distorted, undersaturated and sickly. I'm not able to see Sarah's eyes behind the glare of her glasses as she tilts her head. "She went missing only a little more than a year ago. She gave up her home, her car, and her job. Why?"

"Stop, please." Spiders in my stomach are fighting their way up my throat, a thousand prickling legs, and I cannot escape them. "Don't provoke him."

But she presses on, and the spiders spill into my mouth,

scuttling across my tongue, my teeth, my lips. "What do you think?" she asks. "If you had to guess what became of her…what would you say?"

Something like laughter emerges from his creased lips. The empty eyes turn toward the ceiling as he pantomimes contemplation. At least now I'm certain Sarah can see through his charade as easily as I can. This is not a question he needs to ponder.

"Personally, and this is just my opinion…" The eyes drop back down to meet Sarah's, and I lower myself into the seat at her side, as though I can defend her, as though my presence might be enough to make him shy away. "She had a mental break. Like I said, there was something not right about her, and that Christmas she fractured, and just…got up and left."

As though timed to his words, rain began falling on the word *fractured*. A few drops at first, tapping the roof, colliding with the windows. The lamp is not enough light. It feels as though our world has shrunk into this tiny circle. Sarah, me, and a monster in human skin.

"Patty warned me first." The words are velvet. Rehearsed. "She said Leigh was up all hours of the night, pacing. Behaving strangely."

Sarah is still leaned forward, too close to him. "Did you see any of that?"

"I did. I walk my dogs along the street twice a day. She kept her curtains closed but I could still see her silhouette behind them—and she wasn't herself. Constantly moving. Not with any purpose, either. Just moving. Around and around, for hours."

Sarah lets a breath go, and it comes out as something like a sigh and something like a hum. "You couldn't tell what was disturbing her?"

"No. And I didn't ask." Those limp, too-long strands of hair slide over one another as he turns his head. "I tried to look through her window once, to see if she was all right. She caught me. And I figured it would be better to stay well away. She left not long after."

The rain grows heavier, and it feels as though each drop swells my own emotions. I want to cry out. Fear. Humiliation. Sarah still isn't looking at me, her attention fully absorbed by Cliff.

"So if I had to guess, she'd be in another state. Maybe she picked herself up and found a new job. Maybe got the help she needed. I hope so anyway." He moves the mug up to his lips and draws from it. "I don't like to think of what might have become of her otherwise."

The rain has turned steady. Light but dense, it drips from my eaves and flows into the cracks, and the longer the conversation lasts, the deeper it sets in. It intends to make its mark, not through brute, abrupt force, but by steady persistence, and I'm certain the backyard must be flooding by the time Cliff says his goodbye.

I stay in the immaculate white seat while Sarah walks him to the door. She switches on more lights as they go, and I'm so adjusted to the gloom that I flinch. Then the door opens, and the steady rush of falling water breaks from the drone of background noise. Cliff makes small talk about the weather while he puts his shoes on. Sarah offers to let him stay until the rain passes. He thanks her but says he has dinner in the oven and needs to check on it. The door closes. A beat of silence settles over us, threatening to last forever, and then Sarah's shoes scrape against the floorboards as she returns to the archway. I keep my eyes on the coffee table, where two empty mugs rest between the stacked magazines.

"Leigh—"

"It's a good theory," I manage. "Mental psychosis. It would explain why I left so abruptly. Could explain my death, too. If I was behaving irrationally, I could have walked into a lake, into a mine shaft—anywhere."

She leans her shoulder against the archway. I still don't meet her eyes, flashing lights that they are.

"Still…" I'm fighting with everything I have to keep my voice level, stable. "We shouldn't just take his word for it. He could be covering up his involvement. It's a convenient red herring to throw the police."

"Mm. At least it confirms the accuracy of the journal entries. He *was* watching you. Only now the motive is in doubt."

"The police probably read my journal and interviewed Cliff." The realization comes hard. "He gave them that same story of me behaving strangely. And they believed him. And that's why their main theory is that I left of my own free will."

"To be frank, my dear, I'm inclined to believe him as well."

Fire across my face. Scorching. Setting into my pores, bleeding into my skull, consuming. She must be able to see what it's doing to me. I grab for the mugs on the coffee table and knock one over. A trickle of coffee runs out, but I right the cup. Carry them to the kitchen. Into the sink. Turn the tap on. Detergent. Suds. I'm scrubbing furiously, hard enough to break the mugs, when Sarah's hand touches my forearm.

"Don't be angry," she murmurs.

"I'm not." A mountain of bubbles has developed around the tap's flow. The cups are clean, but I keep washing, knowing that having a task is the only thing that's really keeping me there.

"I believe him because I heard the same thing from Patty." Sarah rests against the kitchen counter and seems to lose some stature. "She said you were incredibly restless in those last few weeks. In her words, it was like you never slept."

My hands are submerged in the cold water, and there are now no longer flames across my cheeks but ice, turning my features hard, making every movement stiff.

"She said you seemed frightened, but you didn't want to talk to her when she knocked on your door."

"No. If something went wrong in my life, Patty is the last person I'd confide in." I rinse one of the mugs and put it onto the draining board. "I've found that a problem is rarely improved if everyone on the street knows about it."

Sarah chuckles. "Except for this problem."

"Well."

"Even if telling Patty couldn't keep you alive, it would have made my job so much easier."

I'm not ready to laugh, but I do smile as I drop the second mug onto the draining board.

"Either way, it leaves us in an interesting situation. We know your journal was accurate. And I believed Cliff when he said you were behaving erratically. One person can manufacture a story to protect themselves from the police, but it's another matter to convince a neighbor—even if they're friendly—to go along with it."

Each nod feels as though it heaps shame onto my head, but at this point I'd be a fool to argue.

"Though…I do *not* believe him when he says you had a psychotic break."

My heart catches. I look at Sarah. Her glasses flash white, and she reaches up to remove them, the clawlike fingers curling around the lights to peel them away. Her true eyes seem too small by comparison, and she blinks moisture out of them as she carefully folds the glasses and places them into her dress's pocket.

"No," she says, and squints at me. "I don't think you died from an accident. Whatever happened to you was *done* to you. Which means, perhaps, your behavior in those last few weeks was not so erratic after all."

I make a show of draining the water and brushing the suds away to excuse me from meeting Sarah's contemplative look. "Thank you."

"Well. Don't thank me yet. I'm running low on avenues to explore. Perhaps my last one is your next-door neighbors. They've been avoiding me."

"Which ones?"

Sarah nods behind herself, toward the house to our left. When I first moved in, that old brick building was occupied by a middle-aged couple and their teenage children. Now, it is home to an older man who uses a walker to reach the letter box and a tiny woman with stooped shoulders. Their evolution from industrious parents to quiet retirees happened so far out of sight that I sometimes forget they are the same people.

"Mr. and Mrs. Moreno. They're quiet," I note. "I think they like their privacy."

"Mm. They certainly do. Or perhaps I've just had the repeated bad luck to call on them when they're not home. Even though the car is in the driveway." Sarah shrugs. "I'll keep trying. I noticed the wife likes to work in the yard some mornings, so an ambush may be in order. Perhaps tomorrow morning. There should be enough time if I'm quick."

"What's happening tomorrow?"

"It's Saturday, sweet thing." Her face brightens, worn skin rising, eyebrows lifting, and in the span of a second, she sheds a decade. "My family will be visiting. Sylvia, my oldest, and Adam, my second, and eight of my grandchildren. I hope you'll join us. I won't be able to introduce you, but I'd still like you to see them all."

"I'd like that, too."

I silence the writhing dread in my stomach. Eight grandchildren. Surely the house cannot be so dangerous that Sarah is not allowed to see her relatives.

A watchful eye will go a long way. I'll stay present during the visit. I'll ask Sarah to make sure none of them stray too far.

Sarah returns to the living room to collect the mugs, and too late, I realize the draining board is empty. My body feels weary, as though simply standing is drawing something vital out of me, and I circle through the dining room to avoid having to face Sarah again. My companion's company has become something I treasure, but tonight, I just need quiet.

As the sink turns on, I move from the dining room to the hallway and face the door under the stairs.

Sarah has blocked the door, but in the cold moonlight, it appears as I always saw it: a panel set into the wall, indistinct and uncovered.

There is nothing remarkable about this door. The wood matches the paneling. The handle matches those elsewhere in the home. But this plain rectangle of a door holds something so ominous that bile rises into my throat and my toes curl.

I reach to touch it. The skin around my nails seems to writhe as it nears the barrier. Every pore convulsing, every sweat gland flooding, and before my skin even touches the wood, my hand is moist and cold.

The house moves. Nothing visible changes, but my balance falls away, and I am left reeling for purchase on planks of wood that are no longer truly flat. The cracks running through my home widen. Their tremors travel through my body, carving a path into what feels like my soul, and I gasp, mouth wide, searching for oxygen that will not come.

I back away, my heart rate too fast, and put my shaking hands behind my back as I leave the door behind.

# THE HOUSE BREATHES

15

PERHAPS THE MOST FAMOUS OF AESOP'S FABLES IS THE TORTOISE and the hare. The story appears in more children's picture books than I can remember, and before the age of ten, I'd internalized its morals. The hare and the tortoise get into an argument about who is faster and agree to settle it with a race. They're seen off by the forest's denizens with cheers and waving banners. The hare quickly leaves his competitor in a cloud of dust, and laughing at how thoroughly assured his victory is, he lies down to take a nap.

The warm sun lulls him into sleep, but meanwhile, the steady tortoise continues plodding along. Past the dozing hare. Past the halfway mark. Up to the finish line.

The hare is woken by the cheers of the forest animals as they celebrate the tortoise's victory. Slow and steady wins the race.

The lessons are pleasantly easy for children to grasp: arrogance leads to humiliation; perseverance will ultimately lead to success.

But there's a different interpretation to the story. Several hundred years after its inception, the writer Lord Dunsany proposed an alternate ending. One that I have never seen in the hundreds of renditions of the story that include pastel illustrations of deer and frogs and birds throwing confetti across the gently smiling tortoise.

After the tortoise wins the race, he's crowned the fastest animal in the forest, to the hare's chagrin. Sometime later, a fire breaks out. It spreads. Quickly. The forest animals rush to alert the tortoise. As the fastest creature among them, it's his job to warn the rest of the animals and save them from the fire. He sets off, slow and steady as always, plodding into the trees.

By the end of the day, the forest has burned to the ground. The only survivor is the hare.

This version of the fable teaches a different set of lessons: that facts can be misleading and reliance on data over common sense can have horrendous ramifications. Yes, the tortoise won the race, but was it right of him to accept the title of the fastest in the forest when he himself had passed the sleeping hare and knew his victory was unearned?

Perched on the edge of my bed, my toes buried in the rug and my hands resting on my own hand-quilted hare and tortoise, I cannot help feeling that my knowledge is just as great a poison.

I think I understand my situation…to some degree. But I continue to battle an intractable fear that seeps out of my very house. The cobwebs want to stick to me. The gnawing dread I try again and again to dismiss.

I'm already dead. What else is there that can hurt me?

And yet, with all this knowledge, my body still squirms at the sight of that door. Turns cold as the cracks running through my home widen.

The forest animals thought they understood. They had facts. Data. Proof, even. And all that knowledge led them to a scorching death.

My bare feet feel too vulnerable where they rest on the floor. It's childish to fear something might lurk under the bed. I have a lifetime of evidence proving that nothing will come from that dark gap, that there is no reason to mistrust it.

Still, I draw my feet up. With my back to the headboard and my knees under my chin, I stare down at the woven fables I conjured. The hare and his arrogance, believing so greatly in his own superiority that he doesn't take a competition seriously. The tortoise, often presented as the humble alternative, is perhaps the only animal in the forest with more arrogance than the hare.

Those two tragic creatures intertwine with a maze of varied, fallible animals. The fox and the stork, who torment each other with soup served in containers that the other cannot drink from. Owl, praising the grasshopper's singing so generously that he climbs onto the branch next to her and is eaten. The crow, trying to wash his feathers as white as a swan's and growing thinner each day.

Their beady eyes stare at me, horribly lively in the muted light of my lamp. Another irrational fear rises: that once I close my eyes, they will come alive, writhing across this bedspread, gnashing teeth and sharp beaks gouging at one another, twining together, dying together.

The bedroom door isn't closed properly. A cold wind moves outside the window, pulling on the stagnant air inside my home, and the door drifts open several inches.

The light from my bedside lamp is barely enough to see the wall beyond. Smooth paint, dulled from age, due for a fresh coat. It transfixes me, making it hard to look away, even when a sound comes from deeper in the house. A metallic grind. A click. Hinges, crying out as they rotate.

The door under the stairs has opened. That is impossible: even if it weren't locked, Sarah has placed a shelf in front of it. And yet, it *has* opened. I feel it in my blood and bones.

My arms tighten across my knees. As I exhale, a wisp of condensation leaves on my breath, curling and evaporating before my eyes.

Something moves through that downstairs floor. Heavy footsteps. Slow, elongated, irregular. Not Sarah. I know her sounds well enough; she doesn't walk like this. It's moving toward the stairs.

The air undulates through the open pane of my window, pushing the door back until only a crack of the white paint is visible.

Something climbs the stairs. One or two steps at a time, pausing, then climbing again. I can tell when it passes the bend in the stairs because the sound becomes louder, clearer.

The door slides open again, revealing more of the wall. The

shadows have changed. My lamp is not as strong; like a flashlight dying by increments, its light grows weaker with every second. I breathe out. Mist floats from me. No longer a wisp, but a burst, the warmth of my lungs robbed by the freezing air.

The stranger reaches the top of the stairs. I can't move. Can't look away. We are both still for an agonizing minute. Then it steps closer. One pace, two. Then it stops. Just out of sight. A narrow slice of a foreign shadow grazes the edge of my vision.

The door drifts closed as the house breathes. It steals my own breath out of me, a rush of condensation that evaporates before I can draw it back in. I'm so cold. My knees press to my chest, my arms coiled around them, pulling myself into the smallest space I can manage as I fight to conserve warmth.

Another step closer. Then one more. It stops again.

There is only a sliver of a gap in my door. A hairline fracture, running from the baseboards to nearly the ceiling, exposing a paper-thin line of the hallway beyond. A line that is now filled with something dark.

I hold my breath, and the house holds its. We are trapped on a precipice, waiting. Waiting for me to breathe. Waiting for the *house* to breathe.

*Not yet*, I beg it. *Don't expose me yet.*

There is an eye pressed against the gap. Small and glittering.

A sharp cry stabs the night air. It's so much like a scream that I have to fight my own urge to cry out. The noise falls to silence for three or four perfect seconds, then repeats as the phone on my desk rattles. Mournful. Horribly loud. The burnished receiver glimmers, and I almost believe it is covered in frost.

I look back to the door just as it drifts open. There is nothing outside. Only the white wall and its collection of unnatural shadows.

The phone rings again. I unfold myself carefully, as though my limbs will crack if I move them too quickly. Time has treated me unfairly. I thought I had only been sitting for minutes, but my joints have grown stiff with disuse.

My feet extend over the edge of the bed, toes rolling, the hem of my nightdress grazing the rug. The rotary phone shudders on its stand, beckoning me. I press my soles into the carpet. In the moonlight, they truly look like a corpse's feet. Pale, bleached of all color save for the snaking blue veins. They're translucent, the unnatural effect highlighted by the dark rug. And by the darkness that comes from underneath my bed.

It seeps out like ink, bleeding into the room, deepening the gloom. And my feet are so unpleasantly close to it. Exposed.

I close my eyes and breathe deeply, forcefully quelling the anxieties. There is nothing to fear. This is my room—the same room I have slept in for the last fifteen years of my life. I don't need to dread the darkness.

The phone rings once more. I begin to rise.

Pallid fingers emerge from under my bed. They shoot forward and close around my ankle. My breath catches before it can leave my lungs. I try to lurch forward but can't break free. Long fingers, disturbingly tepid, tighten. Hard enough to bruise. They begin to pull. Dragging me with them, forcing me to the floor.

My cheek hits the carpet. I dig my fingers into the floor, grasping, but all of my muscles cannot compete with the thing under my bed. I writhe to twist my ankle free. The skin is already slick with sweat, but the hand is like a chain, unbreakable, unstoppable. My leg disappears into the dark gap beneath the bedframe. Past the ankle, past the knee.

"No." I can't breathe, not even enough to scream the word. It's a whisper, and I'm struck with fear that this is how I died—not with a fight, but with a meek whine. That thought is more repulsive than the thing under my bed, more repulsive than the idea of death itself, and I become a wild beast, fighting, kicking, screaming as my hips are dragged into the dark chasm.

The bedframe is low enough that it scrapes my torso as I disappear under. I scrabble for a hold on the mattress, and instead my hands come away full of the quilt. A drowning person's instinct has taken over. The blanket is useless, but I cannot let go. It's all I have. All that is within reach now, as my shoulders brush the edge of the bed. There is no longer just one hand dragging me under, but dozens of them. Cool, fleshy, bony, they grasp at every inch of my body to draw me into the blackness. I tilt my head back, a final effort to pull in enough air to scream. I can't. My head goes under.

All light is extinguished. My heartbeat is magnified, pounding, deafening. I can't tell which way is up, only that the hands are everywhere, pinching, scratching. I coil in on myself, the quilt clutched to my chest.

This is another dream. Another delusion. My mind, fractured by death, hallucinates nightmares to torment me.

I know this. My evidence is that it has happened before. My data says that I will resurface.

My heart screams that I am wrong. It pounds faster and faster, starved for air, crushed by the weight of the darkness. The hands are no longer distinct things, but a cocoon of pressure, pushing on me, driving me further down. Through the floor. Into the house's very foundations.

I can taste it. The rot. The black, sickening thing that corrupts my home. It runs through the fractures. It festers inside the walls. I have been breathing poison in every day as it spreads, and thickens, and decays. I know its nexus. The door. The toxic, hideous door, disguised so mundanely. It devours all.

It will devour me.

"No." I cannot hear my own voice under my booming heart rate. The pressure will not let me move. I am trapped—under floorboards or under concrete or even under the earth, I cannot tell, but trapped so desperately that there is not even an inch of give.

My shoulders ache as I push them against the barrier. My hands are coiled at my chest and I cannot squirm them free. The angle of my neck is a sparking pain.

"No." There is not enough room to breathe. Panic takes hold. I fight for an inch of give and find none.

This will be my final resting place.

The thought comes like a knife into my chest. I've discovered the thing I needed to fear, the thing that supersedes even death: an eternity spent trapped.

My lips try to form words, but even they are reluctant to shift. "Please, no."

The words echo through my head, around and around, trapped, like I am.

*Let me go.*

*It can't be like this.*

*Not while I'm conscious. Not while I can feel it.*

*Please.*

*Please.*

*No more.*

A sound comes through the raging tempo of my heartbeat. Sirens? No. Too irregular, too broken. Crying.

Meg, mourning for me. It has to be. No one else noticed I was missing…or cared when they were informed.

My dry throat cracks as I force a whisper of air through it. My hands are too tightly coiled, wrapped in the quilt, to beat against my tomb. I have no way to call to her. No way to tell her where I am, to ask for help.

And her sobs are growing quieter. Swallowed up by the rot, consumed, like everything else, like me.

The sounds fade until they no longer exist. Then it is just the dark and the silence. Deep, bone-aching, drowning silence. I would give anything for it to be broken but it only stretches and stretches until my ears ring from a lack of noise and my throat vibrates from a scream that has no way out and I cannot survive even a second more, but it stretches even further, this smothering dark and the silence that is driving me to insanity.

My eyes open. Sudden light hurts them. Retinas that have been confined to blackness struggle to cope with abrupt oversaturation, but I don't let my lids close. There is light. I will not take it for granted again.

My arms lay at my sides, legs draped across the floor messily. Above is a white ceiling, and in my peripheral vision, familiar walls. The wooden floorboards underneath me have been freshly swept and seem to shine in the sunlight.

I tilt my head to the right. The door looms over me, and I feel its presence across my body like a shadow.

Frost clings to my skin. It aches as I scramble back from the door. My legs lack the strength to carry me, but my forearms drag my body to the white-painted wall, so I can sit against it. Propped up like that, I feel like a boneless doll that some oversized child has discarded.

The door is less than four feet away. Too close. Its camouflage of wooden facade is interrupted only by the bronze knob. As I stare at it, the handle jostles. Just a fraction.

Seconds pass as my heart's desperate rate begins to ease. I watch the door, waiting, but it seems prepared to bide its time. At least for a while longer.

The sound of crying hangs in the air, as though it bled out of my unconscious mind. It's soft, muffled and distant, and I use the wall for support as I gain my feet.

"Meg?" She couldn't have come back to the house, surely. But who else could be crying for me?

I blink, my vision spotted with bleeding grays and flashing

whites, as vertigo wants to drop me. The sensation clears. I let go of the wall.

Having the under-stairs door to my back is uncomfortable, but I follow the sound of crying into the kitchen. My legs are stiff, my feet extended at odd angles, as my body remembers how to move. I clutch the nearest kitchen counter and hang over it as I try to catch my bearings.

Someone has stacked cups on the countertop near the sink. They're topside down, as though waiting to be distributed. Behind them are a matching stack of plates. And…party hats? Twelve of them, stacked near the toaster.

The house is empty, save for me. The walls are too quiet for anything else. I can no longer hear crying.

Movement comes from outside the kitchen door. I coax my legs to work as I cross to it.

Sarah sits on the wrought-iron bench that faces the oak tree. Her head tilts in my direction as she hears the door open. "Leigh. Good. I was hoping I'd see you today."

There's something not right about her voice. I hesitate in the doorway, blinking against the harsher light, trying to reconcile what I'm seeing. A cake rests on the bench beside her. Store-bought white frosting peppered with edible confetti and buttercream roses, it sits on a black plastic base, the lid discarded on the ground.

"Is it one of your grandchildren's birthdays?" I ask.

"No. Mine." Her smile is brief. "Eighty-five."

"Congratulations." The word is stilted, uncertain. This doesn't feel like a celebration.

I move closer, and Sarah withdraws her glasses from her pocket and puts them on, hiding her eyes. "Come and eat some cake with me," she says. "It's too much for just one person."

I slide onto the bench with the cake resting precariously between us. Sarah has already carved one corner away with a plastic fork. She fishes a fresh one out of a bag and hands it to me and indicates that I should do the same. No slices, no plates, just chiseling away at this slab of sugar as we see fit.

"It's Funfetti," she says. "I'm partial to red velvet—the good, homemade kind, not the cheap dyed stuff you get at the shops. But it's less of a crowd-pleaser. Avery thinks it's gross. No one complains about Funfetti, though."

The cups were stacked upside down. Clean. The plates were untouched. My heart sinks. "It's Saturday. They were supposed to visit."

"Sylvia had a surgery run late. Complications with the anesthetic, I gather. And Millie has a dance recital at school at five. That left them with really very little time. What's the point in driving two hours if you can only stay for twenty minutes? They all agreed it would be better to try again another day."

"Were you a part of that decision?"

She touches her glasses, ensuring her mask is still firmly in place. "Go on, dig in. This cake won't eat itself."

My appetite is nonexistent, but I push my fork into one of the buttercream flowers and flake off a corner of the cake. It's painfully sweet, with an undercurrent of fake vanilla. I go back for another bite.

"I'm glad you're here," Sarah adds. "I was starting to worry you wouldn't show up today. Do you remember me saying that I was going to try to catch Mrs. Moreno while she was gardening? Well, it worked."

"Oh?"

"And you were right. She's very reserved. She didn't want to talk about you at all, and it took nearly twenty minutes of small talk to warm her up enough to even broach the subject. But it was worth it."

I nod, encouraging her to continue, while I chip away at my side of the cake. She's more enthused on the topic than I am, but I don't want to stop her. She seems to need the distraction. I need one, too. I don't want to talk about the door and the prison of darkness and silence. I don't even want to think about it. It's a relief when Sarah begins to speak.

"We narrowed down your likely disappearance to the night of January the third, based on the last entry in your journal and on what we gathered from your other neighbors. But Mrs. Moreno told a different story. She says she saw you walking through your home for weeks afterward. Her bedroom window faces your living room, you know. She says you always kept the curtains closed, but sometimes she would see a light shining through, and you pacing inside. Always late at night."

"That's a lot like what Cliff said."

"Yes, exactly. Except Cliff told me the last time he's certain he saw you was in early January. Mrs. Moreno says you were pacing inside your home well into late January. Maybe even right up until February."

"That's odd." I speak without conviction.

"It is! That's the thing. You didn't show up to work when it resumed in the second week of January. You didn't collect your mail—Patty said it was overflowing by the time she noticed. Your car didn't seem to have been moved. If you really, truly were still living in your home until late January, that raises a slew of questions. Of course, Mrs. Moreno might have been remembering wrong. It was over a year ago after all. But she seemed haunted by it. As though she's been fighting with the same conundrum ever since you were discovered to be missing. Which means…"

Her words flow around me without registering as deeply as they might otherwise. Birds fight over the feeder, which is overflowing with seeds. The oak tree seems older than it did the last time I faced it. The washing line lists.

Scents and sounds that I might never have paid attention to abruptly overwhelm me. The stuttering shrieks of the birds. Dew soaking through my shoes. The taste of this sickly sweet cake—not even the flavor Sarah likes. She's eighty-five. She's sitting on a cold, dirty seat and sharing her birthday cake with a dead woman for lack of better company.

And by her expression, this is the highlight of her day. It's too much. I stab my fork into the cake and rise, interrupting her. "I want to give you something. Come with me."

# 16
ROT

I SHOVE THE KITCHEN DOOR OPEN AND MOVE INSIDE. BY THE time Sarah is out of her seat, I'm already waiting at the base of the stairs, my skin crawling from being so close to the door, but too resolute to step away. She comes after me with shuffled steps. "What is it?"

"Not much." I let her catch up before climbing the stairs. The light still doesn't work, and that sticks at me unpleasantly. Sarah isn't young and she doesn't know the house like I do. This tunnel that rises through my home is treacherous. She should get the wiring fixed.

Again, I wait at the top of the stairs for Sarah to catch up, then lead her into the rumpus room. The area was used for storage. Old sewing machines that needed spare parts to be repaired. Boxes of crockery that I didn't need. Boxes of old clothes waiting to be donated.

I stop by one particular shelf near the window and point to a large cardboard box. "Open this one. Please."

Her expression is impossible to read behind the reflective glasses, but she only tilts her head before pulling the box free from its confines. It thuds as it hits the floor. I kept a pair of scissors in a tray on the shelf and point them out to Sarah so she can cut through the tape.

"It's not much. And I don't have any way of wrapping it." I rub my forearms, alive with gooseflesh, as she pulls the flaps back to reveal the blue material underneath. "And I'm sorry it's not personalized. I would have made you something more specific if…well, if I weren't dead. But this is my favorite one. I was saving it for something special. And I want that to be you."

The quilt spills free, layers of intricately sewn inch-sized pieces of fabric creating a mosaic of animals, plants, and stone walls. I themed it off a quaint yard. The first impression is of a pond surrounded by flowering bushes, but I buried dozens of small details into it: a fox sneaking around the distant gate, waterfowl descending to land in the pond.

Sarah runs her fingertips over the border, a design of brambles with hares darting between them. She opens her mouth, then closes it again, and I have the horrible idea that she's searching for a way to politely decline the gift. Then she peels the glasses away from her eyes and lets me see how red they are. Moisture pools at the corners. Her jaw trembles. "It's so lovely. Thank you."

I reach for her before I can second-guess myself, and Sarah closes the distance, pulling me into a hug, the quilt trapped between us. She feels so warm. Bony and soft all at once, and smelling of cotton and perhaps a hint of mildew, and it is wonderful.

Disengaging is awkward, and we both laugh, and Sarah folds the quilt into a bundle that she holds against her chest. "I'll put this on my bed. It will be especially nice with the nights as cold as they are. How long did this one take to make?"

"Just a bit over three hundred hours." I push the empty box back onto the shelf before following Sarah back into the hallway.

"Mercy, sweet thing. That's almost a second job."

"Well…you already know I didn't have much else happening in my life. This was how I relaxed."

"Still. Are you sure you want me to have this? Don't misunderstand, I'm grateful, and I think it's beautiful, but I'm not sure even the appreciation I feel can compensate for how much you put into this."

We're at the stairs, and I let Sarah go first while I test my answer on my tongue. The words are more vulnerable than I like being, even with how much I've begun to trust Sarah. "There's not much I can do now. For *any*one. Not my sister, not my coworkers, not even you. And I guess it feels good to put something into another person's life. If that quilt keeps you even a bit warmer at night, that will make me happy."

The idea has been growing day by day, and I don't like how uncomfortable it makes me: that I am the definition of dependent. I'm a guest in another person's home, incapable of leaving. I'm reliant on Sarah to speak to neighbors, to piece together timelines, to find out how and where I died. In return, I can't even wash up after she makes our drinks.

That quilt—the last quilt I ever made—is the only part of me I have left to give.

"It is very lovely." Sarah descends the stairs, holding the quilt in one hand while she steadies herself against the wall with the other. "It's a wonder you hid it away instead of putting it on display, like the other one. Or putting it on your own bed."

That makes me chuckle. "I have the Aesop's quilt. I've been using that one for at least eight years, and even though it's a little rough around the edges, I couldn't replace it."

"I don't think I've seen that one."

"The quilt covered in animals? It's in my room."

We reach the turn in the stairwell and pause, making use of the narrow space to search each other's expressions.

"There's no quilt on your bed, sweet thing."

"No, it's definitely there. It's in neutral tones. It has the hare and the rabbit, and the stork and the fox, and—"

"I'm sorry, my darling. Your bed only has sheets and a blanket. I think we just found another item that the police didn't realize was missing."

The stairwell is a tunnel. Where we stand is dark, but when I look up, I can see a rectangle of light signifying the merger with the upstairs hallway. As I stare up at it I feel as though I'm in a pit, trapped, stuck in this two-foot-by-two-foot hole, with nowhere to go.

That quilt was so integral to me. So core to my life, both

before and after my death, that it feels impossible for it to be gone. I shake my head. I didn't want to talk about the images and sensations that tormented me, but now they're too relevant to ignore. "I had a dream last night where I dragged it off my bed."

Sarah's voice floats out from the dining room. "You can still dream?"

"I think so. At least...it's *something*. Maybe a trance. Time shifts, and sometimes I see things and hear things."

"Tell me about that."

I reach the base of the stairs and lean in the dining room's archway. Sarah has opened the curtains and is spreading my quilt out over the dining table to examine it in detail. I'm grateful her attention is divided; explaining this would be impossible if I had to meet her eyes.

"Sometimes the house seems to age. There will be cobwebs and dust all over. Sometimes I see another person in the building. I think it's supposed to be Cliff, but I never get a good look at him. Sometimes there are ropes. From your macramé, I think."

"I didn't realize my macramé would manifest in your world." Her glasses are back in place as she pores over the details on the quilt's edge, but her head tilts just far enough that I suspect she's watching me. "I can take them down if they bother you."

"No. It's okay. Just...sometimes unnerving. I don't like how smooth the ropes are."

"Oh?"

Now I'm certain of it: she truly is watching me. As though she's waiting for me to elaborate. When I stay silent, she crosses into the kitchen and returns seconds later.

"Are these the ropes you see, darling?" She holds out a woven design. It's not made of the thin, sleek material that has been tormenting me. These ropes are rustic: soft and brown, with a slight give under my fingers.

I should have known. Those synthetic ropes didn't belong in a crafter's crate. They're too oily, too alien to decorate a home with. Just like with the furniture and just like with my own death, my mind was pushing for me to ignore obvious warnings in favor of easy delusions. "This is your macramé?"

"They're all in the same material." She pushes her glasses higher on the bridge of her nose. "I think you should tell me more about these dreams, sweet one."

We sit side by side at the table, facing the windows overlooking the street, as I recount as much as I can remember. Sarah interrupts with questions. She's especially curious about the experience in the shed, and the sense that the house is rotting.

"You said it was spreading out from one location," she prods.

I fidget with the overlapping green and brown squares at the quilt's edge. "Yes."

"Tell me."

I don't want to. Somehow, speaking about the door feels like a bad omen. As though I would be inviting something horrendous into my home. Worse than what is already here. The door is something that shouldn't exist, and it draws power from the attention given to it. Don't think about it, don't talk about it, and maybe, if we're lucky, that will slow the spread.

Sarah grips my hand, pressing hard enough to snatch me back down to reality. "Leigh, I need to know. I've run out of neighbors to speak to, and anything else I do from here is like throwing darts into the dark. If your subconscious is offering us any clues, we can't ignore them."

"Okay. But you can't go near it. There's something bad inside, and we can't risk letting it out."

She presses closer. "Something bad? What?"

"I have no idea. It just—it feels *horrible*. Being near it. Touching it. I'm already dead; things can't get much worse for me. But you have to promise you'll be careful. We can't open that door."

"It's a door, is it?" Her eyes light up. "Which one? Not your bedroom. Not mine. Not the pantry…"

The stream of guesses puts pressure on the back of my skull. She'll reach the right solution eventually, so I cave. "It's the door under the stairs."

She takes a deep breath. Before I can gather my wits, she's left my side, and I have to run to catch up.

We come to a stop in the hallway, facing the door. Having Sarah at my side helps me see the display table. Sturdy, stacked with books, it's a welcome barrier between us and the under-stairs compartment, but I still feel sick to my stomach at being so close.

One of Sarah's clawlike hands rubs her chin. "This is it, huh? That little door is causing all of your stress?"

I swallow and taste bile. "Some. Not all."

"Mm. How remarkable. I barely noticed it. You know, when I lived here as a child, my siblings and I would play hide-and-seek, but I don't think any of us tried to hide in there. Maybe it was locked even back then. Or maybe we just didn't think of it."

It's good at hiding. I walked past that door every day, never registering that it so much as existed…until it started leaching poison.

She tilts her head, loose strands of gray hair falling around her ears. "I can't even picture what the space behind it looks like. Peculiar."

What feels like insects squirm under my skin. I'm cold and burning hot all at once. Even being close to the under-stairs door feels precarious; like radiation, like spores of a deadly fungus, it spreads its corruption further than the naked eye can detect.

"Well," Sarah says, and shivers prickle my spine as I register the certainty in her voice. "Let's have a look inside."

"No!" I grab her arm. She smiles up at me, bemused, and some of my fear is hardened into frustration. Not at Sarah, but at the house itself, for presenting this trap that she cannot ignore. "We're not going to. It's dangerous."

"It's only a door."

There are no words to explain my certainty, but it bites deep in my soul. This barrier must stay closed.

"Think for a second, sweet thing." She rests her hand over mine, where I grip her cardigan. "This door is deeply significant to you. What could be on the other side?"

I can't imagine. Don't *want* to imagine.

Her voice is soft, quivering, as she leans closer to me. "Do you think that this could be the answer? That perhaps, behind this door, we will find *you*?"

Rushing in my ears. My heart is tearing itself apart, my veins on fire. I have no avenues left except to beg. "Please don't."

Her hand is a caress. She bows her head, letting her round spectacles slide down on her nose to give me a glimpse of her eyes. The lids crease, the skin bunching up to either side, red capillaries drawing mazes around the pupils. There's so much compassion in those eyes that I almost can't stand to meet them. "I need to do this. And I hope you'll stay with me."

She eases her arm out of my grip and approaches the side table. I don't immediately react, my mind empty, an animal lulled into compliance by their handler's gentle touch, and my trance only snaps when Sarah puts her fingers behind the display and begins to pull.

"No." I'm at her side again, planting my hands on the display's edge, holding it in place. "You can't open it."

Laughter sparkles in her features. She gives up on trying to pull the display, overladen as it is, and begins unloading the photos and books that adorn it. "See, from my perspective, this is my home and by extension my door, and I should be able to get it unlocked with enough elbow grease, and no judge would ever convict me."

She doesn't understand. She still thinks this is paranoia or perhaps my mind trying to block out the reality of my situation, but it's not. It's pure fear. We're standing on tracks, and she can see they're clear for miles ahead, but a train is hurtling toward our backs, and only I can hear it.

She stacks four of the novels onto the floor nearby. I put myself between her and the display. "My body can't be in there. We would have smelled it."

"Except the house was empty for more than a year while the bank foreclosed on it. I don't know much about how bodies decompose, but it's not unreasonable to think you'd be a skeleton by now, is it?" She reaches around me to remove another chunk of fiction.

"The police. They searched the house. They would have opened this door."

"Sure. Except they would have already spoken to Cliff, who told them you seemed to be on the edge of a mental break and had likely left town, so maybe their search was more of a formality than anything else." She hooks her hands on the edge of the display and pulls her body weight against it. This time, it moves, wooden legs scraping painfully across the floor.

I lean on it, putting my own weight in opposition to hers, but it doesn't affect the display's movement in the slightest. "I don't believe that. Remember the two officers who visited not long after you moved in? They looked at this place as though it was a curiosity. They had months to conduct their investigation, and the first thing they would have done is check inside every door. Anything else would be negligence."

Sarah's panting from the effort, shuffling her feet back in

increments, beads of moisture forming on her brow and upper lip. "And yet, I tried to open this door when I moved in, and it was still locked."

A gap has been formed between the display stand and the door, and my panic rises another click. I snatch at Sarah's arm, but she shakes me off. She moves around the stand, putting her back against the door so she can push instead of pull, and I want to beg her not to touch it.

"Oh, wish I'd asked the movers to put this somewhere else." Sarah huffs, her hands spread against the stand's back, cardigan rolled up to her elbows, as she forces the display toward the opposite wall. The scrape of wood against wood is like a scream. The train is coming, its horn a deafening blast, and she still cannot hear it.

Whatever this fear is, whatever my subconscious has been warning me against, I can't allow it in the house with her.

The display now fills the hallway awkwardly, but leaves enough room for the door to swing open. Sarah relaxes, stepping back, rolling her shoulders as she examines the edges of the inset wood panel.

The rot is spreading, ravenous, eager. The cracks pulse under my feet. I try one final time. "Please."

"This is for both of us, sweet thing." Sarah smiles at me before approaching the door. She touches the handle. The house shudders, and I imagine the train tracks under our feet vibrating with the force of an unstoppable behemoth, too close to escape, too close for anything except a final gasp of air.

She turns the handle. It rotates smoothly. The latch clicks. Unlocked. She pulls, and the door shudders, sticking against its own frame, then comes free in a rush.

# 17
# UNNATURAL SHADES

THE DOOR STANDS OPEN AHEAD OF US. I FELT THE INSTANT IT unstuck from its frame, like a tooth being pulled from my socket: insurmountable pressure followed by a blinding pop of relief as it comes free.

The air that rushes out is colder than the house's temperature. Stale, as though it had gone untasted for decades. That should be impossible. Even with the door locked, the gaps underneath and around its edges would have allowed enough transference. And yet, this air tastes like something out of a tomb. Neglected. Old. No longer fit for humans.

That rush of air lasted for a heartbeat, maybe two, then dissipated, but not before leaving a lasting imprint on my lungs. My eyes don't want to see inside the door. They're averted toward the ground, unwilling to obey my instructions, stuck.

The train has hit us. But seconds pass. The world continues

on. The sounds of birds trilling at the feeder's edge bleed into the hum of a car passing along the street. Sarah, at my side, breathes deeply.

Finally, I force myself to look. The door hangs wide, exposing the concealed space beyond, the place that has filled me with fear, the source of the rot.

It's a storage area, as I'd always imagined. No more than four feet deep and six feet wide, its ceiling slanted to accommodate the stairwell above, it forms a tiny walk-in cupboard. A lone light bulb is suspended from its ceiling, a pull-cable hanging beside it.

Five rows of white shelves ring the area, covering three sides, leaving barely enough room for a person to stand inside. Behind them is a plain white wall, discolored even though the cupboard never sees sunlight. Most rooms in this building have seen three or four layers of paint since the home was built, but I suspect this might be the cupboard's original coat.

The shelves hold several items. Two boxes, a scrap of cloth, a book with rumpled pages. Even with those contents spaced about, the shelving looks bleakly empty.

There is no body. It takes a second to register that the digging, sour emotion I feel is disappointment.

"Oh." Sarah presses one hand to her hip, the other holding on to the door's edge for support. Her head turns, first left, then right, then back again, as though the closet's contents will make more sense if she only looks at them properly. "Not what I expected."

She steps in. An idea hits me that the door might close on her, locking her inside, and the only way I can assuage the fear is to physically hold the wood panel open.

Sarah pulls on the light's cord. It doesn't respond. It probably failed at the same time as the stairs'; the same wiring must feed all three switches. Enough light still flows in from the living room windows to illuminate the space, though, so Sarah picks at the boxes. As far as I can tell, they're filled with old clothes. Then she reaches between the shelves, pushing against the walls, as though there might be a second larger room hidden just out of sight. Finally, she picks up the book and flips it open. The old paper is thin and weak, nearly falling out of its binding.

"I can't believe this." Sarah pulls her glasses off and tilts her head back, blinking at the ceiling. "This is Peter's."

The name sparks something in my memory, but I can't catch what.

Her lips are shaky, but their corners quirk up. "My brother. Looks like one of us found how to get into this closet after all. He probably wanted to hide his grades from our father."

She offers the book to me, and I realize it's a school workbook, filled with equations and words painstakingly written in a child's hand.

Sarah reaches for the cloth, and as she pulls it down, I recognize limbs. It's a sewn rabbit. Long ears flop past its blue trousers. One of the button eyes is missing, and the other is dulled with dust.

"Ruth's." Sarah holds the rabbit almost reverently, but her eyes are hazy, and I doubt she's truly seeing it. I let her indulge in the memories, but she places the toy back on the shelf and holds out her hand for the book. "I'm sorry. I truly thought we would find something for you here."

"It's okay." I pass her the book, and she returns it to its place before stepping out of the closet. She doesn't react as I close the door. Energy has left her, and she seems smaller than I remember.

For a minute she stands in the hallway with her back to me, staring toward the kitchen. Then she chuckles and lifts her head. "Well, I had better go and rescue my cake from the birds, if there is any left. Thank you again for the quilt. It truly is special."

As Sarah leaves, I put my back against the display unit, facing the under-stairs door. I don't know what to make of it. The room inside was so mundane, so plain, that it seems laughable to remember how badly I feared it.

Laughable to think that such a nondescript, forgettable door could hide more than a nondescript, forgettable room.

And yet, the fear isn't gone. It starts in my legs and rises through me, prickling my skin, turning my mouth tacky. The idea that the room should have stayed closed. Those shelves and their contents didn't need to be feared, but something else did. And we released it. Like a curse inside a tomb, we ignored the warnings, and now it has been let out, and there is no way to put it back.

My home is still rotting. And the black poison spreads faster and worms deeper, filling my stomach until I am sick with it.

I don't see Sarah through the remainder of the day, and I can't tell if I'm avoiding her, or if she's avoiding me. At some point the cake was returned inside, abandoned on the kitchen sink, two of its corners carved away, a straggling band of ants creeping over the soft, moisture-beaded icing.

Later that afternoon I pass the hallway and notice the display stand has been moved again. Sarah has propped it neatly against the wall and replaced its books. She left the cupboard door free, perhaps in case we need to visit it again. I will do anything in my power to make sure that doesn't happen.

A cold front moves across the region. It brings spits of rain and a gasping winter wind. The sun fails behind rough-edged clouds. A streak of violent red sunset slices the horizon for no more than five minutes before it, too, is absorbed into night.

I remain restless, pacing the lower floor, expecting to run into Sarah eventually but finding myself alone at every turn. The party equipment is packed away. The remains of the cake peek out of the trash. There is something bad about this night, as every time I pass the door underneath the stairs, I'm forced to stare at its bare wooden facade.

Such a mundane door, hiding such a predictable secret. I'm ashamed and angry and confused in alternating beats, the emotions taking turns to pilot me, none remaining in charge for more than a minute before being replaced. Only two lights were switched on in the lower floor: the kitchen's bright bulb, and the living room's more subdued lamp. They create islands of light for me to land in before my restless legs force me back into a sea of black. The door's handle gleams from both, one in each direction, and if I stare at it without focusing, it looks unpleasantly like eyes.

The dining room's large window panes rattle as cold air buffets them. It's not going to rain tonight—not properly, anyway. A few spots of water will linger on the roof and the walls and the yard, enough to make the world feel damp but evaporate into the frigid air before anything can be truly wet. A bad omen. And I cannot stop walking, although I am driving myself insane.

When I pass through the living room I stop by the window and stare into the night. A small LED light flashes through the dim outer world, passing along the exterior of my brick fence. I know that light. It's wielded by Cliff and highlights his sagging face, brought into relief in unnatural shades, alternating with the swishing tails of his two dogs: a golden retriever and a terrier. People say he loves those dogs. Why else would he be braving such an unpleasant night to walk them?

But in the glittering LED light, I see his face turn, just a little, to watch my house. One eyebrow is pulled up to clear skin from around his eye. Dead eyes. Black, like beetles, shining from inside his skull. They rove over my home, fastening on each window, passing over where I stand like a spotlight.

Perhaps those dogs are not so beloved but valued for the convenient excuse they afford him. I wait until his attention returns to the footpath, then drag the curtains closed.

If I were still alive, I could find some distraction to occupy the hours. Beginning plans for a new quilt. Or cooking dinner, although it always feels like a waste to cook for one. Even cleaning could keep my mind busy for a while.

But I am not alive, and the minutes grind by, measured by the sluggish hands of the kitchen clock. Only a little past seven. The house feels too still, too quiet, to be that early.

There is perhaps only one relief afforded to me in this new state: I can embrace oblivion. Hours, perhaps even days, will pass in the blink of an eye, and I won't know which until I wake again.

I have to pass the door to reach the stairs, but I refuse to look at it. My hand finds the banister, which swings me onto the steps. Five of them pass under my feet, and I turn, facing the upstairs hall. A hint of light grazes the ceiling. It's only when I reach the top of the stairs that I find its source: a thin line of it emerges from beneath Sarah's door.

The night is still early, but my body feels tired, and I wonder if Sarah is affected in the same way. *It's the door*, a dark part of my mind whispers. We let something out. We can't see it yet, but it's here, it's poisoning us, and it's already too late to escape.

I pass my own bedroom door and approach Sarah's. She calls a greeting in response to my knock and I let myself in.

The spitting rain adorns her window, little beads shining like baubles in the light of her bedside lamp. They vanish as quickly as they are placed—never enough to wash the dust away, just gathering it and letting it reform in tiny circles.

Sarah sits on the edge of her bed, back to me, as she watches the glass. Her long hair is loose across her back. It contrasts with the burnt orange of her nightgown. She must be cold; she's not wearing anything else, not even slippers.

"Just wanted to say good night," I murmur.

"Thank you, sweet thing." She gives me a look over her shoulder. Her eyes seem small without her glasses, and they crinkle as they watch me. "Sorry we couldn't make much progress. We'll try again tomorrow. Okay?"

I shrug. At some point, without me even noticing, I lost hope that my body will ever be found. Perhaps our first theory was correct after all. I could be in some remote nature trail, my flesh being converted into food for the surrounding trees, my bones a jungle gym for insects, never to be found. "Maybe."

"We'll figure it out. We will." She turns back to the window. Her hands lay in her lap, and I wonder how long she's been sitting there, on the edge of her bed, watching spits of rain form and evaporate.

"Sarah?"

Her shoulders rise a little, then fall again. "I'm fine. Just tired. That cupboard was a surprise, and not even in the way I expected it to be."

Neither of us had expected relics from her first stay in the home to still remain, least of all her siblings' possessions. The door must have gone ignored by every family in the intervening decades.

"I was eleven back then," she notes. "And today I'm eighty-five. That means it's been seventy-four years. It doesn't seem right, but I keep doing the math, and it always comes to the same number. Seventy-four years."

"Since you left?"

She turns her head again—not far enough to fix me with her gaze, but to catch me in her peripheral vision. There's a weary smile pulling at her lips. Something bittersweet except the bitterness has overridden all else. Then she says, "I'm very tired, dear one."

"Then I'll see you tomorrow."

My last glimpse of her before closing the door is her head bowed, staring down at her bare feet, as a gust of wind paints baubles of light across her window.

My own body is cold and clammy as I step into my bedroom. Now that I know there is no quilt on my bed, my eyes don't try to see it. There are only sheets and a layer of blankets, and my room appears sadder because of it.

I sit on the edge of bed, mimicking Sarah's posture. My bedside lamp doesn't do as much for my window, which is latticed by shadows from the oak outside. But it lets me see the desk and its contents. My beautiful rotary phone. The penholder. The place where my journal belongs.

The sheets are unforgivingly cold as I push my feet under them. I curl onto my side, the pillow turned around so I can rest my head on one end and hug the plush body at the other. I won't be able to fall asleep until my feet are warm, but I don't care enough to go in search of a hot water bottle. I leave the light on, though. It's a luxury I feel is justifiable, at least for this damp, unfeeling night.

For a long time, my eyes only stare into the layers of light and dark scattered across my room. My vision blurs until I begin to see shapes that don't exist: a head thrown back in a scream. An arm reached up, clawing. When I blink, they resolve into the most mundane items. My coat. Shadows cast from my bed stand. But I can only hold that clear vision for a moment before my gaze falls into nearsightedness again.

Then the lamp begins to stutter. Like a flame exposed to a brisk wind, it begins to fade in spurts. The long fingers of my oak tree scratch at the window. I hold my pillow tighter. The bulb catches, regains some strength, then stutters again.

Deep in the house, on the floor below me, a lock clicks and hinges turn. I picture the under-stairs door gliding open. Somehow, though, I am unable to visualize the plain white shelves that I know belong inside it. As the door opens, it's like a mouth with nothing but layers of black and red reaching out into a throat that never ends.

My own bedroom door groans as though in sympathy. I'm certain I closed it on the way in. Or perhaps I only imagined I did. Now it's open and at the mercy of the wind.

I won't leave my bed. I won't give any credence to these sounds. They exist to torment me, and the only power they have is what I give them.

Another sound comes. A heavy thump. Something large moves along the upstairs hallway. The lamp flickers. The light is fading, dying out like its energy has been sapped.

This is in my head. Always has been. I close my eyes. Perhaps I can fall asleep before the fantasy devolves. The lamp casts shades of soft yellow across my lids, but the glow rapidly sinks toward black. I imagine myself drifting into a void with it, falling into a deep slumber. My limbs are heavy. My head is tired. And yet, I still cannot sleep.

A high-pitched, metallic sound cuts through the night, and my eyes fly open. Someone is coming through the gate. No, no—they're not. I know the sound my gate makes. This is not deep enough. And it comes from the wrong direction, from behind my head, closer than I'd like.

The noise falters and breaks, and I recognize it. The upstairs bathroom tap. Water flows, thick and loud, and it strikes me as being *too* thick, too viscous, as though the pipes have truly filled with blood. The flow abruptly cuts off. The lamp regains some strength. I stare at it, willing it to hold, and as the door at my back creaks closed, the lamp fades until it is only a spark of light, no stronger than a match.

And then the noise starts.

The low scrape of something heavy being dragged along the floor. Along the hallway. Toward my door.

It comes in pulses. A scrape, then silence, then another scrape. Whatever I'm hearing is heavy. It moves in fragments, no more than an inch at a time, pausing to rest in between. Painful, laborious, and as my unblinking eyes stare into the fading light filtered through my lamp's shade, my overactive mind tries to put form to what I'm hearing.

Fabric, perhaps, dragging over the hallway runner. I picture an intruder dragging a sack behind them. A sack that is heavy with something thick and sticky and red. They strain to haul it as it leaks across the carpet. It exhausts them; the gap between each shuffling beat of movement is growing longer. But whatever they carry, they are not going to stop until they reach their destination.

My room. I already know they will not be passing by. I am the destination.

Another scrape, after which they are quiet for so long that I begin to pray they have given up. Then they move again, dragging closer, this rough, friction-filled noise that grates along my nerves.

I pull the pillow up and wrap it around my head to blot out the sound. Soft cotton presses against my ears. It is only partially effective.

*Scrape*, a prolonged pause, *scrape*. It is almost outside my room. The door is still open a crack, and I think if I can only get up and shut it, perhaps I can keep the noise out. Instead, I squeeze my eyes closed and press the pillow tighter against my ears. It's all in my head. I keep repeating that platitude, but the more I think it, the faster my heart pounds and the sicker my stomach becomes.

Another sound mixes into the dragging noises. I'm terrified to hear it but more afraid to ignore it. I lift the pillow. Almost nothing of my room is visible now: the faint outline of the door, the gleam of the rotary phone, the sharp edge of my bed. The lamp is nearly gone. I hold still, ears straining to hear this foreign sound.

Air passes through a throat: thick, phlegmy, and rattling. It sounds as though it is trying to speak.

Coils of repulsion run through me. They're like snakes in my stomach, insects in my veins, and I'm desperate to squirm, but I don't allow myself the luxury of movement. Not now. Not when the stranger is right outside my bedroom door. I don't even turn my head to look.

*Ignore it. Pretend it isn't happening. It will go away.*

My eyes close, and as they do, I feel the last light fizzle out of the lamp. We're submerged in the darkness, lost together. The rain clouds aren't dense enough for a full downpour, but they are plenty to smother the moon. The oak branches rattle, and the stranger's breath matches it, and I press my hands across my face so I don't have to hear or see any more.

The door groans. Not from the wind, but from a hand pushing it inward, letting themselves into my room.

*Scrape,* right across the threshold. A pause, during which I hear their breath. They're choking on it. Gurgling. A mouth full of saliva—or perhaps blood.

Another scrape. Inching closer to my bed. Closer to me. Noise struggles through the saturation in their mouth. A fragment of a word: "Ee—"

*Go away,* my mind whispers. *Go away, go away.*

A soft thump. Dragging sounds. Coming around the corner of the bed. If the lamp were on and if my eyes were open, I would have no choice except to stare at them. I stay still. I don't want to see.

A gagging, choking noise. The wet smack of lips working together. Then, again, "Ee—"

My heart is galloping, my palms leaving sticky sweat across my face as my fight-or-flight instincts churn my insides. I cannot endure this.

*Thump. Drag.* That rattling breath. That gulping, panting noise. And the smell. Mildew. Dust. Decay. They are so close. At the side of my bed. They could touch me. Drag me out from under my blankets. Take hold of my ankle and pull me down the hall in slow, scraping measures.

My blood is fire. Static fills my ears. I take my hands away from my face, but the room is so dark I cannot even see my own fingers.

The voice, cracked, broken, comes again. "Ee—"

My body shakes. My throat hurts.

A wet gulp. A thud. Then, again, "L-eigh—"

I grab for my lamp. My hand finds the base. I lift it and slam it back onto the bedside table, and the light flickers to life, saturating my room with color.

# 18

## DENIAL

Sarah is on the rug, not standing but lying limply on the floor, strands of hair sticking to her sweat-dampened face. She gazes up at me. One eye is swollen and deformed. The other is half-closed by a sagging eyebrow. That side of her face droops. No longer the sag of age, but of muscles that no longer respond to movement. One arm is curled uselessly at her side. The other reaches forward, grasps at the floor, and drags her limp body an inch closer.

My scream strangles in my throat. I drop from the bed to kneel at her side. Her nightdress has bunched up and stretched around her throat uncomfortably. The clawlike fingers on her left hand are turning blue. Her lips are wet, strings of saliva stretching to the rug, and her tongue flops behind shiny teeth as she tries to speak.

"Don't try to move. Don't—oh." I stare about us, frantic. The rotary phone on my desk glitters in the lamplight. I leap for it, moving around Sarah's prone form, and snatch up the receiver. The dial makes a sharp chiming noise as I spin the numbers. "I'll get an ambulance. They'll be here soon. Just stay still."

Eight minutes. That's how far we are from the nearest hospital. Sarah's wet breath rattles as she struggles to draw air. I crouch at her back, the receiver trapped between my head and my shoulder, and gently pull her head back to clear her airway. I brush strands of hair out of her face. She's burning and clammy all at once, and the panic boiling in my stomach only intensifies as I belatedly realize the phone is silent. No voices. No ringing. Just dead noise.

Because I myself am dead. Because every time I called someone on this phone before, I hallucinated their answer.

The panic spills over, and I want to scream again, want to beat my fist against the desk. The receiver makes a chiming noise as I slam it down, then I drag the whole device to the floor, stretching its cable taut, and position it within Sarah's reach. "You have to call them. I can't. You'll need to turn the dial."

One eye—the swollen one—meets my gaze. The other is lost, buried under loose skin, unfocused. Her jaw works, trying to make noise.

"It's going to be okay." I reach for her good hand—the hand she used to drag herself to me—and pull it to the phone. "Even if they can't hear you, they'll still send someone. Just turn the dial—"

But there is no dial. There's no phone. It's still on the desk. From where I'm positioned, crouched on the carpet, I can see a fine sheen of dust coating it, as though it has not been touched in months.

This time my scream comes out as a stuttering, frightened noise. It reverberates through my teeth. I seize the phone again and drag it back down. It's so perfectly tangible; I can feel the smooth walnut wood, polished to a shine, beneath my fingers. The bronze dial, cold enough to send sparks through my nerves. I can touch every little scratch, every nick, every imperfection. I hold it down and focus on it, willing it to be there on the floor as I take Sarah's hand again.

Her fingers feel so fragile. Wrinkles wrap around them, excess skin on the knuckles, but underneath they seem so thin and so delicate that I fear holding them too tightly. I place those fingers over the phone, my eyes fixed on the shining rotary dial, and I let her hand go. It drops to the floor, melting through the phone, and in a heartbeat the image fades away, like a reflection in a pond that has been disturbed by ripples. It is just the two of us huddled together in the center of my room, with an unmovable phone on the desk above us.

My mind swims. Sharp thoughts pierce through the fog of panic, but they are erratic, unreliable. "Can you…can you reach the phone? Even if you can just get to the cord and pull it down—"

Her breathing is shallow gasps. The good eye, the swollen one, is slowly drifting closed. Again her jaw works, trying to form words. "Ov…oo…"

"No, no, it's okay. I'm here. I can help."

"Ohr-ee…ov…oo."

*Sorry. I love you.*

I want to scream, to howl. I am here, I have heard her, but for all of my will to help, there is so little that I can do. I turn back to the desk again, the frustration pitted so sharply in my throat that it feels ready to tear through. My hands fasten on the edge of the desk and I hurl the table over. Pens scatter, flying from the holder. Papers cascade around us. The phone bounces against the wooden floor, a satisfying clattering noise, and for a second I feel violently gratified, but then the pens and papers begin melting away as the imagery fades.

There must be something I can do. Some way to get help. I cannot carry her. I cannot get her the rotary phone. We have a second phone—the handset downstairs, in the kitchen—but trying to bring that to Sarah will only have the same result.

Sarah can see me. Perhaps she is not alone in that gift. It's a thin hope, a desperate hope, but it's all I can think of. I crouch at her side again, gently stroking her hair back. "I'm going to call for help on the street. Please—we'll figure this out. This will be okay. Don't be afraid."

She moves her head, just a little, and I think she is trying to shake it, to tell me not to bother, that it is too late for that, but this is the only thing I have, the only thing I'm capable of doing.

I fly from the room, feet barely grazing the runner as I dash for the stairs. They disappear under my feet three at a time, and it's only when I hit the colder downstairs floor that I feel the tears marking my face.

The front door bangs when I hurl it open. My bare feet sting as they hit the cold stones leading to the gate. Water comes off the grass and clings to my gown's hem. My hot breath shoots out like smoke, billowing behind me before evaporating into the night.

I reach the gate and lean over it. Since I died, I have never been more than a step beyond this barrier, and I think there is a reason for that. I'm only able to have a form inside the place I considered my sanctuary, my home. If I were to leave my yard, I fear I would fade into the night, like my breaths. Instead, I lean over the gate, hands clutching the wet metal, and scream for help. I scream until my throat burns. Until the spits of rain have painted my face and until my nightgown clings to my shivering form.

Every house around me is dark. It is the deep of the night, well past midnight, and none of our neighbors are even awake any longer.

I move along the perimeter of the fence. Every inhale hurts, a mix of icy air and burnt vocal cords, and each step drives wood chips and dead sticks into the soft undersides of my feet. I pick up a fistful of pebbles from the decorative yard and don't stop moving until I'm facing my neighbor's home: the gentle Moreno woman who Sarah spoke to just this morning. She said her bedroom window faces my living room. She said she saw me pacing through my home after I died.

I rise onto my toes to see over the fence. Two dark panes are opposite me, hiding—I hope—sleeping occupants.

One arm reels back, and I throw the first pebble. It pings off the glass. I throw another, then another, the intensity growing with each projectile until I am sure I must be throwing them hard enough to put a hole through the window. No one responds. There is no light, no sleepy voices. I empty my hands and yell for them one final time, frustration breaking into my voice.

Then I put my head down and rest it against the damp wood of the fence and cry freely. I am so weak. So *tired*. I feel consciousness slipping away and fight to cling to it, but it's like catching water in my hands. The tighter I hold, the faster it drips away, until there is none left.

When I come back to myself, my head is still resting on a wooden surface, only it is no longer rough and rotting but smoothly polished. Time has passed. I can't say how much, only that it is significant. Perhaps a week. Perhaps two.

Gradually, I straighten. My body feels weary. Little movements tax me more than they should. I'm in the kitchen. It's an overcast day, but even with the cloud cover, I can tell it's sometime after noon.

My heart beats strangely. I clench my hands on the table, then slowly relax them. The clock's rhythmic clicks subtly disturb the stillness, but there are no sounds of birds in the yard.

A breath enters my lungs, stuttering. A part of me wants to sit at the table forever. If I never get up, I will never have to know the outcome of that night of spitting rain.

My face is dry and clean again, and I refuse to let tears drip over it, even though they threaten. The house's air smells musty.

As though the windows have not been opened in some time. Sarah would have closed them before that rainy night. The thought twists something in my stomach, and I fear that I am going to be sick.

Slowly, almost against my will, I push my chair back from the table. Adrenaline has filled my legs not with energy, but with unsteadiness. The trash needs to be emptied. The remains of the cake still fill it; mold has grown in abundance, and something squirms around its edges. I turn away.

The hallway creates a straight line to the front of my home. I move along it with halting steps. The under-stairs door is deceptively still. I watch it as long as I can, until I need to step onto the stairs. The first five steps come easily, until they turn and I catch a glimpse of the upstairs hallway. I stagger to a halt.

Something small and dark circles the ceiling on the second floor. It's too small to see clearly, but its hum is distinct. A blowfly.

My mouth is parched and full of a sick taste. My shoulder hits the wall as I collapse against it, and I try to coach myself to breathe, to not fall into hysterics.

I don't expect an answer, but I must try anyway. "Sarah?"

The blowfly hits the ceiling twice in succession before spiraling out of view.

When I died, no one reported me missing until more than a month later. I'd isolated myself, preferring my own company to having friends. Sarah was far more social. She had a family. She spoke with her neighbors.

But she had only lived in the house for a few months—not

long enough to form deep relationships in the area. And her family were yet to visit her. Her absence might not be noticed for just as long.

A strange, inhuman noise forces its way out of me. I knead at my aching sides. The tunnel to the upstairs hall seems impossibly far, but I drag myself up one step, then have to stop again, fear and nausea sticking me to the wooden stair.

The blowfly reappears, spinning as it searches for an escape.

It might have come from outside. It could even have spawned in the cake. Faint hope. I take another step up, bringing more of the hallway into view.

At the top of the stairs, doors hang open. Long stripes of light pass through them to create pillars along the opposite wall. At the end of the hall, Sarah's bedroom door is ajar, but the curtains are closed and I can't make out more than the edge of a table and the glittering eyes of a figurine.

The blowfly hits the wall and spirals through the doorway to my room.

I stagger back down the stairs, my heart rate out of control, a strange, whistling static in my ears.

I hit the wall where the stairs turn and press my face into it. Tears flow hot, dampening the paint. The house accepts my offering. The moisture absorbs into the wall, and by the time the sun sets, I have no energy left to cry. I stay slumped in that corner, knees pulled to my chest, a headache raging and my eyes burning, listening to the broken whir of the blowfly as it beats itself against a window.

If I don't visit upstairs, I will never have to know. Not for certain.

It's a pleasing lie but a lie nonetheless.

My soul knows what I would find in that upstairs bedroom. I left her there to die alone.

Night fills the house and muffles the outside world. Unsteady feet carry me into the kitchen. I take two painkillers, as though they will help, as though it is even fair that I could experience migraines after death. The lights stay off. I fold myself over the kitchen table and wait for oblivion to take me again.

As the night progresses, the homes around me switch their lights off, until the only illumination that makes it through the kitchen window is from the moon. Still, my eyes burn, and still, my head throbs.

She died alone because I was afraid. It was easier for me to expend my energy on a fool's errand, to leave the house, to scream into the night, than to sit with her.

How long was she alive after I left? I press my hands over my ears in a futile effort to block out the thoughts. Did she lie there for hours? Or for days?

"No. No." I kick the chair away and stand. The blowfly's buzzing is still audible, even though it shouldn't be. I pace along the hallway, into the living room, and back. But I don't approach the stairs. I don't dare.

Back in the kitchen, I turn on the sink's tap and force my face under its icy flow. It's a blissful salve. The migraine abates, but only for half a minute, until my lungs are hungry enough that I have to lift my head.

The moon's light is a sickly blue. It transforms everything it touches, turning my home into an environment I don't quite recognize. I rest my forearms on the edge of the sink, water dripping from my nose, as I try with every nerve in my body to not examine the situation I have found myself in. It will not hurt so much if I do not think about it, I tell myself.

The tap water continues to rush, spiraling around the drain. My breathing is a ragged, irrational thing. And another noise fills the space between it.

A scrape. And then a thud.

My reflection is barely visible in the window's glass. Just the outline of my head, limp hair dragging over my shoulders, and the whites of my wild eyes.

The noise repeats. A scrape, and then a thud. It comes above and behind. From the stairs. Something is coming down them.

"Sarah," I breathe. I remained in this house after death because I loved the building, because I was not ready to die, because I had unfinished business. Couldn't all of the same be said for Sarah? With a twinge of bitter irony, I realize that *I* would be her unfinished business. Toward the end, she cared more about finding my body than even I did.

A scrape, and then a thud, closer than before. I turn to face the hallway, my hands clenched together until my fingernails threaten to score holes in my skin. The hallway is darker than the kitchen; I can see the edges of the archways to the living and dining areas, the edge of the stairwell's railing, and a line of something dark that might be the hateful door.

An arm reaches out from the gloom surrounding the

stairs. Thin and birdlike, it grasps for the floor, searching for purchase.

I rush toward her, my body quivering, fear and hope and shame choking my voice. "Sarah."

The clawlike fingers dig in between the wooden boards and the wiry muscles strain as they pull her forward. She emerges from the stairwell. A deafening noise surrounds us, and I only realize the screams come from me when my voice breaks.

My legs fail and I crumple to the floor. My shadow spreads ahead of my form, the bowed head and limp hair shivering in a gust of cold air. The shadow extends nearly to Sarah.

One cold, swollen eye fixes on me. It is pure white, bleached, like the eyes in her family's portrait, but it is not blind. It bores into me, seeming to see past my shell and into my soul.

The left-hand side of her face has melted. It is far, far worse than the visage I saw when she pulled herself into my room. No longer simply limp muscles, but flesh and tendons that have begun to separate, held together by a casing of thin skin. That side of her swings as she moves, inches of swollen jowls, like a balloon filled with water. The left eye has fully disappeared beneath the sagging brow.

Her nightdress is stretched thin, the fabric torn, and strips of discolored flesh are visible beneath. Black flesh, uneven flesh, a body that has bubbled and come alive with bacteria. The dress's color is almost unrecognizable under the staining.

She reaches that birdlike hand toward me. The nails dig into the floor. They are chipped and caked with blood. Her other arm is coiled at her side, frozen, and her legs trail behind her as she drags herself nearer.

My body won't respond. I'm boneless, limp on the floor, close enough that I can smell her—a sticky, repugnant odor of rot. My jaw hangs open as I fight to form words. An apology? A plea for forgiveness? Even I don't know.

Her body slides over the polished wood. That bleached eye shines in the blue light. Her lips form cracks as they widen, showing a row of yellow teeth and something horribly black behind them. Her tongue. Her legs don't work, but her body squirms, writhing to me, closing the gap, and I cannot respond, not even when the cold, clawed hand fastens around my ankle.

She pulls. My breath catches as she drags me nearer, and the smell intensifies, flooding my nose. Decay, and mildew, and greasy skin, and something worse.

"Please." It's the only sound I can make. She doesn't respond. Scabbed fingers and bloodied nails dig into me, cutting through my clothes, as she hauls herself along my body, until we lie side by side on the hallway floor, in the door's shadow.

She puts her head next to mine. The bloated jowl hits my ear. Her slimy gray hair hangs over my face. She is cold as ice, her skin spongy and splitting and filled with pockets of movement.

A blowfly crawls over her lower lip and onto my cheek as she exhales, and then she whispers, in a voice that should never have existed, "You…left…me…to…*rot*."

# 19

## FLIES

SARAH'S WORDS LINGER IN MY EAR LONG AFTER THEY'RE SPOKEN. I convulse, limbs thrashing, and my knee hits the wall. That spark of pain pulls me back to awareness. I'm alone.

Sickness bubbles through me as I sit. I'm still underneath the hateful door. My migraine burns, my vision blurs, and I drag in quick breaths while I can.

The scent has faded. I'm no longer surrounded by the blue light of nighttime, but a tired, dusty gold of midmorning.

Noise comes from the front door and I swing toward it, but it's only the rattle of a car leaving one of my neighbors' homes. My mouth is full of a tacky, unpleasant saliva, and I force myself to swallow.

"That wasn't Sarah." Speaking the words gives them more authority. I think I'm right. I think the vision was a manifestation of guilt and fear, not a reality. The alternative is too terrible to comprehend.

My fingers rest on the wooden floorboards. I know my house. How it feels, how it behaves, and I search it now, seeking any hint that it is harboring another presence.

None. For better or worse, I'm alone.

Knowing that doesn't stop the sticking dread, nor the guilt. I'm safe right now, in the tepid morning sunlight. But once night falls again, my mind will revisit this. It will use it to torment me. And the longer I try to hide from it, the worse it will become.

There is one cure for fear. I push myself off the floor and move to the stairs. Every step adds weight to the dread living in my chest, but I respond by moving faster and faster until I hit the hallway running and tumble recklessly toward my room.

No time for trepidation. I shove through the door, my mind full of static, my nerves on fire. I stop at the edge of my rug.

The black blowfly crawls along the window in twitching motions. My bed is neatly made, the way it must have been when I went missing.

And the rug is empty.

I drop to my knees, gasping, as layers of misery flake away from me. She was found.

How soon, though? The irritatingly hopeful part of me insists that it's possible she was discovered on the same night she came into my room. Maybe someone *did* hear me. Maybe I achieved something by throwing rocks at my neighbor's window.

More realistically, it would have been the day after or perhaps the day after that.

I press my hands into the rug. When I close my eyes, I can

delude myself into thinking I feel warmth. But as my fingers push in between the rough threads, I detect something more. Moisture. Tacky, old, as though the rug were rolled up wet and never given the chance to fully dry.

The sensation sticks to my skin as I pull back. I wipe my hands on my clothes as I rise.

I can't take any more. *Won't* take it. I go back along the hallway, my hair flying behind me, my bare feet glancing off each step as I flow downstairs. Back to the door that has cost me everything, back to the door we never should have opened.

I grasp the handle. The house seems to shift subtly, every wall and every floor tilting just one or two degrees, all turning in different directions. Not a house but a Rubik's Cube. Each room, each doorway, shuffling around, moving, preparing to contort around me. The handle clicks under my hand. Hard metal scraping metal. The latch gives way, but the door is stiff in its frame. I'm too far gone to listen to prudence. I heave, and the door bursts open with a bang.

Dust floats around me. Dust and flies. Six of them: fat, heavy creatures, spinning off the shelves and flashing past me before I can fix my eyes on any of them. One grazes my cheek. Its body is moist but its wings are desiccated. I flinch as it passes, and it disappears into the kitchen, where it will join its brethren in fighting for dominance at the window.

I wipe my sleeve across my nose, which has grown wet. The house's chill is invading me in increments beginning in my bare feet, which have turned numb, and inching into my fingers and face. I could swear the hallway closet is colder than anywhere else in my home.

Otherwise, it remains unchanged from when I last saw it. Plain white shelves. Two nondescript boxes. A child's schoolbook. A child's toy.

There must be some logic here. It's not coincidence that I lost Sarah on the night we opened this door. I drag the nearest box out. A line of tape runs across the cardboard flaps but it's lost its stickiness a long time ago. It comes away with a reluctant cracking noise, and I pull the flaps back. Several moths had wormed their way inside and died on the top layer of fabric. I shake them off.

Layer upon layer of material comes out of the box. All blankets, all child sized.

At the box's base is a small cloth with a hemmed edge, the kind you might place into a crib. The blue material is decorated with faded gold stars. Its edges are dirtier than decades of storage should have left them, and I imagine some toddler from a long-ago time sucking on the material.

I draw the second box down and peel it open. It's more of the same, except this time it also contains two pillows and a coloring book.

By the time I'm done, the boxes' contents are spread about me in a semicircle. I've gone through them twice. They are old enough that I'm sure they must have come from Sarah's time. Many of the cloths were irreparably damaged by the moths, and all of their colors have faded and their seams worn to bursting.

The coloring book is filled with crayon and pencil scribbles. I expected these relics to contain something significant: some kind of answer or, at least, a sign to show me where to look next. All I found were mementos packed away when their owner outgrew them.

The little plush rabbit from the highest shelf stares at me with one doleful button eye. I turn it over in my hands. The stitches are sturdy, if a little rough. It was likely made by a family member. It's small in my hands, but I imagine it would be the right size for a young child to hold at night.

The schoolbook is the only remaining object. I turn the pages carefully to avoid damaging the fragile paper. Even though it only spans a year, it shows a steady progression as the letters grow tighter and cleaner and the math problems grow steadily more challenging. There are many mistakes. On one page, swear words are written in the margin, created in a variety of hands. I can imagine the book's owner gathering his friends around to compile a list of the worst words they knew. On another page, he has doodled an old man with an enormous nose and exaggerated scowl: his teacher.

I want to laugh at the drawing, but the book also holds a sense of melancholy that I can't fully express. This would have belonged to Sarah's brother. And from what she intimated, this child would have passed away many years ago.

The pages are slipping free from their binding. I close it carefully, straightening what I can, and return it to the shelf, along with the doll. Then I repack the boxes. I can't remember their exact order, but I do recall that the baby blanket went in first.

I stare at those near-empty shelves for another moment before closing the door. They have been there for upward of seventy years without being touched. They might last just as long, concealed by this forgettable door, unless the house is torn down or consumed in a fire.

My head aches, pulsing in time with my heart. The door groans as I close it, and I make a slow, shuffling path to the living room. As I sit in one of its pristine white chairs, I wait. What for is a question that I can't answer. The end? I would be relieved if my spirit chose that moment to untether itself, if I never woke in this house again. It doesn't matter that my body hasn't been found. Existing in such an empty space is painful.

The light fails in increments. I don't care to turn on the lamp, so the gloom consumes me.

In some ways it might have been kinder if I'd never met Sarah and never found out the truth. I would still have my routine at least: believing I'd just arrived home, I'd go through the motions of warming up dinner and taking my tablets. Now, I have nothing. No respite. No escape, not even the delusion of work.

A jingling noise comes through the window. I recognize it and coax sore muscles to rise. The night is exceptionally still. I stand on my front step for a beat, the open door to my back, and stare along the footpath that bridges the road and the homes.

Cliff is coming. His two dogs move eagerly, mouths open, tongues flitting behind their teeth as they lead their owner. The metal chains sound almost cheerful, bouncing between the dogs' shoulder blades.

I approach the rusted gate, stopping there just a moment before Cliff himself arrives. A strange static fills my ears, making it hard to think, hard to breathe. The air is more than still; it's stagnant, refusing to cycle even as my lungs work to pump it in and out.

Cliff slows as he nears me. He tugs on the leashes. The dogs obediently fall into line until all three, human and pets, are at a standstill.

Unbrushed hair ruffles around Cliff's gaunt face. He looks so different when he's not smiling. Colder. Full of bitterness. His skin droops more than I remember. As though he is aging faster than his years warrant.

We stand facing each other, the low metal gate a poor barrier between us. My bare feet curl on the stones. The air is still enough that I can smell him. Old, oily skin, disguised under cologne. A striking parallel for what he is: rotting but wearing a pretty mask.

His bleached-white eyes stare at me. Chills travel through my bones.

"What did you do to me?" My voice seems too loud in the claggy, heavy air. It sticks around us, refusing to travel, and I'm sure, if I wait long enough, the reverberations will gradually fall to the ground. "What did you do to *my body?*"

His eyes don't blink. His expression doesn't change, not even to twitch. We are close enough to embrace if we just leaned toward each other, but he shows no reaction.

I step to one side. My feet sink into the smooth grass surrounding the path. Cliff's line of sight doesn't change. He wasn't looking at me; he was watching my house.

The dogs pay attention, though. Two sets of wide, eager eyes follow my movements. Their ears are pricked forward, but their tails don't move.

I follow Cliff's line of sight toward my home. Dead windows, lightless, lifeless. He would have heard about what happened to Sarah. And now he's come to sightsee. To gaze across at the home that has claimed two lives in one year.

"I don't want to be here any longer." I stare at him, willing him to hear me. The smaller terrier takes a staggered step nearer, its nails scratching on the concrete. "Whatever you did to me…let me go."

He takes a long, slow breath. Then he clicks his tongue, urging the dogs forward. They seem relieved to pass me by, and though their heads turn back to glance in my direction, Cliff doesn't look back.

I put my hands on the cold metal gate and bow my head. The air is suffocating. My words swim in my head. *I don't want to be here. Let me go. Let me go. Let me go.*

After that night, the days begin to blur.

My empty home feels more and more like a tomb. I pace the halls in endless loops. Although I'm not conscious of losing time, it slips away from me regardless. The kitchen clock registers one in the afternoon as I pass it, but by the time I've circled through the dining room and back along the hallway, it says it is five.

Phantom images tease at the edge of my eyes. Smooth, acrylic ropes hang across doorways like cobwebs, but only for as long as I don't look at them. Sometimes I imagine I hear Sarah on the second floor again. A slap, then a scrape, as she drags herself to the stairs, but whenever I move closer, the sound stops and the stairwell is empty.

Other times, I hear what I believe are my own footsteps, coming from another room. No matter how intently I follow myself, I can never catch up. It's almost poetic: with no one else to haunt, I am haunting myself.

The house ages around me. Dust gathers across surfaces. The windows collect spots. Eventually, the living room clock's batteries die, and with no one to change them, they remain stuck at twelve twenty.

Most nights Cliff passes by my home. Sometimes he stops to watch it; sometimes he simply keeps moving. Sometimes I go into the yard to stare into his face. Other nights I stay behind my curtains, knowing he cannot pierce the gloom that spreads through my home.

The cake in the trash rots until there is nothing left to sustain life. A generation of flies are born inside and feast upon the remains, but they, too, die, gathered across the windowsills and twitching their last in the hallways I endlessly walk.

And I still cannot leave. It is hell.

Often, during the depth of night, as I pace my home like a wolf in a cage, I search for any escape there might be. A door I missed. A sign to show me what I'm supposed to do. Anything. If my home holds the answer, it is reticent to share it.

Then, finally, on a cold and overcast day, my gate sounds its alarm.

I'm at the kitchen window when the metal screams. Birds occasionally drop down to the feeder to see if the seeds have been replaced, but those visits grow less frequent as their hope dwindles. The old oak branches seem heavier. The washing line is empty, but it still lists, rocking on its base with every gust of wind.

It's been so long since I heard the sound of my gate that it takes a second to register. I turn, already doubting myself. Feet crunch along the pathway to the front door.

I'm not ready for strangers to be in my home. For how lonely I've felt, I still squirm against the thought of unwanted company. Not that I have much say in the matter.

They're at the door. A woman speaks, but her words evaporate into the air before I can parse them. My sweaty palms leave imprints in my nightdress as I clench the fabric. Keys jingle, then scrape as one is forced into the lock. I step closer, stopping near the under-stairs door, my tongue dry, my skin crawling.

The lock turns. The door opens. A woman nudges it in using her shoulder, and I glimpse bobbed blond hair and a riotous scarf wrapped around her throat. She enters the house backward, struggling with something still outside. Something large, being dragged into my home.

"Almost there. I'll tilt you back as we go over the step. One, two, three—"

The woman grunts as she pulls the shape into my home.

Rubber wheels creak on the floor. The woman continues to back toward me until she is clear of the door, then shuffles in an arc, turning the wheelchair she has been maneuvering.

My voice catches in my throat as I stare into round, lamp-like eyes.

# NEVER SHOULD HAVE OPENED IT

## 20

SARAH SEEMS EXCEPTIONALLY SMALL, EVEN SWADDLED BY blankets. Her hands lay in her lap. Her long hair is braided over her shoulder, the ends grazing a shawl. The flashing white glasses obscure her eyes, but her face is both familiar and changed. One cheek droops, pulling on her lips and seeming to melt into her neck.

The stranger busies herself with closing and locking the door, chattering in a way that seems to rob her of air. "Let's get you somewhere comfortable. Is that the living room over there? It looks cozy. Let me just…"

She finds the wheelchair's handles and pushes. I step back as the chair glides past me. The stranger is tall and broad shouldered, dressed in block colors, but with feet that seem far too small to support her. Each step ends with a slight bounce. I follow in their wake as she positions Sarah near one of the white couches, facing the window.

Sarah's head turns slightly toward me, though I still can't see her eyes behind the glasses. One hand rises. The fingers have lost their dexterity; they twitch, but not far, as she gestures to her helper. "Would you do something for me, Allie?"

"Sure, love."

"My favorite cardigan is in my room upstairs. Last door down the hall. It's rose pink."

Allie tugs at the blanket around Sarah's shoulders, adjusting it. "Course. It is a bit chilly. Let me get that for you."

She leaves through the hallway, and her footsteps grow slower and heavier as she climbs the stairs. As she enters the second-floor hall, Sarah's clawlike hand feels around her glasses and carefully peels them away.

One watery gray-green eye fixes on me. The other is covered by her drooping brow and a lid that twitches when she moves.

I'm struck by the image my brain conjured of her: bloated with decay, her face seeming to melt off the bone, filled with fury that I allowed her to become that way.

But then she speaks, and her voice is all warmth. "Hello again, my darling. I wanted to find some way to tell you I was coming back, but it's hard to convince people to deliver messages to empty homes."

Tears rise as I move closer. My hands reach out without me realizing, and she offers me hers. I clasp it, holding tight, afraid to let her go again. "I'm sorry. I'm so sorry."

One side of her mouth rises in amusement. "Well now, what for?"

I lower myself onto the coffee table's edge, where we're close enough that our knees nearly bump. "I couldn't help. I swear I tried—"

"You did plenty, my darling. Don't you remember? You knocked the table over. The phone landed next to me."

My head swims. I remember hurling the desk over, but that should have been a mirage, just like everything else I did. "But…"

"I believe that sort of thing is called poltergeist activity. Though I doubt you would be truly classified as a poltergeist. You don't normally affect things. Just, it seems, when you're very upset."

"And you were able to call for help?"

"Yes. Took me a few tries, but I managed. They said the symptoms might have been reversed better if I'd called in a few hours earlier, but, well, I never expected to have a stroke in my sleep."

The new woman's strange, bouncy footsteps move above us, creaking on floorboards, as she searches Sarah's room. I glance toward the ceiling, but Sarah's clawlike hand squeezes mine. "Don't worry about Allie. She'll only be here part-time. And we should still have a few minutes. I sent her searching for a cardigan I don't actually own."

When I smile, I feel the moisture on my face and swipe my forearm across my cheeks to clear them. "I'm just happy you're back."

"As am I." Her one good eye rises to look over the walls and windows. "I missed this place. And I missed you."

"I'm bad at tracking time. How long were you gone?"

"A shade under three months. The first few weeks in the hospital, the rest spent in a nursing home. Most people seemed to want me to stay there for whatever years I have left, but I can't imagine anything worse. Allie is a compromise. She's a personal caregiver, and she'll be spending part of each day here to cook and clean and make sure I don't tumble out of my chair and kill myself for good."

Laughter chokes in my throat, but Sarah doesn't seem fazed.

"I'm eighty-five. That's a good age to die, I decided, but it looks like the universe has given me a bit more. Mercy willing, that will be enough time to see you set free as well."

Allie's footsteps are on the stairs again, no longer bouncing, but hard and snappish. Sarah smiles her lopsided smile once more before replacing her glasses and leaning back in her chair.

"I couldn't find anything pink, just lots of greens." Allie comes through the archway bearing one of Sarah's cardigans. It's my first chance to get a good look at her face. It's long, with a sharply pointed jaw, and her cheeks are flushed with agitation until they almost match her ruby lipstick. "The pink one must be in the wash. You'll have to make do with this."

"That will be fine. Thank you." Instead of letting Allie put it on her, Sarah takes the cardigan and drapes it over her lap.

Allie bites on a sigh as she turns toward the kitchen. "How about I make you a cup of something before I start setting up your bedroom?"

"Tea would be lovely, thank you."

I don't get another chance to talk to Sarah through that afternoon, but I stay at her side. Together we watch Allie work, like spectators to some strange game without rules.

The upstairs is no longer practical for Sarah, so Allie converts the empty office into a new bedroom. She carries in parts of a hospital bed and assembles them against the wall—the same wall Sarah's family portrait was taken in front of all of those years ago—then lets Sarah instruct her on what other furniture she'd like added.

She's an efficient worker, and a strong one, maneuvering a bedside table down the stairwell as though it weighs nothing.

"We'll get a plumber in to install a shower in the laundry," she notes, "but that will take a few days, so it will be sponge baths until then."

"My favorite," Sarah responds, though Allie doesn't seem to be listening.

"Now, you're going to be a good girl and wear your bracelet, aren't you?"

Sarah raises one arm, shaking her sleeve back, to reveal a band fixed around her wrist. A red button stands out of the silver design. "Of course," she confirms without joy.

"Excellent." Allie finishes tucking sheets into the bed and straightens, flexing her shoulder muscles.

Finally, come seven thirty, Allie leaves. Plates have been cleared away from dinner, the garbage finally taken out, and even the dead flies removed from the sill. Sarah waits until the front door closes and the gate heralds Allie's departure, then releases a deep, weary sigh.

"She's a force to be reckoned with," I note.

"That she is." Sarah places stiff hands on her chair's wheels and turns herself toward the new bedroom. "She's supposed to help me save energy, though I wonder if I'd feel this tired if I'd been by myself. Will you come with me?"

I follow her along the hallway. The under-stairs door is to our right, but although I watch it warily, Sarah pays it no attention.

She wheels into her new room and peels the blankets back from the bed. My quilt forms its top layer, something she specifically requested from Allie. Sarah rises from her chair. She can still stand, at least, though the movements are halting and pained, and she sags as she lowers herself onto the bed's edge. For a moment she just sits, hands braced at her sides, head bowed, her long braid swinging. Then she shakes her cardigan back from her right hand and unfastens the emergency alert bracelet.

"Is it uncomfortable?" I ask.

She tosses it toward the room's opposite side. Allie placed a small round table under the window at Sarah's request, along with two seats. The bracelet misses the table and skitters over the wood floor, disappearing into the room's dark corner. "It was one of their conditions before they'd let me return."

"I think it's smart."

"It's patronizing. I'm already old. How many more years do my children expect to string me along for?"

"As many as you can give them, I imagine."

She gives me a sharp look, but a hint of amusement lights her eyes. "Well, at least I made it as far as here. Sylvia wanted me to move into her home. Again. After buying me this place just months ago."

The bedroom door is closed, but I can still picture what's on the other side, just a few steps away. I pull one of the table's chairs out, turn it to face Sarah, and sit, my steepled fingers between my knees. "Maybe that wouldn't be a bad idea."

"My dear, if my children's wheedling and my grandchildren's emotional manipulation couldn't sway me, you certainly won't. You'll have to put up with me for a while longer."

"I'm not putting up with anything. I'm just worried."

Sarah kicks her slippers off and sighs as she rotates her ankles. Like everything else, they appear stiff.

I already know she won't listen, but I have to try. "There's something wrong with this house. It's been warning me this whole time, through the dreams and the visions, but we ignored them and now…"

"And now what?" Her one good eyebrow rises. "Are you talking about the closet under the stairs?"

"We never should have opened it. I think we let something out."

"I had a *stroke*. Something that is not unheard of in a person my age."

"The same night after we unlocked the door, though?"

"Medical things do seem to love dramatic timing. We could just as easily blame the Funfetti cake."

I try to laugh. It makes my chest hurt. Even after what the house did to her, she still can't see how dangerous it is. Because, to her, it simply looks like her home. She can't see the rot. She doesn't feel when it tilts. "Will your family be visiting?"

"As soon as they can." She rolls her shoulders and grimaces when something catches. "Sylvia wanted me to wait until she could get time off work and settle me in herself, but I threatened to riot. I wanted to get back here."

"Because of me?"

"Silly girl. *Of course* because of you. You don't think I love this house enough that I would agree to *Allie* just to live here, do you?"

My nose is inexplicably wet. I drag my sleeve over it, leaving a dark patch on the fabric.

"Now, I need you to do me a favor. Bring down the portrait from my room. You remember which one, don't you?"

"Of course."

"Good girl."

Sarah wants me to believe the door under the stairs is just what it presents itself to be: the entryway to a storage closet. But as I slip from her new bedroom and pass the wood panels, I feel something spreading from it. The rot. Spores, floating in the air, sticking to my skin, spreading through the house. I hold to the wall opposite as I pass it. Sarah doesn't believe because she doesn't see. She doesn't know how powerful the building truly is.

It's my first time seeing the bedroom since Sarah became ill. The sheets have been half wrenched off the bed. Chairs are tipped over and several of her figurines are smashed on the floor. That would have come from her struggle to reach me. Fresh guilt presses onto my back.

The closet doors are wide-open, and that would be from Allie's search for the cardigan that doesn't exist. Some items fell to the floor, and she left them there. Likely because she believed no one except her would be venturing into the upstairs. She thinks Sarah lives alone.

The portrait is in its usual place. I linger over it, fingertips running across its frame, as a wry smile forms. Sarah knows I cannot carry it. She took advantage of my mind's willingness to ignore my state and sent me on a pointless errand.

It feels real enough to me, though. And Sarah seems able to see the items I manifest, even temporarily. This errand is a fiction, but one that I don't mind participating in. I cradle the photo to my chest as I carry it back to the ground floor.

Sarah has managed to remove her cardigan and lie down in bed. She breathes heavily, her back propped up against the pillows as she waits.

"While I was in the hospital, one thought kept circling my head like a bad fly," she says as I pull my chair closer. "Something I should have told you. I nearly did, a couple of times, but it always felt…too personal. And too raw, even if it's been seventy-four years. But I've started to truly appreciate how little time I may have left, and, well…you deserve to know."

She nods to the picture. The mother, sitting, her feet crossed at the ankles, hands in her lap. The father standing behind and slightly to the right, wearing a weathered and heavily repaired suit. And the four children; two boys, two girls.

Their faces are all disturbing to me. Blank eyes. Empty faces.

"That portrait is special to me. It's the only one I have of my whole family. Before things changed."

"Your father left."

"Yes. But there was more." Her inhale rattles at her chest. It's a strange sound. A frightening one. "It affected all of us in our own ways. My father left. My mother couldn't handle what remained of her family on her own and moved in with her own mother. She passed away when I was twenty-five."

"I'm sorry."

Sarah makes a slight noise. "She was growing weaker every year. Sometimes I'm surprised she made it as long as she did. As soon as they were old enough, my brothers found jobs. We all had to grow up quickly." She indicates the older boy. He looks about twelve; his dark hair is combed to the side and his face appears slightly pinched. "Peter fared the worst out of any of us. He got into drink early. Then drugs. I suppose he was grasping at anything he could to make life feel sufficient, but the more he used, the more he faded away. He stopped talking to the rest of us around the time my mother died. I don't know what became of him."

She indicates the younger boy. His hands are held awkwardly at his side, as though he doesn't know what to do with them. "Hugo kept in touch with Peter longer than I did. Every year or so he would go looking for him and find him in a house crowded with strangers or, sometimes, under a bridge or sleeping in an alley. They lost touch for good around the time Peter turned forty.

"For most of my life, I thought Hugo fared the best out of all of us. He became an ad campaign coordinator for some large brands. They paid him well and he even won some awards. But he had his own demons; he was just better at hiding them. He passed from alcohol poisoning when he was in his early sixties. Left behind a widow and two children."

Sarah's eyes are wet. The left one, the open one, jumps over the photo, as though trying to hold on to every detail, to seal it into her mind. "That's me." She points to the older daughter, a head full of ringlets, around eleven. "I married. I struggled. I survived. Here I am at eighty-five, and as far as I know the last of my family."

"What happened to your sister?"

Her good eye turns to the youngest daughter.

"Ruth. She is *why* everything went bad. Why my father left. Why my mother fell apart, and Peter got into drink, and Hugo escaped to the city as soon as he could. She went missing, in this home, shortly before her fifth birthday."

# 21
## MORSEL

SARAH TILTS HER HEAD BACK TO REST IT ON THE PILLOW. I LOOK down at the portrait in my hands only to realize it's no longer there. My fingers are held stiffly in the air, shaped around a frame that must still be upstairs. I try not to let my frustration show as Sarah's soft, sad voice resumes.

"On the eleventh of March 1946, Ruth vanished sometime between four and six in the afternoon. I was eleven at the time, and after school I went across the street to play with my friend. Hugo stayed late at school. Peter went fishing for tadpoles at a pond a few blocks away. They drained it years later to make room for more developments.

"My mother was delivering laundry, as she usually did in the afternoons, and came home at six to find the house empty. Hugo, Peter, and I returned, but Ruth never did. We couldn't figure out what had happened to her. She was at home when

I dropped off my schoolbag, but sometime after I left, she vanished.

"When the police arrived, they said it was already too dark to look for her, but they'd start a search in the morning if she hadn't turned up. I don't think any of us slept that night. At dawn, my mother started walking up and down the street, knocking on doors. By midday, half the neighborhood was involved in the search. It was my job to sit by the phone and see if anyone called. A lot of people did. Prank calls, mostly kids, but a few adults, some saying horrible things, saying they'd taken Ruth and we'd never see her again.

"The search lasted for weeks, and the longer it went on, the more convinced I became that Ruth had never left our home." Sarah reaches one hand out and rests it on the wall closest to her bed. "I had this idea that the building had gotten hungry and swallowed her like a morsel. While everyone else searched the ditches and the ponds, I searched the house. Again and again. Inside closet, under beds, in the attic. This was the last place I'd seen her. It just made sense that she would still be here."

My heart beats too fast. Every word seems to be hurting Sarah more, but my head is hot and my fingers are cold, and I can't leave it alone. "Do you think…is it possible…that whatever happened to Ruth also happened to me?"

"You both vanished without a trace." Her fingers trail over the wall before she pulls the hand back to her chest. "But I'm afraid, my dear, Ruth's story had an ending. For slightly more than a year my parents searched and begged for tips and tried to keep

Ruth's image alive in the news. But she was eventually found. A hiker stumbled across small human bones in what is now known as Hampton Park."

I know the park. It's a twenty-minute walk away.

"Back then, the area hadn't been developed and it was all forest with a few trails through it. We were lucky to find enough of Ruth's bones that they could identify her teeth."

Sarah shrugs, though she still won't look at me. "That's when things really fell apart. We'd been held together by this thread of desperate hope for more than a year, and suddenly it was cut. My father went to work one morning, got on a Greyhound bus, and never came back. My mother couldn't look at her three remaining children without seeing the one she lost, and it broke her."

"It sounds horrific."

"What I hated the most was how drawn out it was. A year is a long time to a child. I forgot what a normal life should feel like. Moving in with my grandmother was good for us, I think. It got us out of this house. Changed our routines. Got us away from the things that kept reminding us of Ruth."

"Did you ever find out what happened to her?"

"No. A lot of people thought she'd wandered into the forest and froze to death overnight, but I don't believe it. Ruth was shy, and she was not yet five. She wasn't like Peter, who was always looking for an adventure. Mostly, she just wanted to be at home and play with her toys."

I think of the rabbit in the under-stairs cupboard and remember the look of devastation on Sarah's face when she found it.

Seventy years should have been enough to remove every trace of her baby sister from the house, but somehow, that one memento was left behind.

"Most likely, someone knocked on the door, and Ruth answered, and they took her away." Sarah's voice is dispassionate. "No one saw anything. Even though I jotted down notes about every bogus phone call that came in, none could be matched to Ruth. And that was that. After more than seventy years, most witnesses are gone or their memories no longer work. She's joined all of the other children whose deaths will never be solved, and there's nothing to do to change that."

The back of my hand aches, and I realize I've been rubbing it compulsively. I lace my fingers together. "I'm sorry."

"Nothing for you to apologize over, sweet thing. This is just how life goes sometimes."

"Is it painful to live in this house again?"

She doesn't immediately answer. Her one good eye traces over the ceiling; the faint cracks around the light, the window's edge, the door's frame. "Yes. And no. This is the only place that has ever felt like home to me. Mostly, I think, because every home after that was post-Ruth." She looks at me, then diverts her eyes. "To be truthful, when I saw it was on the market, a part of me wanted it for selfish reasons."

"Because you hoped you might find answers."

"Yes. On my first day moving in, I sensed a spirit. And I thought it might be Ruth, still here, after all that time."

"And you got stuck with me instead." I smile, but my voice cracks.

Her hand flicks the words away. "I'm glad, actually. She didn't spend the last seventy years trapped here. And if I can help you, it's perhaps a little bit like helping Ruth, don't you think?"

During his visit, Cliff had dropped a hint that the house had something darker buried in its past. Sarah had breezed past the comment, and now I understand why. No matter how much Cliff knew about the house's past, Sarah knew more.

It would likely also explain why the officers who searched the home displayed more curiosity than the situation warranted. The house was associated with not just one, but two cold cases.

Sarah seems to be shrinking into her pillows, growing smaller with every minute. "I don't know how much use I can be to you now. With some work, I should be able to get out of the chair and start using a walker instead, but I'll still be tied close to home. Allie will do the shopping and run errands for me from now on, but I don't know if I'll be able to convince her to look into your past."

"Or know where to start," I add. "We were already running low on options."

"There must be something. An avenue I'm overlooking or a clue that's just under our noses. It's impossible for a person to vanish into thin air. There must be something…" Her voice trails off into nothing as her eyelids dip lower, pulled down by invisible weights. Sarah is asleep within minutes. Her blankets are crooked, so I adjust them where I can, then pick up the emergency bracelet from where she threw it and leave it on the bedside table, next to the lamp. They'll vanish once I look away, I know, but I can't stop myself from trying.

Early evening is only sliding toward true night, but the world has taken on a still, quiet cadence I associate with the hours after midnight. As I move through the lower floor of my home, I trail my hands across the white-painted walls.

"What did you do?" My words are soft, but I know my home can hear me. I move into the dining room and then toward the kitchen. "What did you do to Ruth?"

Soft bumps run under the whorls marking my fingertips. These walls seem so smooth and uniform from a distance, but as I touch them, I taste their flaws. I imagine rot inside them, bubbling at the other side of the paint, splitting it away from the drywall and bricks underneath. My beautiful, proud home is crumbling from the inside, and no one else can tell.

Synthetic ropes crisscross the barrier between the dining area and the kitchen. My eyes fall closed as I walk through them. The cool coils trace over my exposed skin: my throat, my face, my arms. Tangling me. Tightening. Threatening to squeeze further, to cut into my skin. But I keep walking, and then I am on the other side of them and facing the window overlooking my backyard. The oak tree is dying under its own weight. It must have still been small when Ruth died, perhaps not even broad enough to shade the lawn.

My hands run over my shoulders to brush away loose coils of rope. They create slithering noises as they fall to the floor, like snakes too weak to do more than writhe. The cold bores into me, and my breath plumes as I turn back toward Sarah's room.

I take up sentry in the seat under the window and watch as

the rectangle of moonlight crawls across the wall. I count each of Sarah's breaths, making it as far as four hundred before I lose track and have to start again. The creeping exhaustion cries out from every fiber of my body. I'm ready to close my eyes and fade back into the nothingness…but not just yet. Not until I see Sarah through to the dawn.

The room seems smaller than it did before. I was sure there was more of a gap between the door and the bed. The ceiling appears a few inches lower. When I turn to face the window, it takes up more space than it should.

It gives the strange sense that the house is breathing, but instead of drawing breath, it only lets it out. Further and further, exhaling, shriveling in on itself, the walls bubbling as they lose the tautness necessary to hide the decay. When I stand, the ceiling brushes my head. The bedside table scrapes, in agonizing fractions, across the floor as the wall pulls inward. My mouth is dry. Sarah doesn't wake, not even when I touch her cheek, but there is not much she could do either way. The doorway has crumpled. The walls are nearly at either end of the bed. The small round table at my back crowds me, and I crawl onto the chair so my legs don't become trapped. I have to bend my head at an angle to avoid the ceiling. Knees pressed to my chest, arms wrapped around them, I watch with growing nausea as the ends of the bed fracture under the pressure.

I close my eyes. There's a sound of splintering wood, then only the rapid staccato of my own heart, racing out of control. The ceiling will be on me in a second, flattening me, and I squirm down further to avoid it. Something metal buckles. My teeth ache from how hard I clench them.

And then I open my eyes, and the house has breathed in again.

The room is back the way it should be. The bed is untouched. The door is broad and sturdy. And dawn has come. Sunlight filters through the blinds, distinct stripes painted in a map of air-suspended dust.

I'm still hunched on one of the chairs, my knees held under my chin, and it takes me a moment to feel safe enough to return my feet to the floor. The room is fine again. Except for the small round table, which now bears a deep crack.

---

Allie arrives at ten that morning, heralded by the shrieking gate. She helps Sarah wash and change, then prepares her food, chatting as she does so. She's having problems with her neighbors and their dog that barks through the night. She makes a joke about needing to invest in some poison. She laughs. Sarah doesn't.

She's easy to keep track of at least. Her odd bouncing footsteps paint a trail of her progress through the home, and she rarely stands still for long. I get an hour of respite as she goes shopping to refill Sarah's fridge shortly after lunch.

Sarah and I don't talk much, even when we have the chance. She tires easily. Sometimes she stares into the distance, not seeming to see or hear much. Allie parks her at the kitchen table for most of the day with a cup of rapidly cooling tea and a book of crossword puzzles that she doesn't touch.

"We need to get you a TV," Allie notes, sifting through a basket of washing that has spent the last three months in the laundry.

"I never cared much for TV." Sarah's hands lay in her lap as she stares toward the kitchen window. Through it, I watch a lone sparrow flit down to test the bird feeder, then disappear in a whir of wings. "I guess Leigh and I are the same like that."

I dip my head in agreement. I'd listen to the radio often, but TV either tired or depressed me.

"Yeah?" Allie asks. "Who's Leigh?"

Sarah turns her head just enough to give her caregiver a secretive smile. "A friend."

Allie doesn't appear interested in pressing further. Sarah lets the silence hold for a minute, then draws a breath into herself, as though bracing for something.

"Can you get me a walker? I'd like to start practicing with it."

"Is that right?" There's something in Allie's smile that I don't quite trust. "Well, how about we give it a bit more time and then see how you feel, okay?"

"I've been in this chair for three months. That's plenty."

Allie laughs as she folds a dishcloth. "Don't think I'm arguing, love. But I've been doing this for years, and I've seen how these things usually go. I'm just trying to save your money."

Sarah's good eye doesn't waver from the window. "Neither of my feet are in the grave quite yet. And I'd like a walker."

"All right, then, I'll see what I can do."

Sarah sinks back in her chair. She's bundled up, blankets over her knees and over her shoulders, and they dwarf her. I'm struck by the idea that she has grown smaller in the time I've known her. It was only months ago that I shrank away from her in fear, seeing her as something immense, something that could fill a doorway.

As Allie flicks a new cloth out of the basket, I lean close to Sarah's ear. "You don't need to put up with her if you don't like her, you know."

Sarah tilts her head toward me, angling it so that our companion won't be able to hear. "She was the compromise. My family picked her because they trusted her."

"Tell them you want someone else."

The corners of her mouth twitch up, but it's a sad kind of smile. "I've already caused enough trouble. Allie's all right. I could do a lot worse."

Allie folds the last of the towels and puts them into stacks, which she begins to ferry about the house. She stops partway along the hall, head turned toward the space under the stairs.

I rise from my spot at Sarah's side. Allie faces the door, her eyes narrowed, her vividly red lips slightly parted. For a moment she doesn't move, then she calls, "What do you keep in this cupboard here?"

Sarah's expression doesn't so much as flicker. "It's just storage. Don't bother with it."

"Huh." Allie makes to move away, then hesitates.

I stop at her side, and together, we stare at the indistinct bronze doorknob hidden in the wall of paneling.

"It's just—" Allie rolls one shoulder. Her frown deepens. "I thought I heard it rattle just now."

"It's the wind." Sarah is only in the kitchen, less than ten steps away, but her voice is distant.

Allie holds a stack of towels against her chest. One hand leaves them as she reaches toward the door.

"Don't," I whisper, just behind her shoulder.

She stops. A shudder runs through her. She turns, and her huge eyes fix on the space just a few inches to my right. Then she returns to the door. Her hand finds the handle. She twists it, but it catches, budging less than a millimeter.

My relief escapes as a sigh. Allie rattles the handle, then steps back, turns on her heel, and climbs the stairs, her bouncing steps faster than normal.

A strange routine is established over the following week. It's something that all three of us seem to want to resist but snares us despite our protests.

Sarah naps in the afternoon. She tells both me and Allie that she's not tired, but her whole body droops, accentuating the loose muscles on the side of her face, until she can't deny it any longer. She's asleep within minutes of being placed into bed.

While Sarah sleeps, Allie cleans. She's good at it. She attacks the grouting in the kitchen and the dust and stray webs that gather in corners with gusto. Our house becomes a whirl of brushes and microfiber cloths and buckets of soapy water.

My routine, on the days I have the energy to be present, involves staying at Sarah's side while she's awake and following Allie when she's not.

At least Sarah was respectful. But Allie treats my home as

her own, moving my furniture and rifling through my drawers. She sighs a lot, especially when she finds something she doesn't like: the wrong order for the cutlery or the mess in Sarah's old bedroom or the crowded pens in the cup on my bedroom desk. She takes twenty minutes out of a day testing each of the pens on a sheet of paper and throwing out the ones she deems as too old.

And I, the person who purchased each of those pens, am forced to stand beside the desk, my insides boiling, my hands pulled into fists at my sides as I stare her down.

Sometimes I think she can sense my presence. She looks over her shoulder often, eyes narrowed and lips pursed just slightly. That's good, I decide. She should feel on edge in this house. I am the least of its dangers.

She tests another pen. It's one of my favorites: a memento from the natural history museum gift shop, which I could have gotten for free but insisted on buying anyway. It still has plenty of ink. But it apparently doesn't satisfy Allie because she places it on the growing pile to be thrown out.

"No," I say.

She picks another pen out of the cup and removes its cap.

The lava in my stomach is unbearable. I slap my hand across the stack of discarded pens, my voice booming. "I said *no*."

The natural history museum pen rolls off the edge of the table and hits the floor with a sharp ping. Allie startles but only takes a second to recover. She picks the pen up and returns it to the pile.

There is ringing in my ears. I'm breathing fast enough to hyperventilate, but a surge of vindication courses through me, and the lava in my stomach is no longer eating me alive. I place my hand on the pen. Cool and solid, metal and wood, its beautiful textures alive under my fingertips. I push. It slides to the desk's edge and then tumbles over.

Allie drops the pen she was testing and takes a step back, staring from the door, to the closed window, to the pen on the floor. Her tongue darts out to taste her lips. Her eyes are wide and blind with something akin to fear. She tugs at her shirt's collar, then turns and leaves the room at a trot.

Elated shivers travel along my limbs. The pen moved at my command. Not just as a figment of my mind, but something Allie saw, too. It was real. I feel drained, as though I've survived some kind of endurance test, and every atom of my body has been wrung out. As I slide to the floor and retrieve my favorite pen, I can't stop smiling.

I may be dead, but I'm not yet gone.

# 22
# BEHIND THE WALLS

ALLIE HATES THE HOUSE. SHE ARRIVES AT HER DESIGNATED TIMES and leaves the second her shift ends, apparently intent on fulfilling her commitments while spending as little time inside the building as possible.

I'm glad for it. She exhausts Sarah just by being present. And she continues to be too eager to touch and rearrange everything in my home, even after the pen incident.

But I don't think I'm the only part of the house that unnerves her. Occasionally she'll stop in the hallway and stare at the door. There's real fear in her eyes, and I wonder if she hears something I cannot.

One night, I approach the door myself and press the side of my head against the cool wood. Since Sarah came home, I've given it as wide a berth as possible, and recently, I've even begun taking the longer route through the dining room just to avoid it.

But avoiding the door doesn't make it better. Whatever infests the house multiplies each day, and although it stays hidden behind the walls, it's poisoning Sarah. Rot or mold or spores of some kind that can't be detected by my eyes—it's there, and it's spreading, and the more I ignore it, the worse it grows.

So I press my ear to the door, this nexus of poison, this source of my home's corruption. And I hear it.

It's quiet, like it comes from a great distance away, and I push the soft flesh of my ear against the wood as I strain to make out the sound. Like dead branches, scraping together. Or like a husky voice whispering to itself. Or like insects. Thousands of them. Millions. Teeming, writhing. The noise swells like a wave coming in, then abates, and I am left with weak legs and breathless lungs.

The handle is cold to the touch—colder than the house's ambient temperature warrants. I apply pressure. Not enough to open it, but just enough to test the fastening.

It's locked. The knob grinds to a halt before I can shift it more than a millimeter.

I tell myself it doesn't matter, that even if I could open the door, it wouldn't reveal anything that I haven't already seen.

But I hate that I don't even have the option. And I don't know what to make of this door that ignores the rules, that chooses when it can be opened.

The house is tilting again, and I fear it cannot tilt much further before things begin to cascade out from the cracks. The kind of things that should never be seen. The things that are better kept a secret.

That abhorrent scratching, whispering noise follows me through the house. When I place my hand against the walls, I feel the reverberations come from within.

"I used to love you once," I say to the doorway that leads to the kitchen. "I was prepared to fight for you. Why did you turn on me?"

The reverberations grow heavier until my palm is tingling and I am forced to snatch it back from the wall.

When Allie arrives the following morning, she hesitates on the front step, and I wonder if she senses the changes, too. Her eyes dart across the walls and toward the ceiling, exposing more of their whites than seems natural.

"I'm going to open up some of these windows," she tells Sarah, setting her bag down on the living room couch. "It's getting stuffy in here."

"Mm." Sarah sits in her bedroom's doorway, hands limp in her lap, her eyes dull as she gazes at the view from the window. "If you like."

Allie pushes the curtains back and forces the windowpanes as far open as they will go, and I want to tell her it's futile, that extra air won't fix what's worrying at her, but I doubt she would listen even if she could hear me. I'm familiar with this kind of desperation. I've felt it growing like a steady, gnawing thing inside my chest over months. Once it sets in, you will try anything to relieve it, no matter how feeble the efforts.

Allie wipes her hands on her skirt as she steps back from the window. Strands of blond hair stick to her forehead, and not from exertion. "How long have you been sitting there, love? We really need to get you that TV. Give you something to watch."

Sarah's mouth twitches. "I'd prefer the walker."

"I spoke to my manager already. You need to be patient."

"It's been three weeks—"

"Honestly, don't start on me this early in the morning." Allie tugs her jacket off in sharp motions and discards it on the chair. She's breathing too quickly, trying to divert a quiet fear into frustration, as though that will make it go away. As her rapid clicking footsteps move into the kitchen, I kneel at Sarah's side.

"Call your family. Tell them you want someone else."

She stares at me, but with her flashing glasses in place, I can't fully read her expression. There's a bittersweet angle to her lips that hurts me deep inside, and when she places a hand on my head, I'm shocked by how cool the skin is. "I can handle Allie. You don't need to worry about me so much."

I want to ask if she truly believes that, but she already has one person disagreeing with her choices, so I bite my tongue. Allie bangs cups onto the kitchen counter with enough force that I'm worried they'll crack. It feels like any small thing could set the house off. We have to tiptoe, we have to whisper. It doesn't take much to spark an avalanche.

Sarah sleeps after lunch, and as has become my habit, I follow Allie. She spends some time in the kitchen, wiping down the counters and scrubbing at a stain on the cupboard doors that I never managed to eradicate during my time in the home.

Then she takes up her bag and moves to the stairs, only pausing momentarily by the door before turning her head sharply enough to flick her hair. She takes the stairs quickly. I follow at a slower pace, always keeping her in eyesight.

Allie has already cleaned every upstairs room. My least favorite days were the ones she spent in my own bedroom, pawing through my belongings, rearranging my furniture. But today, she aims for the room at the end of the hall.

Sarah's collection of porcelain figurines have been clustered onto one surface. Allie prefers the tables and vanity to be left empty, so she can dust them more easily, and that's what she does today. A cloth comes out of her bag and runs over every surface, digging into the corners and edges, even though they were aggressively polished just a week before.

Once she's satisfied, she sits down at the vanity and begins pulling out drawers.

"You can't treat this house like you own it," I say, moving to stand behind her. The vanity is old and its glass has grown fogged, and our dual reflections shimmer in the mirror.

She lifts her head long enough to glance at the open bedroom door, then opens another drawer.

"I know why you're doing this. Sarah can't come upstairs anymore. So you think it won't matter if you rearrange her belongings because how would she even know?"

The second drawer holds several small boxes. They're wood, well made, with tiny bronze latches. Allie's fingertips trace over the lids, then she hooks her fingers down to open one.

"It still matters." I lean over her shoulder to whisper into her ear. "Whether you do it in public or in private, it matters."

The delicate blond hairs on the back of her neck rise. Inside the box is a pair of pearl drop earrings. She lifts them out, draping them over one hand to admire them in the light.

"Don't." My voice has grown raw. Her expression is angled toward me through the mirror. There's a light in her eyes. Her lips twitch into a small cautious smile. She holds one of the earrings up, dangling it beside her lobe, watching how it shimmers against her wax-colored hair. The smile grows larger.

Again, she glances toward the open door. We both know she doesn't need to fear being disturbed. Sarah won't be coming. Sarah likely won't ever know what she does in this room.

But perhaps she can feel me. Some part buried deep in her knows that she's being watched, and it puts her on edge.

Her lips rub together, smearing the ruby lipstick. Then her hand wraps around the earrings. She pushes them into the handbag at her feet, burying them deep, and straightens, breathing slowly through her mouth, before turning back to the vanity.

My anger is not hot this time. It's blisteringly cold. A gnawing ache that comes from the deepest parts of me, spreading, my blood freezing in my veins.

"Get out of my house," I spit through clenched teeth.

We are captured together in the mirror. Her broad shoulders and long face with its coy smile. Me slightly too tall, my hair limp, my face bloodless in my anger. She tilts her head at her own reflection, as though asking it a question. Her eyes trail down toward the open drawer, which still holds another two boxes.

My anger breaks through. Like ice cracking to allow a fissure of dark water to flood out, it bursts from me, too powerful to stop if I even wanted to try.

My voice is something unnatural, something broken, as I scream, "Get out!"

The mirror cracks. A long, jagged line runs through it, smaller spiderwebs branching out, cutting the glass in half, dividing our reflections.

She draws a sharp breath as she looks up. Our eyes connect through that screen of fractures, and I know she's truly seen me for the first time.

Allie's cry chokes off as she jolts away. The chair hits the floor hard. She presses against the wall opposite me, one hand against her chest, the other to her mouth. Wild eyes switch from the mirror to the room, darting across the shadowed recesses between the furniture. Although we're facing each other, her gaze passes through me. The color has bled from her face, and her skin strikes me as dangerously fragile, like paper.

My anger flowed out of me when the mirror cracked, leaving me cold and numb. I lower myself onto the end of Sarah's bed, my breathing labored, my head throbbing. I'm on the verge of fading, but not yet. Not until she leaves the room.

Allie stands beside the dresser, held in place by locked muscles. One hand grips her blouse. The other presses so tightly across her mouth that it will carry a smear of lipstick when she takes it away. Light glitters across beads of sweat as she bends, stiff and awkward, to look into the mirror a final time.

I have a clear view of her through the jagged cracks, but her eyes stare through me as she scans the room. She draws a carefully controlled breath as she lowers her hands, then circles the desk to catch up her handbag. She refuses to look back but holds the bag to her chest as she leaves the room in long, stilted paces.

A weak "ha" escapes me as I droop, forearms braced on my knees.

Every other time I've viewed myself in a mirror, I've been shown a familiar image. A long, pale face, its expression a little too intense. Dark eyes. Straight, plain hair.

But I've been nurturing a suspicion that Sarah sees a different version of me. Sarah, who removes her glasses when I'm around for my benefit, but perhaps also for her own. Sarah, who will not give me a direct answer about what I look like to her. Sarah, who believes without a doubt that I was murdered.

In the brief second when the mirror cracked and Allie saw me, I also saw myself. My face was still long. My skin was still pale. My hair was still straight. But those details were all that remained of my past self.

My corneas had bleached in death, leaving a foggy off-white layer across my iris and pupils. My skin was ashen, blue veins mapped across it, but not as many as there should have been. I'd lost a lot of blood. Much of it stained my chest, running from the angular gash that cleaved my throat. More marked my face, clotting in my hair and trailing over my cheek.

Sarah was right: I did not die peacefully.

I lift shaking hands and drag them across my face. The skin feels smooth. There is no blood nor any gap in the clear line of my throat. That small movement drains the last of my strength, and I fade.

The darkness holds me for a long time. I'm heavy, my limbs bloated, and they refuse to move at my command. Even fitting air through my swollen throat is an impossible challenge. I lie in the dark, my body contorted, gurgling with each failed breath. Part of me wonders if I will be trapped here forever, and yet I don't even have the energy to feel proper dread. It just *is*. I broke my body with the anger. As it flowed out of me, it tore me apart, and now I must endure the consequences.

Gradually, I begin to realize that I can feel the house. Not any one specific part, but the building as a whole. It presses on me from every side: above and below, against my tongue, against my fingertips.

I feel footsteps move across the floors as clearly as if they stepped on my bloated, stiff body. Voices reverberate around me. The doors slam and I feel it in my bones.

I'm a seed planted inside my home, and I have grown through it. The pipes are my veins. The walls are my skin. I spread through the building as thoroughly as the mold. Perhaps I *am* the rot. The thing that poisons my home. The thing that chokes and kills all other life.

Over time I shrink again, pulling back to only myself. My senses end at my fingertips. My tongue cannot taste anything more than my own mouth, tangy with blood. I breathe, and I no longer choke on it.

As my eyes open, they twitch against the sudden light. Weeks of darkness have made me blind. Shapes blur across my vision and slowly, in fractions, resolve themselves.

My house stands ahead of me: tall, steady, a tomb disguised among this quiet suburban street. I'm at its gate. My hands rest on the crusted, aged metal. Cool air snatches at my dress, whipping it out behind me.

For a moment I can't tell whether it's dawn or dusk, then I realize it is neither: the late-afternoon sun has been corrupted by brewing rain clouds. The air tastes dusty and dry, but the sky is poised to break open.

The gate's hinges struggle when I push it open. My feet feel unsteady, so I place them carefully, crunching over the stone path I have walked thousands of times before. Toward my house. I feel energy in the air as I near the door, though it doesn't come from the storm, but from the building itself. It has been growing worse. Far, far worse. I hesitate before opening the door, knowing that whatever this building is holding at bay must be released soon and that it is something to be feared.

But no matter what, it is my destiny to be here. I cannot escape this home, for better or worse. I turn the handle. The energy buzzes around my head like a swarm of flies, and then it passes and I step over the threshold.

Voices come from near the kitchen. One I recognize: Sarah's. She pauses and is answered by a man I don't know.

As I shut the front door behind myself, I sway. Stepping into this home is like stepping onto a ship on rocky seas. The floor tilts, then turns in the other direction. I wait until the sensation fades, then press forward, toward the rear of my house.

My path is blocked by a tall, thin man, silhouetted by the light. I flatten myself against the wall as he sweeps past me and catch just an impression of curls and pale skin, then he's gone, jogging up the stairs.

Sarah isn't in the kitchen, as I'd thought, but sitting in the backyard. A scarf wraps around her neck, like the ruffles on a fancy pigeon, glasses hung on one of the loops. She turns her head a little as I approach and her left eye—her good eye—lights up. "Leigh. I was wondering when you might be coming back."

"Was I gone for long?"

"Fifteen days, I believe. You tend to pop in and out, but you usually don't take that long."

I settle onto the metal bench at her side. Maybe it's the lighting or maybe my memory is unreliable, but she looks better than she did before. Her right eye still sags until it's virtually closed, and she still rests in her wheelchair, but there's more color in her face, and instead of lying limp in her lap, her hands are clasped onto a mug of what looks like hot chocolate. "Who was that man I passed?"

"That's Troy. My new aide."

My heart rises. "You called your family."

"Oh, no, my darling, this one's on you. Allie left halfway through a shift and point-blank refused to come back. She said the house was possessed. The agency had to scramble to find a replacement. You should have heard them apologizing. They sounded truly embarrassed, kept swearing that this had never happened before. What did you *do* to her?"

"I lost my temper. She stole your earrings. I'm only sorry I couldn't stop her sooner."

Sarah exhales a cackling laugh. "You mean the ones in the box in my vanity? Oh, what a poor prize. Those are fake pearls. I got them years ago so I'd have something to wear to weddings and funerals."

A cautious smile forms. "Really? I was worried you might have inherited them or your husband might have given them to you."

"Mercy, no. And I'd have told him to return them if he had." She lifts her hands in an open-arm shrug, and I watch the hot chocolate teeter dangerously close to spilling from the mug. "Do I look like the kind of person who likes jewels? Allie can keep them for all I care. It's a small price to pay to have her gone."

"I won't argue with that. What about the new one?" I lean over the chair to glance through the open kitchen door, but I can't tell where he's gone. "Is he okay?"

"Oh, yes, I like Troy quite a lot. Apparently he only just completed his training. Poor thing's eager to please and isn't afraid to show it. Look at that." She waves one hand toward the kitchen, and I notice a walker placed beside the table. "He got that for me within two days. I'm still shaky on it, but making progress."

"Good."

"My family wasn't especially happy. They liked Allie because she'd been working there for so long. But apparently, Troy swore up and down that he didn't believe in ghosts and wouldn't be scared even if he encountered one, so the agency put him forward." Sarah's smile is lopsided but vivacious. "I told him he'd have nothing *to* fear as long as he behaved himself."

I can't help myself; I laugh. To think my life has turned into this. A point of gossip for an office and a new measure to vet candidates against. I almost pity Allie. She knows what she saw but has no way to prove it.

"The house isn't as clean as when Allie was in charge," Sarah continues. "But he plays cards with me and reads, and isn't trying to park me in front of a TV like some overtaxing toddler. He'll do very well."

Footsteps clatter through the house. I'm used to how every pair of shoes sounds against my floor, and I'm surprised to realize I recognize this set. I heard them, again and again, during the weeks when I wasn't strong enough to be fully present. A man appears in the open doorway, his arms full of blankets and pillows.

"Sorry, sorry, I thought I remembered you had a fleece one, but I couldn't find it, so I brought these instead. Is that okay?"

"It's lovely, thank you."

I get my first good look at Allie's replacement as Troy places the blankets onto the porch's wooden boards and shakes the top one out. He's tall and gangly, and although I suspect he's in his twenties, he still looks like a teenager. His nose is very large, but then, so is his curly mop of hair and his broad, awkward smile, so it balances out in a way.

He turns that smile on Sarah as he folds the blankets around her legs. "I thought I heard you say something before. Were you talking to the birds?"

The feeder is busy, I realize. Sparrows bicker over the overflowing seeds.

Sarah's answer is cryptic. "Maybe. Or maybe I was talking to the ghost."

Troy laughs, and it's a jangling, genuine noise. "Tell her we don't want any trouble."

"Oh, I think she'll like you well enough."

I move out of the seat beside Sarah as Troy approaches and let him take it. He has a book—one of the paperbacks from the display unit that used to cover the under-stairs door—and he reads from it with all of the stiltedness and bad inflection of a poorly rehearsed high school presentation. Sarah closes her eyes and reclines in her seat, content, and I think she might be right. He will do very well.

The sky darkens as the clouds merge with dusk. I watch the bird feeder as Troy fights through a scene. Three sparrows dance, bickering and fluttering as they revel in their feast. Then, abruptly, they fall still, their heads quirked up to watch something I cannot see. A heartbeat passes. The sparrows explode away from the feeder in a burst of whirring wings. It's not the focused flight of a bird aiming for a new perch, but the terror-pierced flurry of a prey animal that has realized jaws are poised to snap around them.

There's nothing to disturb them, though. I frown, tilting my head back. Two of the old oak tree's branches are lit up. Yellow light bathes them, catching all of the whorls and creases marring the bark.

I've seen the branches like that before but never from this angle. It's how they look when my bedroom's light is switched on.

Troy is wholly focused on the novel. Sarah has her eyes closed, her face serene as she drifts toward sleep. Neither of them notices as I slip away and move through the open kitchen door.

The house is colder than it otherwise might have been. Spots of dirt and dead leaves spread across the kitchen floor, blown inside by the same gusts of wind that snatch at my back.

Something moves on the second floor, betrayed by a creaking board.

My skin prickles as I near the under-stairs door. Something dark bleeds from around its edges. Spots of black, little circles, spreading across the wooden floorboards and wooden walls. It's clearest on the ceiling, where it's contrasted against the white paint. Mold.

I reach toward it but stop myself from touching it. The discoloration has only bled outward by a few inches, but I know it won't stop there.

But what *will* stop it? I'd be a fool to believe that bleach or soap could cure this.

My hand finds the doorknob. I don't intend to open it, only to test that it's still locked, but when I turn my wrist, the handle obeys. The latch clicks. The door is unsealed.

Troy's voice reaches me as a low burbling sound, like something calling from underwater. The words blur together. I glance toward the kitchen, but as the fading sunlight grows paler, it's increasingly hard to see my companions.

The door presents a horrible choice: open it, regardless of the consequences, or step away and never know? My hand moves almost against my own will, tugging on the door, dragging it open.

The storage room has been corrupted. Its tidy white shelves, its plain white walls, its boxes and its trinkets—they have been taken over by the mold.

Dark and dense, it blurs all edges. A thick, mottled undercoat, not unlike the lichen on my gate, crusts the surfaces, but it is smothered in plumes of a steel-gray downy substance. Each tiny thread shivers as the cupboard's still air is disturbed.

I throw my forearm across my mouth and nose, but the spores are already inside me. They scratch my throat until I have to cough, which only sends them deeper into my lungs.

The fur-like growths are thicker in the corners. They run in rivers over the shelves' edges, hanging like icicles. They clump across the boxes, the book, and especially the little cloth rabbit.

I only touched the doorknob, but my hands feel sticky. The gray mold clings to my fingers and palms. A surge of panic shorts my ability to think, and I rub my hands on my dress's sides, urgently trying to get the substance off my hands.

The door's outside is rich wood. Its inside is muffled gray. My foot hooks around the door's edge as I attempt to reseal the room without touching any more of the mold. It slams shut, and I recoil as a plume of spores billows out from the narrow gap.

Above, the floorboards creak as someone walks through my home.

# 23
# LIKE SHARDS OF ICE

MY HANDS ARE STILL TACKY. THEY CLENCH AND RELAX AT MY sides as I move onto the stairs. Outside light evaporates as thick clouds drown out the sunset, and even from the stair's turning point, I can see that the upper floor is dark enough to be night.

Some kind of noise hums at the edges of my hearing. Exactly the same sound as I heard through the under-stairs door. Like whispering voices, like dead leaves blown by a rough gust of air. It comes from a million miles away, until it's reduced to just the idea of noise. The hairs across the back of my neck rise.

I ascend, taking each step carefully. The kitchen door bangs, thrown closed by the wind, and Troy laughs. He and Sarah have returned to the kitchen. Their noises are faint, though, and I feel as though I have been swaddled in a cocoon, trapped where sounds cannot fully reach me.

The upstairs hallway comes into view. Its shadows seem

foreign. My tongue skips across the backs of my teeth and finds a strange taste. Fear?

My bedroom door hangs ajar—not by much, just a crack. No light comes from within. Someone is here, though. I can smell them. It's an aged scent—musk and oil and old clothes. The smell I associated with Sarah when she first came into my home. It hangs in the air, dense enough that the walls absorb it.

I step toward my bedroom, then freeze. Just inside my room— just out of sight—a foot scrapes across the floor.

Voices from the ground floor cut through the cold air. Troy speaks too cheerfully for my comfort. "Anything else for tonight?"

"I'm fine, thank you, love. You head home."

*No*, I want to say. *Don't let him leave.* But the footstep was less than fifteen paces away, emerging from the darkness that floods my room, and my companions sound like they're on another world as Troy lets himself out of the front door. In the space of five short, sharp heartbeats, the gate sounds. Now the house only contains Sarah, me, and whatever exists in these upstairs rooms.

Window frames rattle as the storm settles in around us. I hold myself against one of the walls and move closer to my room. The door drifts inward, then rocks back toward me, the latch nudging against its lock but not fully closing. I hold my breath. The foreign noise—the scratching, fuzzy sound—is joined by heavy tapping across my roof as the clouds release their burdens.

The door shifts again, drawing inward several inches, and I think I see something beyond it. Some sort of shape standing in my room's center, its head grazing the ceiling, its arms hanging limp by its sides, but then the door closes again, knocking against its frame.

Every heartbeat aches as it struggles to push blood through stressed muscles. My outstretched hand touches the door. A light tap—as light as the raindrops above me—and the door drifts open again.

There is no figure in the center of my room. Even in the heavy gloom, that much is clear. I swallow. It catches in my throat. My eyes burn, but I'm afraid to blink as I ease myself across the threshold and feel for the light switch.

The foreign sound is louder. It's not dead branches. And it's not rain. It's voices. Coming from near my bed. A small red light flashes there, standing out among the shadowed shapes. The radio is switched on. And it emits something from my nightmares. Voices, speaking over one another, all monotone. Their whispers sound as though they were dragged through raw throats. The words are sharp, sometimes harsh, but contain no modulation as they form a constant flow of syllables jutting over each other, scrambled.

My numb fingers find the plastic light switch. I turn it. The bulb above me doesn't respond.

*It's the rot. It started under the stairs and killed that light. And now it's spreading.*

The radio's sound is hypnotic. No part of me wants to go any closer, but I still cannot resist stepping fully inside my room. My senses are on high as I approach the bedside table. Something sticks to the underside of my shoes, and I crouch, fingertips exploring the rug and finding it is no longer damp but drenched. The liquid is tacky when I rub it between my fingertips, and the smell is unmistakable. Metallic. On the edge of being sweet in the most abhorrent way. Blood.

The sounds spat out by my radio are growing louder as their urgency increases. I reach for the small black box. Its electricity prickles my skin as we make contact, but I don't let myself recoil. I lift it to my ear.

It only contains one voice: a man's. But that voice is speaking several times at once, not even pausing for breath, as it holds three separate currents of words. It's near impossible to tell the threads apart, let alone isolate the words.

*Didn't want...*

*...too far...*

*...fault...*

*...rot...*

Icy fingers graze my back. Long and cold, they run from my neck down to my waist. I convulse, my whole body shuddering, the radio falling from my grasp. It hits the floor hard, bouncing, before coming to rest half-buried under the bed.

There is nothing behind me. The touch was real, though: my skin still burns from the five lines of contact. I put my back against the nearest wall, my heart in my throat, my eyes wide and wild.

The oak tree branches scrape against my window as the storm thickens. No light comes from the window. Nor does any light float in through the hallway. The house is fully dark. Sarah has gone to bed.

In this pit of black, my eyes strain to pick out any irregularities. I can scarcely see the edge of my bed. To my left is the desk under the window. Opposite and to my right is the open bedroom door.

Something shifts in the darkness. As it falls still, it blends back into the shadows, perfectly hidden. Except for its eyes. Two pinpricks of light, hovering near my ceiling, focused on me.

My mouth opens, but I have no air left in my lungs to call out, even if I had someone to call *to*.

Movement in the darkness. Many shapes, long and thin. Its fingers, flexing at its sides. Fanning out. Contracting again. The pinpricks of light seem closer than they did before. The smell is so much stronger. Oil and musk and age and death. The radio is louder, that harsh, unmodulated voice whispering with greater intensity as the rain lashes the windows and pours off the roof.

The darkness quivers as its form moves, and the pinpricks of light vanish as they turn toward the door. I sense, more than see, its great form shifting into the hallway.

My legs crumple as I fall to the floor. Breathing is a struggle; air whistles as it passes through my narrowed throat. I press my hands to the sides of my head—dirty hands, sticky with spores and blood and dust, but I do not care—and rock gently against the wall.

I've never felt fear like this before. I want—no, *need*—to cry, but nothing can escape me. Every muscle in my body is pulled tight with incredible tension, until I feel that I am on the verge of snapping like a rubber band.

The presence was familiar. I couldn't see it, not shrouded in darkness like we were, but I still recognized it and recoiled from it—with every fiber of my being.

That was my death.

My fingertips dig into the sides of my head. My teeth chatter uncontrollably. I try to move, but the muscles cramp, unwilling to even shift me to the side.

The stairs creak as the presence descends toward the ground floor. Good. The further away it goes, the better—

No. *No.* Sarah is down there.

It killed me.

I am certain, deep in my heart and in my soul, that it took Ruth.

And now it is coming for the home's newest occupant.

My heart seizes, then thumps. That is enough to break the trance. I move, muscles stiff but finally working together, to scramble to my desk. The radio spits vile, angry words at me. I tune them out as I pull desk drawers open, still on my knees, and drag my hands through the contents.

I own a small penlight, useful for seeing inside narrow spaces, and find it inside the second drawer. It's no larger than my finger and the light is narrow and pale, but it's the only source of illumination I can think of on the second floor.

It turns on at my command. The beam filters across the rug, catching on the gloss of red liquid sticking to every fiber. Part of the light slips under my bed. The darkness there has a fuzzy quality. It takes a second to recognize it. Fungus, thick and cloistering, spreads out of the underside of my mattress and through the floorboards.

I use the desk to pull myself up. My legs don't want to work. I need a moment to brace myself, coaxing my lower half to take my weight. Each breath feels like a knife slicing through my throat. My legs twitch, and I push away from the desk, staggering to the bedroom door.

Lightning floods through the window and splashes across the opposite walls. My momentum stills. As the flush of light fades, I try to convince myself that it was an illusion, that this cannot in any way be real.

I raise my penlight and direct it toward the open door. Just like the lightning, it fails to show the white-painted hallway walls. Instead, it reveals a mass of something thick and black.

The rot has reached my room. I hold my left sleeve across my gasping mouth as I stare at the crusts of mixed blacks and grays that glimmer around the doorframe's edges. They are crusty and damp, and I am horribly reminded of split boils oozing pus.

Beyond that is worse. Gossamer-thin threads spread out from the wall. They are delicate, but they are long, rising from the ground and hanging from the ceiling, shivering as air rolls through my window. They grow from the boiling rot that spills out of a multitude of crevices in the walls. I knew my house was full of hairline fractures. I did not expect *this* many. They are like cracks across an eggshell. Like a shattered pane of glass. Running from the floor to the ceiling, crossing each other in jagged dashes. The paint peels back, coiling, and tar-black rot oozes out of the gaps.

Even in the seconds I spent frozen, it has spread another inch into my room. I cannot stand here, watching as it envelops me. This house is as familiar as the back of my hand. I close my eyes and put my head down and step into the folds of the gossamer fungus.

The delicate threads brush across my exposed skin. Snagging, itching, clinging to me as they break away from the walls. My shoes crunch over uneven ground, bursting more of the pustules.

An urge to heave rises, but I fight it. Retching will only drag more of the spores into my throat. And like a body trapped underwater, the urge to gulp in air may very well kill me.

Instead, I hold my breath as I press forward, through threads that stick to me like spiderwebs. My shoulder grazes the flaking walls. I'm nearly at the stairs. The floor is growing denser, like mud, and I realize I can hear burbling water. The bathroom tap runs, and the rot has filled the pipes, causing it to overflow. It floods across the floor, feeding the spores and trickling down the stairwell.

I reach the stairs. Normally I would run one hand across the wall to help guide my steps. Now, the idea is repulsive. I trust in my instincts instead. I know my home. As distorted and broken and wretched as it is, I can still follow the stairs, even when blind.

I find the first step. The floorboards are uneven and slimy. I press down, testing the edge of the step, planting each foot carefully before extending the next. My lungs burn. I take the smallest breaths I can manage until my head is swimming, but that will have to be enough.

Something damp and cold touches my face. Ropes. Hanging from the ceiling, covered in rot, sliding over me like cruel snakes. Irrepressible shudders run through me and I lose my footing. I slide over the edge of the step and am forced to grasp at the walls. My fingers dig into the filaments, thick as a snowdrift, soft and unpleasantly cool.

I gag and taste the fungus. My stomach turns. I crouch over, sitting on the steps, eyes watering and lungs convulsing as I fight to keep my mouth closed. The sensation ebbs but doesn't fully abate. I pull my hand out of the wall and continue down the stairs.

The floor's texture changes as I follow the stairwell's turn. It becomes harder, crunchier. The water from the upstairs tap has flowed into the cracks, allowing this space to dry out. The filaments brushing across my skin become sparser, and I finally dare to open my eyes.

The penlight dances across flaking walls. Strands of white mold hang from the ceiling, low enough to graze my head. The floorboards have split, some jutting up like shards of ice, allowing the rot to seep out of them like dark gray foam. I descend into the hallway. Every step is loud. The boards whine as they strain under my weight.

Lightning comes through the living room windows. It lights up the irregular rivers of mold that pour through the walls…and catches on an open door.

The storage room under the stairs is no longer sealed. The door hangs open, crusted with more of the white fungus, shifting slightly with every gust of air that buffets the hallway.

And that is not the only open door. The entrance to the study now hangs ajar. I turn my penlight toward it, and even though the narrow circle of illumination lights up either side of the doorway, it fails to reach inside.

My legs continue to shake and threaten to falter as I press forward. That strange humming noise—the sound from the radio—now comes from the dark study.

And another sound. Thick, choked gasping. The same sounds Sarah made the night of the stroke as she tried to call for help.

I'm rooted to the floor, terror pressing on my shoulders like a concrete weight, and I cannot move, breathe, think.

Another gasp comes from the dark room, sounding weaker. A thud as a hand hits the wall. She's dying.

A cry drags through my throat, stuttered and broken, as I push myself forward. The fear is so great that I can barely see—just glimpses, cast in the erratic shots of my light. My shoulder grazes the doorframe as I crash through the opening.

Then I'm there. The shape, the man, stands over Sarah's bed. He's a shadow: enormous, head grazing the ceiling, darkness spilling out of him like smoke. It pools over the bed. Over Sarah. Smothering her.

Her eyes are wide and blind in the dark. One hand grasps at the shape over her, trying to push it off. The other reaches toward the bedside table. The bedside lamp's switch is an inch beyond her fingers' reach.

She makes another sound. Gasping, whining. The hand spasms.

The shadow man turns. His pinpoint eyes shine in my direction. Too bright, too keen.

I throw myself at him. Hands snatching, feet kicking—anything to force him to move.

The dark smoke envelopes me. It enters my nose, my throat, my lungs, and suddenly my oxygen is gone and I'm drowning in this inky tide. The penlight leaves my hand but I don't hear it hit the floor. Everything is dark. I can't feel anything except for a terrible, invasive cold. My feet kick helplessly at the air.

Then I slam into the floor. My body convulses as pain sparks along my back, but I force my eyes open and, as a wash of lightning glances through the windows, see the white paint of the hallway's ceiling above me.

I roll onto my side and retch. Directly ahead is the open hallway door. The smoke boils out of it, rolling and bubbling, and the door begins to drift closed in its wake.

"No," I gasp, throwing my hand out. It catches the door's edge. I wrench it back open in time to see the white wall at the back of the closet shiver.

My heart races through a furious staccato beat, leaving my mouth dry. I crawl forward, into the closet. The door drifts closed behind me. It clicks shut and I'm swallowed by the shadows, blind but undeterred. My hands reach for the part of the wall that moved. I find it at the back of the closet: smooth, cool paint that shifts slightly under pressure. Hairline cracks mark its edges, so faint that I never noticed them until my fingertips brushed across the borders. I brace myself, then push. The wall swings backward, like a hatch. Thin, insipid light flows through. It catches over my hands and the strands of hair that have fallen across my face, quivering in my unsteady breaths. The space between the lowest shelf and the floor is just wide enough for me to crawl underneath. I lower my head and squirm closer and see a ladder's rungs appearing at the edge of a cliff.

# 24

# SIXTEEN MONTHS EARLIER

Something lingered outside my room.

I woke slowly, like a body drifting through layers of freezing water to reach the surface. It was a cold night, and a dark one, with wind-torn clouds obscuring a sliver of moon. My quilt formed a weak barrier between my body and the chilled air. Decorated with the denizens of Aesop's fables, it took on a darker, less welcoming visage at night. Animals appeared to scream at the stars. Clawed paws reached toward the ceiling, as though twisted in fear or pain.

As my senses returned, I lay still, watching the wall, uncertain what had woken me. A bad dream? Foreboding lingered over me, as though warning me that a monster from my nightmare might have slipped into reality. But if it had been a dream, I couldn't remember any trace of it.

My shoulders were sore from the angle I'd slept at. I rolled them back, stretching the muscles, and exhaled a deep sigh as I turned over.

The bedroom door was open. Not by much. Just a few inches. I frowned. My door always stayed closed at night; otherwise, the wind would tug at it and disturb me with its knocking.

Something watched me through the gap. I could barely see it, but its silhouette blocked out the white wall beyond. It was tall. Ragged strands of hair hung around what must have been its head.

My body fell still, my mind stunned into silence. For a moment we held our positions. I watched it, and I was sure that it watched me. I didn't dare breathe. Didn't dare move. My heart was a furious rhythm, loud in my ears, so loud that I was afraid *it* would hear.

The silhouette outside my door shifted, drifting out of view. I heard footsteps, heavy, moving toward the stairwell.

My tongue darted out to taste my lips. Dry and cracked. I kept my eyes fixed on the doorway as I shifted my legs toward the bed's edge. The blankets rustled, betraying me, and I silently cursed them.

The phone—that rotary monstrosity I purchased from the secondhand store—was not far out of reach. Patchy moonlight, smothered by the clouds and bisected by the old oak tree's branches, glinted across the rotary dial.

My feet found the rug, and my toes curled into the crisp fibers. Each breath came shallow and desperate. My head faced the door, but my body was turned toward the phone as I rose, moving slowly so the bed wouldn't creak.

I could no longer hear *it*. Perhaps it had descended the stairs. Or perhaps it had come to a halt in the hallway, no more than five paces away, just out of sight. I tasted my lips again, but this time, my tongue was too dry to wet them.

Shivers traveled through me as the cold night air wormed inside my nightgown. It had to be after midnight, but dawn was still a long way off. My feet moved from the rug to the floorboards, and my soles stuck to them, tacky with sweat.

The phone's receiver clinked as I lifted it from the base, and I clenched my teeth. One hand pressed the handset to my head while the other sought out the dial. My index finger burrowed into one of the holes, selecting a number, and began dragging it around. I had to look away from the door to see what I was dialing. Maybe that was my mistake. Or maybe the footsteps, rapidly coming closer, really were my first warning.

The receiver hit the floor with a sharp noise as I swung to face the door. The intruder was two steps away. Then one. In the jagged shards of light, I caught a glimpse of something pale and long. My arm rose to block it, but I was a fraction of a second too late as the synthetic rope pressed across my throat.

His breathing was loud and sticky and filled with the same frantic energy that thrummed in my chest. My open palm slapped into his face, and I felt stubble and creases and aged, dried skin. I pushed, but the loop was already cast around my neck. We were tethered together. My mouth opened to scream, but it had become disconnected from my lungs.

I staggered into the table, pain shooting through my hip as his weight pressed me against it. My hands were still free. I clawed at his face, his throat, anywhere I thought might be vulnerable to my nails. His sharp stuttering breath and the sensation of hot blood across my fingertips told me it was working.

But my oxygen was running out. It raced through my veins, forced to horrific speeds by an overstrained heart, and there was nothing new coming into my lungs to replenish it.

We staggered again. That was my best glimpse of him, when we were poised in the room's center, both fighting for purchase on the rug. His bulging, gray-green eyes, surrounded by folds of sun-pocked skin. Yellow teeth bared behind thin lips. The muscles in his arms were strained to their limits as he pulled the rope taut.

Sparks of light appeared at the edges of my vision and rapidly spread inward. My mouth opened, my chest heaving as I replicated futile motions of breathing, but the cinch around my throat was final.

We collapsed to the floor. The impact jarred his hold on the rope. I dug my fingers around my throat, trying to pull it out of where it indented the skin. A thin breath made it into me. It was both painful and not enough. The sparks of light were being joined by splotches of darkness. If I was given time—time to breathe, time to rest—I could have survived. But that option was never offered to me.

Through the sparkling black-and-white static, I saw him pull a knife from his belt. *My* knife. The one that had vanished from my knife block two days prior. I'd thought I'd misplaced it, that it would turn up in the dishwasher or in some odd drawer eventually.

I barely had the strength to breathe. There was nothing left to fight with, but somehow, I still fought. Arms came up to protect my face. Sparks of sharp pain flashed across them, but on the edge of consciousness, they barely registered. I kicked. I threw my hands at his face, aiming for his eyes. The knife came down again and again. Across my torso. My face. Then, finally, drawn over my throat, across the line of bruises already forming in the rope's wake.

My struggles had faded long before the man slumped back. His own breathing was just as strained as mine had been. He wiped one sinewy forearm across his face, smearing the sweat and blood, then sat, waiting.

Waiting for sirens. Or for lights to come on in the houses around us. Or for someone to knock on the door.

An hour passed. It was just him…and me. Huddled in the dark together, as the last of my blood absorbed into the rug and dripped onto the wooden floor.

First, he wiped the knife on his jeans, then tucked it back into the belt with shaking hands. Then he reached for the quilt on my bed. It went around my body like a colorful shroud. Then he picked up the edges of the rug, near my head, and began to pull.

I left a bright red streak across the floor as he dragged me into the hallway. Like a stroke from a paintbrush, marking my descent down the stairs. He would need to clean it, later, and clean it he would—using the bleach from under my sink and scrubbing for hours, days even, until his keen eyes could not detect any trace of discoloration.

He had plenty of time. My absence was not noticed for weeks.

During those days, he moved through the house freely. The curtains remained closed; occasionally, neighbors saw his silhouette behind them, but it didn't strike them as abnormal.

Buckets of red-tinted water were tipped down the second-floor bathroom sink. His paranoia led him to crouch down, examining the pipes to ensure none of his evidence had leaked free. That was how he found the envelope of money.

My passport and bank cards were taken along with it. He couldn't use them, not without drawing attention to himself, but their disappearance would make my own appear less suspicious.

By the time the police knocked on my door, he had retreated to his own home, the one underneath mine. His work had been thorough. No traces of blood remained. Nothing appeared out of place. The police questioned my neighbors, but there was nothing to indicate that my absence was anything other than self-imposed.

And so he lived as he had for months before that time: leaving in the middle of the night to purchase food from a 24/7 store and emerging from his nest to enjoy the comforts of my home during the workday. That routine would not change for more than a year, until the foreclosure had been completed and a new occupant moved in.

I stand at the base of the ladder. This room—if I can call it a room—is badly lit by a lamp propped on the rough concrete floor. We're in the foundations of my home. The ceiling is low; I need to crouch to move through the space. Concrete walls surround us. The exposed wires hanging from holes in the ceiling tell me that he has provided electricity for himself by rerouting the cables from the stairwell's light.

The room doesn't contain much. A foam mattress, topped with an old sleeping bag, presses against one wall. A stand-up freezer rests against another, humming quietly. A folding table and chair are nearby, and the table contains a stack of magazines and books. Buckets in the corner serve as a bathroom. There is no shower; he likely used mine when he needed it.

I recognize trinkets around the space. The lamp is one I threw out, along with the salt and pepper shakers on the table. Several of the paperbacks came from my upstairs bookcase. One of the blankets I kept in long-term storage is draped over his sleeping bag, and one of my cushions has become a yellowed pillow. The rug from my bedroom is coiled upright in the far corner. The blood has long since dried but its faint metallic scent still lingers. A key hangs from a hook beside the stairs. It's my first time seeing it, but I can guess what door the tarnished bronze opens.

The man paces. Now that I know what he looks like, I can see him clearly. No more smoke, and no more monstrous size. He is a man. An old one. Heavily wrinkled skin covers bands of sinew on his exposed arms. He wears the same pair of jeans as the night he attacked me. They've been scrubbed, but he couldn't completely remove the red mark along one leg.

Shaggy, thin hair covers most of his face. He's hunched, fingers digging into his scalp as wheezing breaths scrape through his lungs.

I'm surprised by how little I feel. Looking at him now, at the way he lives, robs him of any terror. Nor is there anger or grief. Just a strange kind of acceptance.

My bare feet crunch over the dusty floor, strewn with chips of concrete, as I approach the opposite wall. The standing freezer's hum is quiet, like a distant fly that will never be silent. I plant one hand on the lid's edge and, already knowing what I will find inside, lift.

Icy air plumes out of the box. My own face looks back at me. The eyes are pale and blind, bleached by the ice. My knees are drawn up against my chest, the arms wrapped around them, my head tilted to one side to make me fit. My mouth is slightly open. Behind the teeth I glimpse something mottled and dark. Mold. It crusts around the freezer's sides, too, now brittle and dead behind the layers of frost. The power would have been cut to my home after too many months of nonpayment, and the man would have had no choice except to let my desiccated body thaw.

Cuts cover my body: across my forearms, my legs, my cheek. They mark all of the same places that I dreamed I was cut in the shed. Those came from the night of the attack. But there are other, newer holes, too. Their incisions are bloodless and carved down to the bones, leaving broad gaps in my flesh.

He would have become trapped when Sarah moved her bookcase in front of the under-stairs door. He came up often to rattle the handle, but the heavy blockade stayed in place for weeks. He was desperate. Not desperate enough to call out for help…but desperate enough to turn to my body when his hunger grew too great.

The lid creaks as I close it over my body. I put my back against the standing freezer, my heart working too fast, my skin prickling.

The man fills my view. He stands immediately ahead of me, bloodshot gaze boring into me. No. Not me. The freezer unit. He's staring at it, just like I did, both drawn to and repulsed by its contents. As though staring into my bleached eyes for long enough will give him the answers he seeks.

He turns abruptly and resumes pacing, speaking to himself as he crosses the room in erratic, loping strides. The words come rasping and thin. A voice that has whispered to itself day and night for years, until the words lose all meaning and become nothing more than a loop of sound.

"Once more." His lip is twitching as a nerve misfires. He stoops over the small dining table, hands braced on its edge, his body swaying as he fixates on something.

I don't want to be any closer. But I move near enough to hear his thundering heart, to see the scars from my fingernails marking his cheeks and throat, so that I can look over his shoulder.

The knife—the missing kitchen knife, the blade that cut my own throat—is hidden behind the salt and pepper shakers.

"Once more." His tongue darts out to coat those twitching lips. "Once…more."

I tilt closer as I examine him. Watery, green-gray eyes, sunk deep in their skull. Skin, old and paper thin, has moldered against his wiry, bony form for decades. There's something strikingly familiar about his features.

I take a slow, careful breath. The air is rancid. Laced with dust and mold and the something else I first detected on the night I encountered Sarah. "You're Peter, aren't you?"

The eldest brother. The one who left the family and disappeared. It seems too improbable, too much like something out of fables I stitched into my quilt. But I know I am right.

*Once more.* I was the second life taken by his hands in this house. The first was Ruth.

The truth falls together in horrible clarity. He'd told everyone he was out hunting tadpoles on the day Ruth vanished, but he'd stayed home instead. He was only thirteen at the time.

It would have happened quickly. A spat leading to a blow to the head or a shove at just the wrong moment. The sort of childish fighting he might have engaged in hundreds of times before. But Ruth wasn't yet five, and Peter was thirteen, growing fast and not yet aware of his developing strength.

Thirteen. "Old enough to know what you'd done was unforgivable. Old enough to know how to hide her."

He must have found this under-house space while playing one day. No one else knew about it. At least, Sarah didn't. It's possible Ruth did. She might have died in this dim, claustrophobic hole.

Or perhaps he only dragged her body into it, where she remained hidden until the lingering fear of discovery grew overwhelming and Peter moved her bones into the forest.

He was two years older than Sarah; that would make him nearly ninety. His strength held up remarkably for a man who had no permanent home for most of his life. But even his tolerance of the elements must have been waning in the past few years. That was why he'd sought my house out. It had been his childhood home. He knew of the secret lower level: a place he could stay, out of the rain, with easy access to food.

And it worked…for most of a year. Until Christmas break. I always had three weeks off over Christmas, but he hadn't been expecting that. Suddenly, I never left home, and he had no opportunity to slip outside to find food or to even raid my pantry.

"Once more." His eyes, glassy, flicker as he reaches for the knife. The blade looked as though it had been scrubbed a hundred times, but dark patches still discolor the join around the handle.

A thick and inescapable dread wraps around me. Sarah is upstairs. The phone is in the kitchen. Her emergency bracelet is discarded in a dark corner of the bedroom. How long will it take her to reach one of them?

How long for help to respond?

She knows Peter is in the house now. Only one of them can stay after tonight. Only one can survive. Whether they realize it or not, they're trapped in a race where the winner takes all.

"Stop." My words are useless, but I hold to his side as he

moves toward the ladder. The knife presses against his thigh, held by knuckles that glow white in the weak lamplight. "She's your sister."

He may not realize. They last saw each other half a century ago. Would he have guessed his sibling might feel the pull to return to their childhood home just like he did?

At this point, would he even care?

The knife goes between his teeth to free his hands. A bead of red blooms at its edge, drawn from his still-moving tongue as he whispers to himself.

I grasp at his arm and pull. My touch means nothing to him. He plants one shoe on the lower rung of the ladder. The knife clatters between shivering jaws as he begins to climb.

My panic rises, ironclad bands tightening around my chest. Am I doomed to be a spectator in this bitter theater? If I cannot influence events, what else is there to do? I picture myself holding Sarah and whispering what little comfort I can as her life fades, trying to ease her passing in any way possible, and feel as though I am about to be sick.

No. The pen moved at my command. I am not gone yet. It was only a pen, true—but then, I only cared about it a pen's worth. This is Sarah. She is my everything. She can *have* my everything.

He's three rungs up. I throw my arms around his waist, fingers digging into fabric that's dusty and crinkled. My face presses into his back. The smell is overpowering in its intimacy. It's the scent that laced my dying breaths more than a year ago. But I don't shy away. I let the repulsion and hatred and fear ground me, rooting my feet to the rough concrete floor, making my arms strong, every muscle growing taut. Then I pull back ferociously, dragging us both down to the earth.

My arms pass through him. I'm falling alone, my vision blurring from the spent energy as he lifts a foot to rise up one more rung.

*No. I can't fade. Not now.*

My sight goes black as my shoulder blades hit the concrete. I reach for the expected pain, hoping to use it, to wield it like a shield against my body's dragging desire to evaporate, but the pain never arrives.

Instead, cold air touches my face. I'm not lying on my back in the dim basement, but standing in a dark expanse. Rain rushes over me. My mouth is open, anticipating a gasp as I hit the no-longer-there concrete, and water takes advantage to wash around my teeth and coat my tongue.

Harsh white light floods the world. Lightning, gashes of it, cutting across the sky as thoroughly as my oak tree splits the moon. It paints my pale skin and wet dress in polarizing shades. It flows across the earth, sharpening blades of grass into knives and pools of water into mirrors. And it silhouettes a dark, ferocious building.

I'm at my gate. One hand rests on the lichen-garbed metal. This is the same storm that raged when I entered the basement. I did not fade. I simply shifted to the place I most closely know as *arriving home*.

My teeth ache as I suck in water and air. There may still

be time. The gate screams as I throw it open, but the sound is drowned out by the rising boom of thunder. The final spears of lightning fade and the world sinks back into oblivion. The clouds are too thick to let in even a scrap of stars, and the night is too deep for any of my neighbors to have their lights on. I am blind.

But it does not matter. I know my home. I can trace every inch of it in my mind. Long strides carry me toward the front step. My hand rises to meet the door handle. Sarah would have locked it before bed, but the door knows me too well to deny me entrance. It hits the hallway wall hard enough to rattle the hooks where I once hung my bag.

Sarah's bedroom is to the right. I only make it a step closer before catching myself. The rolling thunder is deafening but underneath is something sharper, more metallic. More dangerous.

The rattle of metal as the under-stairs door opens.

I run for it. Wet hair sticks to my face. My dress whips behind me. The house is as dark as my grave, but I can sense the door creeping outward, long fingers wrapping around its edge.

*The door.* That's what I focus on: not the man but the house. I cannot touch him. My words pass deaf ears. But this house is *mine.* It always was.

There's no chance to slow my momentum. It carries me into Peter. I feel the impact even if he doesn't, and I slip past him, into the narrow room. My hand grasps the door's edge. Our fingers are overlapped, calloused skin beneath my own. I pull.

The house knows me. The house listens. The door rushes closed on my demand, reverberating like a gunshot as it hits home.

Peter felt the movement and pulled his hand back a second before it became jammed. Metal clatters as his teeth tighten over the knife.

We're side by side. He's kneeling, just emerged from the hole in the back of the closet, and I crouch at his side, my lips close to his ear. "No," I whisper.

He reaches for the door again. I'm faster. My hand slides underneath, pressing between the door's rough underside and the gritty floor. My fingers wrap up to secure my hold as he turns the handle above us. When he pushes, I pull. The door stays closed.

Peter's breathing becomes erratic, panicked, as he tries again and again to escape. He slams his shoulder against the wood. It bows an inch before I snap it back.

My body is shuddering. This effort empties me until I am nothing more than a shadow, until I cannot even feel my own limbs, but still I hold on. My swimming mind fixes on the only thing I can remember with any clarity: Sarah is across the hall. This door *must* remain shut.

Then Peter falls back and hits the shelves with a heavy thud. I lose my grip on the door and slump, my world swaying as I fight to stay present.

Clothing rustles as Peter feels for something in his pockets. A rasping sound, followed by another, and I see a spark. A third click and a flame dances atop a lighter.

He holds the light in the empty space between us. The closet is narrow to the point of claustrophobia, barely fitting one person, let alone two. We're close enough that our breaths compete to influence the flickering fire. Wet hair falls like sheets on either side of my head. My hands are braced on the wooden floor. Water, runoff from the rain, spreads around me. Drops of blood mingle with it. The blood is mine. Falling from the stab wounds. Falling from the slashed throat. My white-sheen eyes rise, tracing over my killer before meeting his gaze.

He still carries the knife between his teeth. His jaw is clenched so tightly that he can't get it out. Thick cords of muscle and sinew run down his throat, disappearing under his shirt. Bulging eyes fasten on me. *See* me.

The house tilts around us, threatening to drop me out of its embrace entirely. I dig my fingertips into the floor as though that will be enough to hold me there. My words sound impossibly distant. "No more, Peter."

A trail of saliva traces down his jaw. His arm shakes, jittering the lighter so badly that the flame barely hangs on, but he can't lower it any more than he can release the tension in his jaw or look away from my bloodless face. His head jerks back, bumping against the shelf.

"No more, Peter." A slow smile draws over my mouth. Those last words weren't to him, but to myself. He can do no more.

One of his legs twitches, kicking out. His eyes are still fixed on me, but they've lost their focus. I can't hear his breathing any longer. A horrible strangled cry reverberates somewhere in his throat as he convulses again. The spasm lasts and lasts, veins straining, then abruptly loosens as he sags.

The lighter hits the floor first—the knife a second later, its sharpened edge making a dent in the wood. A string of saliva hangs from his mouth, and then it too breaks free, falling between his limp legs.

My eyes close as the last stutters of energy flow out of me. My conscience is bleeding away, and through my fingertips, I feel the house. Immense. Terrible. Wonderful. My home.

I hang on just long enough to hear the sirens converge on my street, and then I fade.

# PATCHWORK

AN ETERNITY LATER AND SOMEHOW ALL AT ONCE, I'M KNEELING in my bedroom, in the place where my rug once existed, in the place that I died.

The afternoon sun paints shades of gold over the walls. The air tastes crisp and clean. I rise slowly, allowing myself time to catch up to my new environment.

The gate creaks. From my room I can barely hear the crunching of shoes across the stone path, but I still close my eyes and try to trace the steps. The door opens. There are voices. Sarah's. And someone else's. A sound very familiar and very distant all at once.

The upstairs floor is growing dusty, and my bare feet gather those traces of neglect as I make my path toward the stairs. The stairwell is dim, as always, relying on windows from the ground and second floor to show the edges of the steps. The voices become clearer as I turn the stairs' corner, but I stop there, still concealed by the shadows, as I watch the two figures before the under-stairs door.

Sarah's hands drape over the edges of the wheelchair's armrests. Her hair is plaited, and the plait tied up into a bun at the back of her head. Bruises mar her throat. Her face is attentive, though, and the liveliness compensates for the way one side droops.

My sister, Meg, stands next to her, a handbag clutched to her chest, as though she won't know what to do with her hands if she doesn't have something to hold. Her eyes are shiny, the lids tinged red to contrast against the shadows under them.

"This is where it happened?" Meg asks, tilting her head toward the open doorway and exposed storage closet. The police must have only finished their work recently; they left behind traces of fingerprint dust.

"Mm."

Meg's jaw twitches. "I can't believe she was here the whole time. It's so horrible."

"You're having trouble sleeping," Sarah guesses.

"Of course." Her fingers dig into the bag's leather. "Every time I close my eyes I picture it. She was in pain. And she couldn't even reach the phone. She must have been so frightened."

"I wasn't," I say.

Sarah's head tilts toward me, and a slow, languid smile develops.

I raise my shoulders in a shrug. "It happened so fast; there wasn't time to be afraid. I didn't think at all. I just fought."

Sarah leans forward to reengage Meg. "I don't think she would have had much time to be scared. It was over very quickly."

Meg rubs her palm across her cheek before returning it to her bag. "Thanks for calling. And for letting me come here. I know it's too little too late, but it still helps."

"Is it really too late?" Sarah asks, her eyes on me.

I descend to the stairwell's base and, holding my breath as though any stray noise could disturb my sister, step closer.

Meg's head twitches slightly, as though she's trying to dispel a bad thought. "We...didn't really talk much in the last few years. Not even at Christmas. And if I'd—if I'd just—"

"It's all right, my darling."

"No. It's not. I could have invited her to visit that Christmas. I thought about it. And I decided...not this time, maybe next year. And that was it. That was my last chance to see her and I didn't and I don't even know why."

Tears roll down Meg's cheeks, and she fights them, bundling her sweater sleeve into her palm and swiping them back as quickly as they come. "That was my last chance to tell her how much I love her."

I'm at Meg's side. My hands rest on her shoulder and back, wanting to hold her, but her only response is a small shiver. My own tears are rising. Sarah makes eye contact, and I nod.

"She loved you, too," Sarah says, her birdlike hand reaching out to hold Meg's forearm. "There's a secret I want to share with you. I have a small ability. Sometimes I can hear people who are no longer here. The dead, you understand? Your sister stayed for some time, and she wanted you to know how precious you were to her."

Meg's tears fall into hiccups. One arm presses across her eyes, hiding them, but her body has gone still. I wait, my heart fluttering in my throat, watching for her response. When she finally speaks, her voice is muffled. "Okay. Thank you. I'd better…go."

Meg tucks her bag under her arm and, head down, turns to the door. I circle around to kneel at Sarah's side and whisper into her ear.

"You had a golden retriever when you were children," Sarah calls, and Meg freezes halfway along the hall. "He was called Freddy. You used to pretend you were knights and he was your horse, and you'd charge with him across fields."

Meg's head turns just enough for me to see her wet face.

"He passed away when you were nine and Leigh was eleven, and you missed him so badly that you pretended he wasn't really gone, but was out battling the monsters in the forest across the railroad tracks and would come home one day."

Meg turns another fraction. "You…"

I continue whispering into Sarah's ear as she relays the words on my behalf. "Leigh said she missed you even worse than she missed Freddy. She wanted to call, but she didn't. And she's sorry for that."

"You're not…" Meg doesn't try to stop the tears now, but there's a fierceness in her face; her eyebrows pull her forehead into hard creases and her lips twitch. "Don't lie to me. Please."

Sarah slowly turns her chair to face Meg. "She wasn't upset to be dead. She said that dying itself wasn't even too bad. She said the only thing she actually regretted was not being closer to you these last few years."

"If you're lying to me, you need to tell me." Meg takes a step toward us, her bag held against her chest like a shield. "I don't want you to make me feel better. I just... You have to tell me the truth right now, okay?"

"Come look at this." Sarah wheels herself into the living room, following my lead. Meg hesitates, then comes after us in short, stiff steps.

I stop beside the patchwork quilt hung from the wall. In its center is a forest scene, bordered by many smaller depictions. "I made this for your thirtieth birthday," I say, while Sarah, sitting on the opposite side of the coffee table, relays. "But I never actually sent it to you. I guess I was ashamed, like it was too personal or like I was trying to recapture something we once had. But...this is the fort we used to play in. The one we found on the other side of the train tracks and never told our parents about it."

"The castle," Meg whispers, staring at the forest scene that depicts a rotting tree house suspended among the trees.

"Freddy," I say, brushing my hand across the images surrounding it. "The lizards that we pretended were baby dragons. That thick patch of brambles that we believed hid treasure. We spent days pulling it back to reach the secret inside, and we found coins."

"I remember," she says, and an enormous tear falls off her chin.

"Those were mine. I came out the day before and hid them

there so that we'd have something to discover together." My chest hurts, but I manage to laugh. "Here are the weapons we made out of sticks, and the scary house on the hill we had to stay away from because the lady living there was cranky, so we said she was an enchantress who ruled our rival kingdom."

"Mrs. Watts." Meg smiles, and it's watery but genuine. "We met her again when we were teenagers and she was actually nice, just a little stressed."

I return to Sarah's side as she continues to relay my words.

"She wants you to have it," Sarah says. "It was supposed to be for your birthday, and she's sorry it's late, but she wants you to have it to remember her by—and remember how much she loves you."

Meg slides into one of the white chairs, unable to stand any longer. "You're really telling me the truth?"

"I am."

Meg glances at Sarah but turns away again almost immediately. "Is she still here?"

Sarah looks to me, and I shake my head. It will be kinder if Meg believes me gone. "She passed over when her body was found. But she knew you came looking for her. She was so grateful that you did."

Meg nods, her head dropping into her hands and her words becoming muffled again. "You said…it wasn't too bad? It didn't hurt her?"

"Only for a minute, and then she moved into a world where there is no more pain."

"Good. She deserves a good ending." Meg chokes on her laughter. "You know the reason I stopped calling her?"

"No, she never said."

"Because I hated how small she made me feel."

My hand tightens on Sarah's shoulder. "What?"

"She had this amazing career, and this beautiful home, and her life figured out, and I was always lagging five steps behind."

"You have a family," I say, but this time Sarah waits in silence, not translating. "You're surrounded by people who love you. I had *nothing*."

Meg brushes stray hair away from her damp face. "But…now I'm proud that she was my sister. I wish I could have gotten my ego out of the way sooner and told her how cool I thought she was. Because she was really the coolest person I knew."

I'm not sure whether to laugh or cry. I have never in my life felt cool. But hearing it from Meg—that goes a long way to making it true.

"She was proud of you," Sarah says, relaying my feelings even when my words fail. "She never thought you were less than her. She wouldn't have given you up for anything."

Meg leaves sometime later, once her eyes have dried enough for her to drive safely. She carries the quilt, folded carefully and clutched to her chest, where the bag had once been. At the open car door she stops and waves at the house one final time. Sarah, in the open door, and I, standing by Sarah's shoulder, both raise our hands in farewell. We don't return inside until Meg's car has left the street and the quiet rumble of the engine is no more.

Footfalls pound through the house. Children's voices swell, chattering over each other, one rising into a scream over some perceived unfairness. I press my back to the hallway wall as they tumble past me, racing onto the stairs to reach the second floor. A girl on the cusp of her teenage years has a unicorn-shaped cookie in her mouth, half-devoured. She's closely followed by a younger girl, and a boy around ten who's trying to grab the bead bracelet off her wrist, and another girl, this one closer to fifteen with glitter spray in her hair, who yells at them both to hurry up.

As they disappear into the upstairs rooms, I turn toward the kitchen. There's a moment of silence followed by a woman's sigh. "It's all that sugar."

"Mm. That's the perks of being a grandmother. I get to load them up on sweets and send them home when I'm tired. All of the aftermath falls to you."

As I reach the kitchen's entryway, I stop, resting one shoulder against the wall, watching the arrangement. Sunlight is warm, sparkling off a freshly cleaned sink. A bunch of flowers dominate the counter, poised in a vase, a riot of color. Sarah sits at the table's head. The wooden dining chair has been permanently removed to make way for her wheelchair, but now she leans forward, one weathered hand wrapped around a half-empty mug.

Opposite her is another woman, thin and angular, her hair cropped short and filled with a decadent streak of gray. When her head is at the right angle the resemblance is so vivid that I imagine I'm looking at a younger version of Sarah.

Filling out the group is a man with sloped shoulders and comfortable clothing. His eyes are enormous behind round glasses and the sunlight catches on a bald circle at the back of his head. His slacks and sweater contrast with his wife's suit and gold jewelry.

"Well, the sugar probably isn't the only culprit," the woman says, and it takes me a moment to remember her name: Sylvia. "They've missed you. I have, too."

Her husband makes a mild noise of agreement. "It's been a nightmare of a month. For all of us, I suppose."

"Oh, I don't know. I've quite enjoyed myself." Sarah catches my eyes and sends me a secretive smile. "It's about time I had some excitement in my life."

Sylvia manages to cut off a laugh by sipping her coffee. "I doubt your doctor would agree."

Upstairs, three sets of feet pound along the hallway, followed by something heavy colliding with a wall. Sylvia leans back in her chair, her face creased with frustration. "Jay, would you—?"

"Don't worry about them." Sarah waves a hand breezily. "Dents can be patched over. Memories are forever."

"Still. They're like wild animals."

"Fresh out of the zoo," Jay replies, smiling.

"And I don't want them making too much mess. Your new caregiver seems to be struggling as it is."

"Troy's doing fine," Sarah counters, and I have a sense this is the bulk of their relationship: Sarah steadily deflecting her daughter's anxieties.

"Dust is getting everywhere. And I think I saw mold in that closet."

"He's not the best at cleaning, but he makes up for it elsewhere. And, best of all"—Sarah raises her mug an inch, tilted toward me—"the ghost doesn't bother him."

I smile and approach the table while Sylvia makes a derisive noise. "Ghosts, honestly," she mutters.

"I could see it being possible," Jay says. "My sister swears her old house had a presence in it, and she's one of the most rational people I know."

"I'd need to see something for myself to even consider it," Sylvia says as I take the chair between her and Sarah. "And even then—"

Something heavy bangs upstairs. I fold my arms on the table, unperturbed. After seeing my beloved home enveloped in dripping mold, a little damage to the drywall seems starkly trivial.

"Well, whether you believe or not, I guess you'll be leaving this ghost behind," Jay says.

Sarah's eyebrows rise, crinkling her forehead. "Why would I?"

"Why?" Sylvia almost chokes on the word, and shocked laughter ripples out of her. "Mum, after they found Peter under the house—"

"But he's gone now, isn't he?" Her lopsided smile moves from Jay to Sylvia. "I see it as a lightning-striking-twice kind of scenario. Someone broke into my house once, so the odds of it happening a second time would have to be much lower now, wouldn't you agree?"

Sylvia rubs her fingertips across her temples while Jay lifts his mug in a cheers. He sends an apologetic smile to his wife. "It *would* save the cancellation fees."

"I can't believe this is a debate we're having," Sylvia mumbles.

Jay turns to Sarah, his shoulders rising into a shrug. "It was supposed to be a surprise, but I guess we may as well tell you. Since you didn't want to live close to us, we thought that we might move nearer to you. It's a good suburb. Good schools. Syl could transfer, and I already work from home. So we bought a house a few blocks away."

"Oh?" Sarah lights up, unperturbed even by Sylvia's glum expression.

Jay shrugs again. "But then, well, *last week* happened, and we thought you wouldn't want to live here any longer."

"This is my home," Sarah says. "Wild horses couldn't pull me out."

"No, I believe that." Sylvia shakes her head, incredulous. "You're sure, Mum?"

"As sure as I've ever been."

"Looks like we can keep the new house." Jay smiles at his wife. Sylvia still doesn't seem pleased, so he nudges her with his elbow. "It's close enough that the kids can walk here. Free babysitting, remember?"

Upstairs, there's a shriek, followed by excited laughter. Sylvia shoves away from the table. "That's it." Her black jacket swishes in her wake as she takes the hallway in long strides.

"Won't be a moment," Jay says as he hurries after Sylvia.

As their footsteps recede up the stairwell, I slide my seat closer to Sarah. "She's a force to be reckoned with."

Sarah smiles, and a tinge of pride lights her face. "Almost as stubborn as I am."

I laugh.

She finds my hand and gives it a light squeeze. Her fingers are cool, the skin loose and dry but not unpleasant. "I hope this isn't an indelicate question for someone who's dead, but I thought you might have moved on by now."

I could. There has been a strange sensation in my bones ever since I stepped foot in the underground room. A feeling of lightness. Fragility. The thing that tethered me to this world has been severed, and now, I only need to let go and I will be allowed to float away.

Not quite yet, though. It strikes me as the kind of journey that might be nicer with a friend.

Footsteps thunder down the stairs, and three children race along the hallway, jostling each other for the lead, and yelling "Hey!" and "Hello!" as they pass the kitchen table. Gleeful smiles light their faces as they flee their parents and disappear through the open door and into the backyard.

In the lull of silence that follows, I place my other hand on top of Sarah's. "I thought I'd stay awhile longer."

Her smile fills her eyes. "Well, I wouldn't mind that at all."

# ACKNOWLEDGMENTS

Immense gratitude to Mary Altman and Rachel Gilmer, the editors behind this book. They've been endlessly supportive, and Leigh Harker wouldn't be the same without them.

Thanks goes to the whole team at Sourcebooks, who have made amazing things happen: Dominique Raccah and Todd Stocke, for taking a chance on me and setting everything into motion. Sean Murray, who has made sure my books aren't just in stores but are visible. Molly Waxman, Mandy Chahal, Caitlin Lawler, Tiffany Schultz, and Shauneice Robinson, the powerhouses behind the marketing. Nicole Hower for her incredible designs, and Heather Hall for managing production and making sure my commas all end up in the right places. My gratitude extends to the rest of the team too, many who work behind the scenes but are no less valued.

Finally, special thanks goes to my mum. She's not a fan of

horror and doesn't really *get* why anyone would want to write it, but she's been my most steadfast supporter. Every weekend, she stops by our local bookstore to count how many of my books are there. Love you, Mum.

# ABOUT THE AUTHOR

Darcy Coates is the *USA Today* bestselling author of *Hunted,* *The Haunting of Ashburn House, Craven Manor,* and more than a dozen other horror and suspense titles.

She lives on the Central Coast of Australia with her family, cats, and a garden full of herbs and vegetables.

Darcy loves forests, especially old-growth forests where the trees dwarf anyone who steps between them. Wherever she lives, she tries to have a mountain range close by.

# THE HAUNTING OF ASHBURN HOUSE

## THERE'S SOMETHING WRONG WITH ASHBURN HOUSE...

Everyone knows about Ashburn House. They whisper that its old owner went mad and restless ghosts still walk the halls. But when Adrienne, desperate and in need of a place to stay, inherits the crumbling old mansion, she only sees it as a lifeline...until darkness falls.

Strange messages are etched into the walls. Furniture moves when she leaves the room. And a grave hidden in the depths of the forest hints at a terrible, unforgivable secret. Something twisted lives in her house, its hungry eyes ever watchful. Chasing the threads of a decades-old mystery, it isn't long before she realizes she's become prey to something deeply unnatural and intensely resentful.

She has no idea how to escape. She has no idea how to survive. Only one thing is certain: Ashburn's dead are not at rest.

# VOICES IN THE SNOW

## NO ONE ESCAPES THE STILLNESS.

Clare remembers the cold. She remembers dark shapes in the snow and a terror she can't explain. And then…nothing. When she wakes in a stranger's home, he tells her she was in an accident. Clare wants to leave, but a vicious snowstorm has blanketed the world in white, and there's nothing she can do but wait.

They should be alone, but Clare's convinced something else is creeping about the surrounding woods, watching. Waiting. Between the claustrophobic storm and the inescapable sense of being hunted, Clare is on edge…and increasingly certain of one thing: her car crash wasn't an accident. Something is waiting for her to step outside the fragile safety of the house… Something monstrous, something unfeeling. Something desperately hungry.

For more info about Sourcebooks's books and authors, visit:
**sourcebooks.com**

# CRAVEN MANOR

## SOME SECRETS ARE BETTER LEFT FORGOTTEN...

Daniel is desperate for a fresh start. So when a mysterious figure slides a note under his door offering the position of groundskeeper at an ancient estate, he leaps at the chance, even though it seems too good to be true. Alarm bells start ringing when he arrives at Craven Manor. The abandoned mansion's front door hangs open, and leaves and cobwebs coat the marble foyer. It's clear no one has lived here in a long time... but he has nowhere else to go.

Against his better judgment, he moves into the groundskeeper's cottage tucked away behind the old family crypt. But when a candle flickers to life in the abandoned tower window, Daniel realizes he isn't alone after all. Craven Manor is hiding a terrible secret...

One that threatens to bury him with it.

For more info about Sourcebooks's books and authors, visit:
**sourcebooks.com**

# THE CARROW HAUNT

## THE DEAD ARE RESTLESS HERE...

Remy is a tour guide for the notoriously haunted Carrow House. When she's asked to host guests for a weeklong stay in order to research Carrow's phenomena, she hopes to finally experience some of the sightings that made the house famous.

At first, it's everything they hoped for. Then a storm moves in, cutting off their contact with the outside world, and things quickly take a sinister turn. Doors open on their own. Séances go disastrously wrong. Their spirit medium wanders through the house at night, seemingly in a trance. But it isn't until one of the guests dies under strange circumstances that Remy is forced to consider the possibility that the ghost of the house's original owner—a twisted serial killer—still walks the halls.

And by then it's too late to escape…

# HUNTED

## HER DISAPPEARANCE WASN'T AN ACCIDENT. HER RESCUE WILL BE A MISTAKE.

Five days after twenty-two-year-old Eileen Hershberger went missing on a hike through the remote Ashlough Forest, her camera was discovered washed downriver, containing bizarre photos taken hours after her disappearance. But with no body and no additional clues, finding Eileen in the dark and winding woods seems next to impossible.

Chris wants to believe his sister is still alive. When the police search is abandoned, he and four of his friends vow to scour the mountain range until they find Eileen and bring her home. But as the small group strays farther from the trails and the unsettling discoveries mount, they begin to realize they're not alone…and Eileen's disappearance was no accident. But by then, it's already too late.

# THE HOUSE NEXT DOOR

## NO ONE STAYS HERE FOR LONG...

Josephine began to suspect something was wrong with the crumbling Gothic monstrosity when its family fled in the middle of the night, the children screaming, the mother crying. They never came back. No family stays at Marwick House for long. No life lingers beyond its blackened windows. No voices drift from its ancient halls. Once, she swore she saw a woman's silhouette pacing through the upstairs room...but that's impossible. No one had been there in a long, long time.

But now someone new has moved next door, and Marwick House is slowly waking up. Torn between staying away and warning the new tenant, Josephine only knows that if she isn't careful, she may be its next victim...

# THE HAUNTING OF ROOKWARD HOUSE

## SHE'S ALWAYS WATCHING...

When Guy finds the deed to a house in his mother's attic, it seems like an incredible stroke of luck. Sure, it hasn't been inhabited in years and vines strangle the age-stained walls, but Guy's convinced he can clean the building up and sell it. He'd be crazy to turn down free money. Right?

But there's a reason no one lives in Rookward House, and the dilapidated rooms aren't as empty as they seem. Forty years ago, a deranged woman tormented the family that made Rookward its home. Now her ghost clings to the building like rot. She's bitter, obsessive, and fiercely jealous…and once Guy has moved into her house, she has no intention of letting him go.